EVERY BREATH YOU TAKE

MIRANDA RIJKS

INKUBATOR
BOOKS

Published by Inkubator Books
www.inkubatorbooks.com

ISBN (eBook): 978-1-83756-407-1
ISBN (Paperback): 978-1-83756-408-8
ISBN (Hardback): 978-1-83756-409-5

Miranda Rijks has asserted her right to be identified as the author of this work.

EVERY BREATH YOU TAKE is a work of fiction. People, places, events, and situations are the product of the author's imagination. Any resemblance to actual persons, living or dead is entirely coincidental.

CHAPTER ONE

TWENTY-EIGHT YEARS AGO

Last week, I turned thirteen. I'm officially a teenager, although as my brother never fails to remind me, I don't look it. I'm small for my age, puberty seemingly years away, and in contrast, my brother with his long limbs and broadening shoulders appears so very grown up. A lazy, long summer holiday stretches ahead of us filled with nothing because Mum doesn't believe in holiday camps and clubs. She thinks we should make our own fun. When I was moping around saying I was bored, she replied tersely, 'Only boring people are bored.'

Today Mum has gone to London for the day, to some doctor's appointment, which means Stephen is tasked with babysitting me. He's lounging around at the front of the house, which is weird because there's a much bigger lawn at the back. But I don't blame him taking advantage of the first beautiful day after months of incessant rain. For now, I'm in my bedroom, lying on my bed reading a book, but I'll go outside when I finish this chapter. The quiet is broken by the repeated sound of a honking car horn coming from the road.

'Stevie!' a female voice shouts. 'You coming?'

I run to the window and peek out. Stephen jumps up. There's a young woman there, leaning against the bonnet of a small, battered silver car. Stephen starts gesticulating, pointing up at the house, but frustratingly, without opening the window, I can't hear what he's saying. Then he turns around and races into the house.

I jump backwards, leaping onto my bed.

Stephen's footsteps are heavy as he runs up the stairs. Mum says he's got the tread of an elephant, which is weird because Stephen is tall and skinny, almost giraffe-like, with long gangly limbs. He flings open my door.

'Get yourself ready! We're going out for the day.'

'What? Where?' I ask, but he just waves away my questions and hurries along the corridor to his bedroom.

About five minutes later, Stephen is standing in the hallway, a big carrier bag at his feet. I notice a bottle of wine poking out of the top. He's obviously nicked it from Dad's stash, but I don't say anything.

'What's happening?'

'We're going out for a picnic and because I can't leave you here by yourself, you're coming with me. But you're not to say anything, alright? If you embarrass me, you can make your own way home.'

A moment later, we're out of the house and my brother is striding towards the small silver car, a big grin on his face. He tugs open the car's rear passenger door and shoves forwards.

'Get in,' he orders.

There's already a boy and a girl seated on the back seat, their brown limbs tangled around each other. There's the strong stench of cigarette smoke, which makes me cough.

'Who's the kid?' the girl asks with a frown. Her hair is braided into long plaits, interspersed with beads, and she's wearing a bikini top and sarong-type trousers in a tie-dyed fabric.

'My sister. Sorry, couldn't dump her,' Stephen says. 'She'll stay out of our way.'

I hesitate.

'Just get in.' Stephen gives me a push in the centre of my back.

'We won't bite!' The girl laughs at me. I redden and I climb into the car. By the time Stephen has squeezed in next to me, I'm literally wedged into the rear seat, trying hard not to touch the girl's thigh with my own, my shoulders hunched forwards and my knees tightly squeezed together. There aren't enough seat belts for all of us so I don't get one.

Stephen directs the young male driver, who drives at a crazy speed holding a cigarette with one hand and the steering wheel with the other. Music blares out of the open windows and I have to concentrate hard not to throw up from a mixture of fear, fumes and car sickness.

'Where are we going?' I ask Stephen, but he ignores me, singing along to the music in his tuneful tenor voice. I'm so relieved when the car eventually stops, parking up onto a leafy verge, but it isn't until we pile out and start walking with all the bags that I realise where we are. At Mum and Dad's special place by the river.

I remember the first time we came here Dad was carrying the wicker picnic hamper, Mum held my hand, while Stephen bounced along the grassy path in front of us. The birds were singing and the sun was hot on my bare shoulders. I was wearing a pale yellow sundress, my favourite. Stephen was in khaki shorts and a T-shirt, his dark hair curling at the nape of his neck, such a contrast to my corn-coloured, flowing locks held off my face with little pink clips. Dad chose a place under a willow tree, a grassy bank that looked down onto the fast-flowing river below us. He placed the blue tartan blanket on the ground and I sat on it, clutching my knees, breathing in the scent of summer.

'What do you think, kiddos?' he asked.

'It's nice here,' Stephen said.

'Nice?' he derided. 'We don't use the word *nice*, do we, Stephen?'

He flinched.

'Yes, it's really lovely.' Mum sighed, pushing her sunglasses onto the top of her head.

'Well, my darlings. This is all ours now.' Dad flung his arms out wide, the sun rays making the little hairs on his arms glisten like gold. 'I've bought the whole estate. Two hundred and twenty acres extending that way, and one day the fields adjacent to the road will be developed into houses, and you, my lovelies, will be rich.'

Mum had kissed Dad on the lips then, and I played with a ladybird. I don't remember what Stephen was doing. We stayed there for a couple of hours, eating Mum's carefully prepared picnic, making daisy chains, until Dad got bored and drove us the few miles back home. But we returned to that spot on the riverbank as a family whenever the weather was particularly lovely.

'WHAT ARE WE DOING HERE?' I whisper to Stephen.

'It's where I come to do drugs, drink and have sex,' he says.

'Really?' I ask, my eyes widening.

'If you say a word to Mum or Dad, your life won't be worth living.' He says that without the faintest hint of irony and I know that he means it. Stephen's friends look old and scary and I'm feeling extremely uncomfortable following the five of them as they saunter along the overgrown path, bulging bags flung over their shoulders, bottles clinking. The girl with short, choppy hair, who looks like she's at least twenty, has her arm around Stephen's waist and when they reach the willow tree, she tugs him to one side, drops the bags and weaves her fingers into his hair before kissing him on the lips. I've never been so close to people snogging and I'm transfixed watching them. The girl pulls away and, holding Stephen's face between her hands, mutters something that I can't decipher. Perhaps she told him that she loves him. And then Stephen's lips are on the girl's once again and he's pushing his whole body up against hers.

'Oi, don't be a voyeur,' the girl with the braids says, her sharp nails digging into my forearm. I've no idea what she means but I turn away and follow her to the grassy bank. She drops a flowery piece of fabric onto the ground and sits down. I follow suit, but then Stephen appears with the choppy-haired girl. There's a daisy tucked behind her ear and her lips look pink and swollen.

'Shove it,' my brother says, kicking my leg with his dirty bare foot. 'Go and play with your dolls or whatever you do. Over there, where you can't see us.'

I hesitate. I don't want to be out here alone but Stephen's friends are all eyeing me and not one of them has a friendly expression on their face. I grab my bag and hurry away. It's muddier the other side of the willow tree and the bank slopes down sharply to the river below. Despite the hot summer's day, the river is rapid, streaming over smooth rocks, making little whirlpools where clumps of branches and grasses have got stuck along the side. A bird squarks somewhere above me. I sit there for a while, annoyed that I've forgotten to pack my book. I've got nothing to do, so I start collecting twigs and chuck them into the river, watching as they get caught under the fast-flowing currents, dragged downwards and occasionally popping up further down the river. One of Stephen's friends has brought along a stereo and they've turned up the music so it's almost drowning out the sound of the water. The rapid *thump, thump, thump* reverberates through me and I don't like it. There's a smooth-looking rock just below me, perfect for skimming into the river. I reach down to pick it up but I lose my footing and then suddenly I'm slipping. I try to scramble upwards, but my fingers can't get traction and all I'm doing is collecting mud under my nails.

It happens so fast. One moment I'm breathing air, the next I'm in the freezing cold water. I scream but the foul-tasting water gets in my mouth, fills up my nose and my airways and I'm coughing, but the more I splutter, the more water gets in my mouth. I try to scream, except I'm sinking, being pulled further and further downwards, the skin of my legs tearing against rocks and plants. Small bubbles appear in front of my eyes and then there's darkness, the heavy water pushing me down. My lungs are on fire and my chest is going to explode. Fear makes my limbs weak and I know that this is it. I'm going to die in this river. I will only be a teenager for a few days. My short life is over.

Suddenly I feel something grab me under my arms. I'm tugged upwards, away from the depths of the terrifying water. Air hits my face and I hear a familiar voice say, *just leave her*. But then I lose consciousness and my world turns black.

CHAPTER TWO

THE WIFE

'I think my head is going to explode.' Nicolette groans. I am fully loaded up with painkillers so my headache has shifted, although my stomach is feeling decidedly queasy. That's what happens when you go to Amsterdam with your three besties and pretend you're still a teenager. At forty, we should know better, yet I think we were more outrageously behaved this weekend than we were two decades ago. Perhaps it's because for most of us, life has become rather serious. Kalah and I have our families and we all have careers.

The engine roars as the airplane speeds forwards, pushing us back in our seats as it takes off. I'm sitting adjacent to the aisle so I can't see out of the windows. That's on purpose. I don't like to look at the vast ocean far beneath us, or in this instance the grey English Channel that separates England from the continent. Angela, who is in the window seat the other side of Kalah, fumbles in the seat pocket and brings out a tattered paper sick bag.

'Really?' I ask, winking at Kalah and raising my eyebrows at Angela.

'Taking precautions,' she mutters. She does look rather green. Kalah edges ever so slightly towards me, her strawberry blonde hair touching my shoulder. It's only Nicolette, who is sitting on the other side of the aisle engrossed in a fashion magazine, who seems as put together on our return as she was on our arrival. Perhaps it's because Nicolette is the only one of us who still parties regularly and is immune to the morning after the night before. She is single. Officially at least, as she's made no secret of the fact she's seeing a married man.

Three months ago, the four of us had gathered in a wine bar, one of our regular haunts, planning our long weekend, all in agreement that to mark our fortieth birthdays, we needed an upgrade on Brighton or Winchester, the towns we'd visited the previous two years. When Amsterdam had been mooted as our city break, I had reservations. With its widespread network of canals, I wasn't sure if I could enjoy it, despite the city's beauty and history. I'd grimaced, slightly embarrassed, even though my girlfriends were supportive of my phobia of water, even though I'm sure they thought I should have grown out of it decades ago, but they were uniformly understanding, taking it upon themselves to protect me from my fear. It's not like I'm scared of water per se, just bodies of water that I might fall into. Brighton was fine because I had no intention of going anywhere near the sea; in Amsterdam, walking adjacent to canals is non-negotiable.

Kalah must have noted the look on my face because she whispered, 'Don't worry. You can walk between us.' And my lovely friend was good for her word. Of the four of us, Kalah drank the least. And thank goodness one of us remained sober and was able to guide us back to our hotel, otherwise we really might have ended up in a canal.

Kalah is always sensible because if she isn't, she faces the wrath of Xavier, her controlling husband. During the weekend, he rang her every two hours, ostensibly asking questions about after-school activities, or where she'd hidden the ketchup (in the fridge, obviously) and announcing that Autumn wouldn't settle without saying goodnight for the fifth time. None of us were taken in by the constant harassment. Kalah is married to a control freak and frankly it was a miracle that Xavier let her come away with us. Having downed several cocktails last night, Nicolette asked her why she didn't leave Xavier.

'I love him,' Kalah said, tears welling in her eyes. 'And I have to do what's right for my daughter.'

I tried to probe a little more, but she shut down the conversation. It makes me sad though, because the sparkling, quirky eighteen-year-old has morphed into a rather dull adult, as if she's shrouded with a grey blanket so heavy, she can never break free. Right now, however, she's on edge. Our flight home has been delayed by nearly ninety minutes.

'You okay?' I ask as Kalah fidgets, pushing up the sleeve of her jumper and looking at her small watch for about the hundredth time since we boarded the plane.

'I'm just worried there won't be enough time. I can't be late.'

'Late for what?' Angela asks.

'Picking Autumn up from school, making supper. Just stuff.' Her voice fades away. Angela throws me a *what the hell* look. I turn away. I hate that Kalah has been reduced to a bag of nerves. I guess we're a little similar in that way, although my aqua-phobia doesn't compare to her coercive husband.

I squeeze her hand. 'I'll collect Autumn from school and then you'll have time to do whatever you need to in the house.'

'But what about you? Don't you have to get supper for Samuel and the kids?'

'I'll find something in the freezer.' In reality I'll probably order a take-in, or message Samuel to pick up some ready meals from Cook on his way home. Today I still want to bask in the freedom of our weekend away, and my family won't mind.

'What have you got Hunter for his birthday?' Nicolette asks Angela.

'He wants a new bike to add to the already massive collection. He'll choose his own.'

'Are you going out for supper tonight?' Kalah asks.

'No. He's having a drink with the lads. We'll go out somewhere at the weekend. Samuel is joining Hunter, isn't he?' Angela asks me. Hunter and Samuel have been best friends since they were children.

'Yes. He's promised he'll be home in good time though,' I say.

Angela snorts with disbelief.

I make it home with just ten minutes to spare before I need to leave for school pick-up. The house looks like a bomb has hit; crockery congealed with leftover food is piled up in the sink, beds are unmade and dirty clothes lie scattered throughout the house. Housekeeping is not Samuel's strong point and I've given up asking him to help. However, he is a great dad and I know Riley and Alfie will have had a fun weekend, packed full of outings and games. One of the many things I love about Samuel is that he doesn't just palm the kids off to keep themselves entertained with computer games and films, but he actually plays with them. I send him a quick message to say I'm home and looking forward to seeing him later tonight. He's joining Hunter at a pub straight after work although being a Monday night, I'm hopeful he'll be home early as promised.

Angela, Kalah, Nicolette and I have been friends since sixth-form college. Angela was the first of us to get married. As chief bridesmaid, I was thrown together with Samuel, who was the chief groomsman. We've been inseparable ever since and married almost a year to the day of Angela and Hunter's wedding. We see Angela and Hunter frequently, both as couples and individually. Our only difference is, they don't have any children; a life choice which I try to understand but in all honesty, I'm not sure I do because I can't imagine my life without Riley and Alfie.

I pick up a load of clothes and shove them in the washing machine, then I rifle through the deep freeze and take out a couple of pizzas. Everything else will have to wait. After locking up the house, I hurry to the garage and reverse my car into the drive. We are blessed to live in a beautiful house, newly built six years ago. Half of the house is constructed within an oak frame, so our huge bespoke fitted kitchen with exposed beams overhead has space for an L-shaped sofa, a dining table that seats ten and a wood-burning stove that belches out heat in the winter. Our views are onto woodland, lending the feeling of being cocooned by trees. It's the sort of house that features in magazines.

Riley and Alfie attend a small primary school twelve minutes' drive away. I've got the timing down to the second, assuming I'm not obstructed by a slow-driving tractor or road works. Kalah's daughter, Autumn, is in Year Six with Riley and they're firm friends. There's something very special seeing the next generation continue with our deep connection. Kalah lives two roads over, so we're in and out of each other's lives a lot.

'Mummy!' Alfie exclaims as he runs towards me, wrapping his arms around my torso. He's a young nine-year-old who, fortunately for me, still loves his mum and isn't embarrassed to show it. Riley, on the other hand, is eleven going on thirty, and any parental affection is deemed gross.

'Did you have fun with Dad?' I ask, placing a kiss on his head.

'Yes, so much fun. Did you have a nice time too?'

'I did, thank you, darling.' Riley is loping towards us, her school rucksack bulging. She's whispering to Autumn, muttering behind her hand.

'Hi, girls. Good day at school?' I ask.

'Yes, thank you, Mrs Simmons.' I've suggested to Autumn on numerous occasions that she calls me Eva, but Xavier expects his daughter to be formal, so I don't push it. 'I'm taking you home as your mum is running a bit late.'

'Can we have a sleepover?' Riley asks, her voice rising with excitement.

'Sorry, girls, it's a school night. Perhaps at the weekend.'

Riley groans melodramatically.

We pull into the DeFonts' drive. Kalah's car is parked at the front, a gleaming white BMW which she has cleaned twice a week. Their house is traditional for this area of Sussex, with a low-slung tiled roof and front door set behind a large porch. The garden, like every aspect of the property, is immaculate. Even though it feels like it hasn't stopped raining for weeks, there are no puddles on the drive, and the lawn, which at most people's houses is long and straggly because it's been too wet to mow, is as immaculate as a new carpet. It crosses my mind that it might be fake.

Kalah swings open the front door. She's changed since she got home and is wearing a neat, if somewhat ageing, navy pencil skirt and white blouse.

'Hello, darling! she says, her face lighting up. Autumn allows her mother to give her a peck on the cheek. Riley pokes her head out of the car window. 'Please can we have a sleepover?'

'I've already said no,' I tell Kalah.

'Not tonight,' Kalah confirms.

'Everything alright?' I ask, my voice low.

'Yes, hunky dory.' Her tight smile suggests she's lying.

'We'll catch up later in the week,' I say, and blow her a kiss.

Back at home, the next couple of hours are a whirlwind of clearing up the house, eating an early supper with the kids, making sure they do their homework and getting them to bed at a reasonable hour. It's only when I've said goodnight to Riley that I check my phone. It's nearly 8.45 p.m. and Samuel hasn't responded to my earlier message. That's strange. He might have had back-to-back meetings this afternoon and hurried to the pub in town where he was meeting his mates, but it's unusual for him not to reply. I can see that he's read the message so I send him another one.

> Hope you're having fun. What time will you be home?

An hour later, I'm in bed, exhausted. I glance again at my phone. The last message I sent to Samuel hasn't been read. I thought he'd be home by now because he had said he'd only stop for one drink, but perhaps I shouldn't be surprised. Hunter doesn't have an off button and as he and Angela don't have children, their lives aren't controlled by school hours and early bedtimes. And when Hunter is on a roll, he makes it nigh impossible for his friends to say no. Samuel is probably several pints down by now and he'll stumble home sometime shortly after closing hour. I send him another message.

> I'm knackered and going to sleep. See you in the morning. E x

It's pitch dark when I wake up gasping for air. I've had the nightmare again, the first time in ages. My heart is pounding and sweat coats my torso. I don't want to wake Samuel by switching on the bedside light. Trying to control my breathing, I strain my ears listening for Samuel's gentle, comforting breaths. I hear nothing so I gently pat the bed next to me except my hand just slides over the cool, smooth bottom sheet. I sit up and fumble for the light switch. My heart is still thudding. The image of me being pushed further and further downwards by a massive body of cold, dark water, unable to breathe, is still too horribly vivid. I let out an audible breath and glance at my clock. It's 1.07 a.m. Where is Samuel?

I listen carefully, wondering whether the sound of Samuel taking a shower in the bathroom woke me, but I hear nothing. I slide my legs out from under the duvet and grab my dressing gown. The house is quiet and when I open the bedroom door the light that I left on in the hall is still lit. I pad lightly downstairs. The front door is locked but the chain isn't across it, just as I left it before I went to bed. Quickly, I stride around the house, but it's obvious that

Samuel isn't here. Switching the outside lights on, I peer into the darkness, hoping to see his car. It's not here either, although that doesn't mean much, as he normally gets a taxi home after a night out with the lads. I run back upstairs and switch my phone on. There are no missed messages or calls and the last two messages I sent him don't appear to have been read. I try calling but his phone goes straight to voicemail.

This isn't like Samuel. My husband is reliable. He tells me where he's going and what time he'll be home. Yes, he's been working crazy hours the past few months, but he lets me know when he's going to be late. My husband is the type of man who messages me when he's on his way home; he's trustworthy.

I know it's nearly 1.30 a.m. but nevertheless I call Hunter. If anything has happened to Samuel, he'll know. Unsurprisingly, his phone goes straight to voicemail too. I make myself a camomile tea to settle my nerves and carry the mug back to the bedroom, shivering underneath the thick duvet. I'm unsettled and worried, images of Samuel lying hurt in a ditch becoming increasingly vivid as I switch off the light and lie motionless in the dark. I'm hyper alert, sitting bolt upright every time I hear a car in the distance or the creaking of our house as the temperature dips. By 6.30 a.m., I haven't slept a wink and a massive knot of worry sits like lead in my stomach. I get dressed and go downstairs to prepare breakfast for the kids. On the dot of 7 a.m., I call Hunter again.

'Eva,' he answers quickly. I can hear the warmth in his voice. 'You're bright and early.'

'Sorry to disturb you. It's just Samuel didn't come home last night. Do you know where he is?'

There's a long silence which I eventually break by repeating his name. 'Hunter?'

'Sorry,' he says. 'It's just that Samuel left us about 9 p.m. yesterday evening. He called a taxi to take him home as he'd drunk three pints of beer. Said he'd leave his car in town and collect it in the morning. I tried to persuade him to stay out longer but he said he wanted to get back as you'd been away.'

'So where is he?' I ask, more to myself than Hunter.

There's a long pause. 'I don't know, Eva. I really don't know.'

CHAPTER THREE

THE WIFE

'Mum, where are my trainers?' Alfie shouts down the stairs. The last thing I can think about is tracking down my children's stray belongings. It just seems so irrelevant. Yet I can't possibly tell them their dad is missing.

'Where's Dad?' Riley asks as she lopes into the kitchen. It's as if she's reading my mind. She's always been a daddy's girl and he's been keen to oblige. It worries me sometimes how lenient he is towards her but I'm sure his attitude will change when she embarks on her first relationship.

'Dad had to go away for work,' I lie, turning my back towards her so she can't see my face.

'I thought he was going out with Uncle Hunter last night,' she says.

'His plans changed. Now hurry up, please, otherwise we'll be late for school.'

Every time the kids are in a different room, I ring Samuel's number but it continues to go straight to voicemail. I try that geo locator app on the iPhone but it whirls around and around before saying a location cannot be found. Is that because his phone is off? Or has it been shattered into tiny fragments next to his broken body? Surely if he'd been in an accident, the police would have notified me?

I'm jittery and short-tempered and when Riley and Alfie start bickering in the car on the way to school, I lose my cool. 'Please be quiet, the both of you!' I exclaim and immediately feel bad for raising my voice. I glance at Riley, who is staring at me as if I'm a stranger.

'What's the matter with you?' she asks, disdain in her voice. Alfie has tears in his eyes.

'I'm sorry,' I say, ashamed of my poor mothering skills. 'I've got a lot on at the moment and it wasn't fair to take it out on you.'

The second I pull up behind other parents' cars, Riley is out of the car followed swiftly by Alfie. Neither of them says goodbye, and I find myself waving limply at my children's backs. I let out a groan.

'Where the hell are you, Samuel?' I mutter to myself. I'm about to pull away from the kerb when there's a knock on my window which makes me jump. I slam my foot on the brake and glance to the side. It's Kalah.

'Sorry, didn't mean to startle you,' she says as I lower the window. She peers at me. 'Are you alright? You look knackered.'

'Probably because I am.' I hesitate for a moment, wondering if I should say anything, but the words just slip from my lips. 'Samuel didn't come home last night.'

She looks at me as if she doesn't understand.

'He went out for a drink with Hunter, left the pub at 9 p.m. and hasn't been seen since.'

'Bloody hell, Eva.' Kalah looks shocked. 'Have you rung the police?'

'Not yet.'

'You need to, in case there's been an accident or a mugging or something.'

In a way I feel relieved that Kalah doesn't think I'm catastrophising, that this is so out of character for Samuel it warrants the feeling of fear that is gripping my stomach.

'Are you going home? Would you like me to come with you?' she asks.

'It's kind but I'll nip home, call the police and the hospitals and then I really need to go to work.'

'Keep me posted,' she says. 'And please send me a text when you've found him.'

Back at home I call 101 rather than 999 because it's not an immediate emergency; or is it? The phone is answered rapidly by an efficient-sounding woman, who asks why I'm calling.

'My husband didn't come home last night and I'm worried something has happened to him,' I explain. 'Are you able to tell me if there have been any reported accidents or muggings in the Horsham area?'

I can hear the clicking of fingers on a keyboard. 'Can I take some information, please?'

I give her my name, address and phone number, and Samuel's details.

'Have you got any reason to believe your husband may be in danger?'

'What do you mean?' I ask, my voice rising in pitch.

'Does he have a history of self-harm or do you think he may have harmed himself?'

'No, absolutely not!' I exclaim. Samuel wasn't depressed, he was just busy. 'He's never just disappeared,' I say. 'It's completely out of character.'

'Has he seemed different in any way over the past days or weeks?'

'No, not at all.' Although if I'm being honest we've been like ships passing in the night for months now. Both of us have been busy with work and I can't remember the last time we went out for supper just the two of us. When he gets back, I'm going to suggest we reinstate date nights.

'Most people who go missing turn up in a few hours. You mentioned he had been out drinking so he probably just stayed over with a friend.'

I open my mouth to contradict her but then change my mind. I reiterate my earlier question asking if there have been any reported accidents or muggings. There's more clicking on a keyboard.

'No,' she says eventually. 'There have been no reported incidents.'

'So what happens now? Will you investigate?'

'In these circumstances, I suggest you ring around friends and family and if your husband hasn't reappeared this time tomorrow, then we will issue a missing person's report.'

Really? That's it? The woman is cordial but firm and swiftly ends the call, telling me not to worry. As if.

I pace around the kitchen, chucking the breakfast things into the dishwasher with abandon. It simply doesn't make sense for Samuel to have disappeared without contacting me.

After a few restless minutes, I ring the three nearest hospitals but they confirm what the police officer already told me. No one by the name of Samuel Simmons has been admitted. I then call Samuel's closest friends. A couple go to voicemail and the others seem as perplexed as me. This is totally out of character. Finally, I call his parents. They are elderly and perhaps his mum or dad has fallen sick and Samuel has rushed over to be with them. They live in Cheshire and we don't see them nearly enough. His mum, Phyllis, answers the phone. After some niceties, I ask, 'Have you heard from Samuel in the last twenty-four hours?'

'No, love. Should we have done?'

'Um, no. It's just he's lost his phone,' I lie, not wanting to worry her unnecessarily. 'I was wondering if someone might have called you from it in the hope of tracking him down.'

'No, pet. Nothing like that. How frustrating,' she says. 'But it's lovely to hear from you. How are the children?'

'They're both good, thank you, doing well at school.'

'I'm so glad to hear that. Perhaps we can FaceTime at the weekend.'

'Absolutely,' I promise.

Finally, I ring Samuel's office. The receptionist confirms what I already assumed: he hasn't turned up for work and no one knows where he is.

There's a horrible leaden sensation of fear sitting in my stomach, the knowledge that something is terribly wrong.

I think back to last week. How was Samuel before I went to Amsterdam? It feels like a decade ago, not just a few days. I flick through my online calendar. He stayed the night in London last Tuesday night, having spent the day working for a new client and then taking them out to dinner. He rang me about 10 p.m. saying it had been a successful day and he was hopeful Simmons Edge would get more work as a result. I recall thinking how upbeat he sounded, more positive than he's been for weeks. On Thursday evening we'd attended a parent-teacher meeting for Riley, a discussion about her moving up to senior school. Stephen, my brother, had babysat Alfie for the couple of hours we were away. In front of Riley's teachers, Samuel had seemed distant, disinterested even, and we'd snapped at each other in the car on the way home. We rarely have full-blown arguments, and a couple of hours later, as normal, we were back in our evening routine, eating supper, discussing the minutiae of our lives. I can't recall anything out of the ordinary.

By the time I've rung everyone I can think of it's nearly 10 a.m. I'm getting changed, ready to go into work, even though it's the last thing I feel like doing. My mobile rings and I grab the phone, hope rising in my throat, but it's only Luke from the charity.

'Did you have a good weekend away?' he asks, without giving me the time to answer. 'I'm just checking to find out what time you'll be in the office. I'd like to go through a few items with you this morning, before the AGM.'

'Shit,' I mutter. I've completely forgotten that it is our charity's annual general meeting this afternoon. How on earth can I have forgotten the most important day in our work diary? In my mind, I turn over the possibility of cancelling it, except I can't. The date is set from one year to the next and several of our trustees come from afar. I glance at my watch. 'I'll be with you in thirty minutes,' I say, swapping the skirt and jumper I'd chosen for a black trouser suit.

Leap Ahead is a charity for young people. It was set up a decade ago by Dad after he sold his energy business for many millions. It was a mixture of tax efficiency and philanthropy that led him to pump a huge sum of cash into a charitable trust. When he died so unexpectedly just two years later, I stepped in to develop the charity. Initially it was going to be a part-time job, something I could run on the side while the children were young. It's grown so much over the past few years, that it is now all-consuming. We support young people, typically aged 14 to 21, who have had a tough start in life. Our community centres help them with addictions or managing difficult family situations. We teach them how to budget and cook and fend for themselves, and offer safe spaces where they can come together to make friends or just seek out support from our large roster of therapists. The need for our services has grown massively and we now have Leap Ahead premises in twelve towns in the South-East of England. Dad would be proud. I'm proud. It's just that today I'm feeling that charity should begin at home. And that means I shouldn't be going to work and rather I should be out there, looking for my husband.

Our head office, which makes it sound grand when it absolutely isn't, is wedged between a pet superstore and a garden centre on the edge of Horsham. We have three rooms – an open-plan room for our five staff, a boardroom, and my small office. Fortunately, I prepared the agenda and my notes before I went to Amsterdam; the accounts are all up to date and Jack, our accountant, tried to explain the numbers to me last week, although I'm not sure I can recall a word he said. It's only when I'm pulling up into the carpark that I remember Samuel promised to collect the kids from school today, prepare their supper and oversee homework. Our board meeting typically runs from 3 to 6 p.m., meaning I won't be home in time. What if I can't track my husband down before then? I need a back-up plan. Groaning, I call my older brother Stephen, hoping he'll answer his phone at work.

Stephen and I are chalk and cheese, although we've remained close over the years. He works in admin for a builders' merchant, getting in at 7.30 a.m. and leaving at 3.30 p.m. The early hours suit him as he's always been a lark.

With his almost pedantic eye for detail, I expect he does well. Just when I think the call is going to click to voicemail, he answers.

'Eva,' he says, slightly breathlessly. 'Did you have a good time in Amsterdam?'

'Yes, thanks. Look, I've got a massive favour to ask of you. Is there any possibility you could collect the kids from school and give them supper?'

'What, today?'

'I'm sorry it's so last minute. Samuel's been called away and I've got our AGM, which means I won't be home until around 7.'

There's a long silence until eventually he sighs. 'I suppose so.'

'Thank you so much. I really owe you.'

Stephen harrumphs. 'I've got Jiu-jitsu at 8 p.m. I really don't want to miss it.'

'I'll be home long before then,' I promise. And hopefully Samuel will be back too, so we can cancel Stephen, but I don't tell him that.

CHAPTER FOUR

THE WIFE

Samuel hasn't come home and the annual general meeting was a disaster. I couldn't concentrate. Midway through the meeting, my friend and co-trustee, Ian, took me to one side and asked if I was all right. I lied and said I had a throbbing migraine. I'm not sure that he believed me. Throughout the day, I've been checking my phone, calling Samuel, all in vain. As every hour passes, the fear increases, clouding my brain, causing my stomach to clench painfully. Where is my husband?

I'm not naive. You hear of people walking out on their lives, except I know Samuel would never do anything like that. We may take each other for granted, but he loves the kids and makes a point of calling to say goodnight to them whenever he's not home in time for bedtime. There is no way that he would go two nights without speaking to the children. Of course, our marriage isn't perfect; what marriage is? We argue from time to time but we always make up eventually. Sometimes we're both so busy we barely speak to each other, but I love Samuel and can't imagine a life without him.

Back at home, Stephen is in a hurry to leave, and the children are hovering around us, so I don't get the chance to tell him the truth. In a way I'm glad. We're siblings and we love each other, but we're not close friends and confidants. I'm not sure how Stephen would react if I told him Samuel is missing. I think he'd be a mixture of sanctimonious, probably because he's a little bit jealous of my long marriage, and controlling, even cloying, sweeping in to assist his poor little sister.

Once the children are in bed, I pace the house, unable to eat or concentrate. I feel like I should be out looking for Samuel, but where? I've called everyone who might have seen him. Kalah rings to check if Samuel is home, and the pity in her voice when I tell her no is almost too much to bear.

I take a sleeping pill because, despite my aching bones and exhausted mind, I know I won't sleep. I leave my phone on, the sound switched up to high, to ensure I'll wake if it rings. Samuel, Sam, my Sammy (the abbreviation he hates) still hasn't come home and I am convinced that something is horribly wrong. I've never been particularly aware of my intuition, but right now my clenching stomach and thudding heart are yelling at me that my husband needs help and it might already be too late. I assume that's the physical manifestation of intuition and it completely terrifies me.

The sleeping pill gives me five hours of sleep until I wake gasping for air, scrabbling with the duvet, my heart racing. That horrible drowning dream, again. I fumble to switch the light on and grab my phone. No missed calls. No messages. It takes a good ten minutes of deep breathing and drinking a full glass of water for my body to still. My brain, however, is racing. At 6 a.m. I call the police again, determined that I won't be fobbed off with platitudes. This time the police officer seems to take my concerns seriously and he promises to send a colleague to our house at some point this morning.

'Not until after 9 a.m., please,' I request. The last thing we need is for the police to turn up when the children are still in the house.

The doorbell chimes at 10.10 a.m. It's pouring with rain but through the deluge I can see a marked police car on the drive and two uniformed officers stand at the door. I open it quickly.

'Good morning. Are you Mrs Eva Simmons?'

'Yes,' I say, stepping to one side to let them in. One of the police officers leaves a long umbrella on the outside doorstep.

The police officers pass me in our wide open-plan hallway. 'I'm Police Constable Sherri Sayed,' the shorter of the two women says. 'And this is my colleague, Police Constable Isla Kendall.

'A lovely house you've got here, Mrs Simmons.' Isla Kendall has red hair tied back into a small pony tail and pale blue eyes, a contrast to the darker features of her colleague. She glances all around, taking in the tall window at the far end which gives a vista onto the leafy garden.

'Thank you,' I mutter. 'Please follow me.' I lead them into the kitchen and watch as their eyes widen as they take in the huge, beamed room. 'Would you like a tea or coffee?' I ask, gesturing for them to sit at the oak kitchen table.

'No, we're fine,' Sherri Sayed says. She has flawless skin

and seems too petite to be a police officer. It feels chilly in here and I shiver as I sit down opposite them.

She removes a small notebook and pen from an inner pocket. 'We understand your husband is missing. Samuel Simmons, is that right?'

'Yes, and it's very out of character.' I clench my fingers together. I explain the circumstances of his disappearance, repeating what I told the officer on the phone.

'And what was Mr Simmons's state of mind before he went missing?' Sherri Sayed asks.

'Fine. There was nothing out of the ordinary.'

'What was he wearing?'

I hesitate because I have no idea. 'I was away at the weekend so I'm not sure. I can check to see what's missing in his wardrobe.'

'Okay, we'll come back to that. We will need an up-to-date photo of him. What transport did Mr Simmons use to get from his office to the pub?'

'I assume his car. He drives to work and then he probably drove into town, although his friend said he was planning on getting a taxi home.'

'What car does he have and registration number?'

And then it hits me. Samuel took delivery of a new company car, a sleek black Mercedes, only three months ago. It is his pride and joy and I recall him mentioning it was so expensive it had to have a tracker installed. There were a couple of emails about the tracker that came into our joint family account – the email that we use for household bills and the children's school, a shared email. I just need to recall the name of the tracking company. I mention this to the police officers and they ask me to find the email.

I hurry out of the room to our shared study and grab the

laptop, returning with it to the kitchen. Placing it on the table, I input our password, open Mac mail and sort through the emails. I find it quickly. TracksterVehicle, and right there is an email with our login details. Clicking the link leads me through to a number of pages until I get to a map that displays the last known location of Samuel's Mercedes. The ignition was last switched off on Monday at 6.05 p.m. And the location was Mallet Street, a little residential side street with rows of terraced houses, two roads over from The Golden Duck pub where Samuel was meeting Hunter.

I turn the laptop to face the two police officers. 'Does this mean the car is still there?" I ask.

'Assuming the tracker hasn't been removed, which is unlikely because the monitoring company would contact you, I would assume yes. We'll check that out,' Sherri Sayed says, scribbling in her notebook.

'Can you get access to your husband's bank account?' she asks.

'Yes. We have a joint bank account, then Samuel has his own account, as do I, and we have a shared savings account. I have access to his banking; we don't hide anything from each other.'

Sherri Sayed purses her lips and a single crease appears between her eyebrows, but then she smiles and the fleeting look of cynicism disappears. I suppose she's seen it all in her job.

A couple of years ago, when I was out with the girls, I remember mentioning how Samuel and I have access to each other's banking. Angela commented how unusual that is, and she should know, being a divorce lawyer. I rather liked feeling my husband and I have something special, that we hide nothing from each other, that we believe in complete transparency. Kalah admitted she didn't even know how much Xavier earns and that he manages all of their finances. Nicolette did nothing to hide her horror, telling Kalah that she was a submissive wife. Later, Angela told me that she spoke to Kalah and told her to siphon off money for herself; a rainy day fund. Kalah was horrified, but Angela has seen enough marriage breakdowns to know all of the warning signs.

Police Constable Sherri Sayed leans towards me. 'If you could look at his online banking, it would be useful to know if there have been any recent transactions.'

'Sure,' I say, logging into our NatWest account on my phone. I pull up the joint account. There are a couple of transactions that I made buying groceries and filling up my car with petrol and the only transaction I didn't make was on Monday at 6:51 p.m. when Samuel spent twenty-two pounds and fifty-three pence at The Golden Duck Public House. I show the details to the police officers. That was a hefty round of drinks, or perhaps they ordered some nibbles too, a plate of cheeky chips maybe. And then I remember that Hunter said Samuel ordered a taxi to take him home.

'There's no transaction for a taxi,' I murmur. 'His friend said he took a taxi home.'

'Could he have paid in cash or used his sole account?' Isla Kendall suggests.

I snort. 'Samuel doesn't believe in cash. He uses a card or Apple Pay on his phone. If he got a taxi it would show up in his account.'

'Can you get access to Samuel's sole account so we can be sure?' Isla Kendall asks.

I use Samuel's login details. The pin code is Riley's birthday and the password, Pushkin, the name of his parents' dog. But the password is wrong. I try again, wondering if I input the characters incorrectly, but the same happens. I feel myself flushing slightly. 'Sorry,' I say. 'He must have changed it.' This doesn't make sense. Why did Samuel change his banking details and not tell me? I try to recall when I last looked at his sole account; it must be months ago when he asked me to transfer funds to our joint account so I could pay for our family holiday to Sardinia.

The police officers share a quick glance.

'Talk to us about your husband's state of mind.' Sherri Sayed shifts forwards in her seat, placing her neatly manicured fingers on her knees. Her black crepe trousers have a sharp line that creases down the centre of both of her legs.

'His state of mind?'

'Could he have been having an extra-marital affair?' Isla Kendall adds.

I pull myself up with a start. 'No, absolutely not,' I say. 'Our relationship is fine and we don't keep secrets.' Except evidently, we do. I've just discovered he changed the login to his banking. Everyone keeps secrets. They may just be little ones such as telling our partner that his hair isn't balding at all, when in fact there's a distinct thinning on the top of his head, or pretending we're late due to a traffic hold-up when in fact we'd been drinking a sneaky glass of wine with one of our girlfriends. But none of that surmounts to a failing relationship. Could Samuel be having an affair? Yes, he's been working long hours, and yes, we don't talk as much as we could or as much as we used to, but that's normal for a fifteen-year marriage, isn't it? I suppose it's possible he's having an affair but I've had no indication that he's any less interested in me. There have been no unusual presents to appease a guilty mind and no unexpected overnight stays. I haven't noticed any lipstick or the scent of perfume on clothes, and he hasn't been exercising more than normal or taking any greater care in his appearance.

'And what about medical conditions? Does your husband take any medication?'

'He has high blood pressure but that's hereditary. His father has it too. Otherwise nothing.' And then I remember his sleeping pills but lots of people are prescribed those to self-medicate occasionally, me included.

'No mental health issues?'

'Absolutely not.' But it does make me pause for a moment. It's depressingly common for a man to take his own life and for his wife to be totally unaware that he was depressed or unhappy. Could Samuel have done something like that? I try to dismiss that little kernel of doubt. He loves the children so much, and there's never been an inkling that he's feeling down.

'What job does your husband do?'

'He's a partner in a marketing agency, Simmons Edge. He founded it with a friend about eight years ago.'

'That sounds stressful,' Isla Kendall adds.

'Not unduly,' I reply, although I'm not sure that's strictly true. Samuel has been working so hard this past year. He said that it's because the market is difficult, although they don't seem to have lost any clients, so I'm not sure what the problem is. Nevertheless, he sounded so ebullient last week after his dinner with the new client. I will talk to Jen, his business partner, find out if there's anything at work that might have been worrying Samuel.

'Can't you track his phone?' I ask. 'Even though it's switched off.'

'Unfortunately, no. We can only see the last location when it was on.'

'But he could be severely injured in a ditch somewhere or in a back alleyway. You need to be out there looking for him!' My voice sounds unnaturally shrill.

'Is your husband's passport missing?' Sherri Sayed asks.

'His passport!' I exclaim. 'My husband hasn't absconded somewhere,' I snap.

She tips her head to one side. 'Would you mind double-checking, Mrs Simmons?'

I hurry back to our little study, which really is only a box room next to the kitchen, with just enough space for a built-in desk and book case along the back wall. I scramble under the desk where Samuel installed a small but sturdy safe to keep our important documents and some of my better pieces of jewellery. Stabbing the buttons, it takes me a couple of attempts to open it. I pull out the pile of documents and am relieved to find all four of our passports. Samuel's, mine and the kids'. I shove everything but his passport back in and close the door.

'It's still here,' I say as I walk back into the living room, holding up the navy blue document. The two officers stand up.

'Most people reappear within a couple of days,' Sherri Sayed says. 'I realise it must be a worrying time for you, but in our experience there is normally a positive outcome.'

'Are you saying you're not going to do anything?' I wring my hands together as I stand in the doorway, reluctant to let them leave.

'We'll file a missing person's report and circulate details on the police national computer; however, at this point we don't consider your husband's disappearance to be high risk.'

'But it is!' I exclaim. 'This is completely out of character. You need to launch an appeal, search Horsham, just do something!'

'Of course, we will start investigating and we will stay in touch with you, Mrs Simmons. If...' She pauses. 'When your husband reappears, please let us know immediately.' She holds out a business card which I take from her and put in my jeans pocket.

I see them out and watch as they get into their car and drive away. They might not think Samuel's disappearance is high risk but they're completely wrong. I know my husband and I know that he's in trouble.

After messaging Luke to say I'll be in the office later, I find Samuel's spare car key in the drawer of his bedside table. I lock up the house and drive the five miles into Horsham. I go slowly, looking out for any skid marks on the road or shoes lying abandoned on the verge, but it's difficult to see anything with the incessant rain. Because I'm driving at a snail's pace, I get hooted at by the driver of a white van who overtakes me and sticks his finger up in the air. Yet I see nothing out of the ordinary. Once in Horsham, I head for Mallet Street. There's a free parking space at the beginning of the street, so I carefully manoeuvre my car into it and buy a ticket at the machine for an hour's parking. Then I stride down the street, glancing left and right, looking for Samuel's black Mercedes. It's parked at the opposite end, outside number 56, and there's a parking ticket wedged underneath the windscreen wipers. Samuel parked his car in a residents-only bay, free parking permitted between 6 p.m. and 8 a.m. Keeping myself dry with a small black umbrella, I walk around the car but it's still gleaming, scratch-free, and every-thing looks normal, except the parking ticket. Taking his spare key from my handbag, I unlock the car and climb into the driver's seat, dripping wet onto the flawless black leather seats. Samuel keeps his car clean and tidy, and other than a receipt for a parking garage in Guildford, I find absolutely nothing unusual. No stray earring dropped by a careless lover; no lipstick-stained tissue; in fact nothing to indicate who the owner of the car is. I inhale deeply and get the faintest whiff of Samuel's aftershave. And then, for the first time since he's gone missing, I burst into tears. When an elderly woman in a mobility vehicle stops adjacent to the car and throws me a look of pitying concern, I wipe my eyes and pull myself together. Then I call Sherri Sayed, who answers on the third ring.

'I've found my husband's car in Horsham, where the tracker said it was. Should I drive the car home or leave it here? It's got a parking ticket.'

'You can drive it home and I suggest you pay the ticket.'

'You don't need to check the car or anything?' I ask.

'As far as we're aware, no crime has been committed, Mrs Simmons. Please let me know when your husband reappears.'

I decide to drive Samuel's car home and when I'm en route, I order a taxi to collect me from our home so I can return to Horsham to get my car. The whole exercise takes about thirty minutes and I'm back at my car just in time to see a parking warden approach Mallet Street. Hurriedly, I get in my Golf and drive to the multi-storey car park in the centre of town.

I spend the next hour pacing the streets of Horsham, getting soaked, despite my hood and umbrella, peering behind dumpster bins, showing Samuel's photograph to a lady selling *The Big Issue* and a young homeless man shivering in the doorway to an office block. I go into The Golden Duck and ask the middle-aged woman behind the bar if she remembers seeing Samuel with his mates on Monday evening. She's non-committal. Says it's a busy pub. And eventually I head back to my car. I'm at a loss what to do next.

Just as I'm starting the engine, my phone pings with an incoming text. I grab my phone and let out a cry. It's Samuel. Thank heavens. He must be all right after all. I wonder if he's just come to in a hospital bed somewhere and I let out a moan of relief. At long last. I jab the Messages button and read.

> I'm sorry I disappeared without telling you where I was going. I've fallen in love with someone else and I'm leaving you to be with her. I'll be in touch soon to sort out practicalities but for now I need some time away to sort my head and heart out.
> Please don't tell the children yet. Say I'm abroad for business. We can talk to them together. S.

The phone slips out of my fingers and slides down into the footwell.

No. This can't be right. Samuel wouldn't do this to me. Surely he wouldn't. My husband isn't a coward, ending our marriage of fifteen years by text message. Stunned, I reach down for the phone and read the message again. I let out a sob. The shock reverberates through my body. This can't be right. Samuel has made a mistake; something must have confused him. Perhaps he's had a head injury or something. I try calling him but as before, the phone goes straight to voicemail. I reread the message over and over until the words are swimming in my tear-filled eyes. He didn't even sign it Sx. He always puts a little cross after his initial.

And what am I meant to do now? Just accept this? Pretend that I'm not devastated and angry and betrayed? Does the bastard really expect me to lie for him to the kids? And that's when I start trembling. Samuel is about to ruin our children's lives. How dare he!

I switch off the car's engine and telephone Hunter. He's an accountant working for a firm in Redhill, I think. His phone also goes straight to voicemail so I leave a message in a shaking voice, asking him to call me back urgently. And then I just sit there and stare, straight ahead, my mind and body in a turmoil, unable to accept the betrayal. A woman carrying two shopping bags frowns at me as she opens the boot of her Volvo. It feels like I'm frozen, yet tears are pouring down my cheeks, my heart splintering. The woman takes a step closer to my car and she mouths, 'Are you alright?'

I nod, wipe my eyes and cheeks with the back of my hand and turn on the engine, driving slowly as I head out of the carpark towards home, my eyes still brimming with tears, a hard, jagged feeling in my chest that veers from dismay to anger to disbelief, the foul weather mimicking my mood. Earlier I'd considered going into work this afternoon, but I'm in no fit state now. Just as I'm indicating right at the end of the street, my mobile rings.

'Eva, it's Hunter.' His voice sounds loud as it booms through the car's speaker system. 'Has Samuel come home?'

'No. He sent me a message to say he's fallen in love with someone else and is leaving me.' My voice cracks.

There's complete silence. Not even any static, just the hum of my quiet engine. 'Hunter?' I say eventually. 'Did you know?'

'No, of course not. What the hell is he thinking? No, I had no idea about this. Nothing at all.'

For a moment I wonder if he's protesting too much.

'Do you know where he might have gone?' I ask. 'His passport is at home.'

'I'm sorry, I've no idea. I'm as floored by this as you are. Let me know if I can do anything.'

Another call is coming through so I end the conversation with Hunter in the hope that the withheld number might be Samuel. It's not. It's Police Officer Sherri Sayed.

'I'm calling to say that we've logged your husband as a missing person.'

I interrupt her. 'He's not. You were right,' I say, trying to stop my voice from breaking. 'I received a message from Samuel a few moments ago. He's leaving me for another woman.'

'Oh,' Sherri Sayed replies. 'I'm sorry to hear that but I'm glad that your husband is safe. In which case we'll close the case.'

'Thanks for your help,' I murmur, before ending the call. Not that they really did anything.

I'm not sure how I make it home, how I'm able to see as the tears splash from my eyes and the sobs choke my throat, but soon enough I'm pulling up at the house I thought I'd be sharing with my husband, at least until the children left home for university. I walk through the back door and sink down onto a kitchen chair, the one that Sherri Sayed sat on only a couple of hours ago. And then I let out a wail and I give in to the feeling of utter betrayal. How could Samuel do this to me?

After a while, my eyes are red and my nose is sore from where I rubbed it with kitchen paper and the sobs ease, even if my chest feels like my heart has been torn out. I go upstairs into our dressing room and I search through every single pocket of every pair of trousers and each jacket that Samuel owns. But I find nothing. No dodgy receipts for hotel rooms or restaurants. I tip our little office upside down, unsure what I'm looking for, and find nothing that might suggest he was having an affair, let alone with whom. Then I go onto the laptop and search through our emails, but I don't have access to Samuel's work emails or his sole bank account. When would he even have time for an affair? He came home to me most nights and he was working crazy hours. Or was he? Perhaps he hasn't been in the office at all, and when he was at home beavering away on his work laptop, perhaps he was conversing with his lover right in front of me. And how long has this relationship been going on? Weeks, months, years even? I think back to our wedding day and those early years when we were so happy. I recall telling him that I would divorce him instantly if he ever cheated on me, but now I think back to that naive young woman and realise that life is more nuanced. We have two children now, a life that is completely interwoven, that can't simply be undone with a single text message. And I think of Kalah and how she perseveres with what most of us perceive to be a broken marriage. Can I be like her?

The front doorbell chimes and I realise I'm standing in a complete mess having tipped the study room upside down. Hurrying to the door, I glance through the side window and see Hunter and Angela standing there, both dressed in dark suits, Hunter holding a large golfing umbrella. What are they doing? It's the middle of the working day, when Hunter should be at his accountancy firm and Angela, who is a family solicitor, helping her divorcing clients.

I open the door, a frown on my face. Hunter can't meet my eyes but Angela is gripping his hand tightly and she yanks him forwards.

'He's got something to say to you,' she says, glowering at her husband.

'I don't know for sure, but I suspected Samuel was having an affair,' Hunter mutters, still unable to meet my gaze.

'I'm sorry, Eva,' Angela says. 'But Hunter rang me from work and told me about the text and that he'd lied to you. I told him in no uncertain terms that our loyalties lie with you, the victim in this, and not your bastard husband.'

I gape at them. Is that what I am? A victim.

'Hunter has to get back to work but I wanted you to hear this from the horse's mouth.'

'Who is she?' My voice is a whisper.

Hunter shrugs his shoulders and meets my eyes for just a nanosecond. 'Sorry, I don't know any detail. It was more a suspicion than a certain knowledge.'

'How long has it been going on for?'

'Again, I don't know, Eva. I'm really sorry. Possibly quite a while.'

'Why were you suspicious?' I ask.

'Just hints of things he said, nothing concrete really.'

I wonder what truths he's hiding and also why he's broken up his working day to come to tell me things he doesn't really know, or is he also lying, covering up for my deceitful husband? I suppose it's the force of nature that is my friend, Angela, who has insisted he talks to me face to face, but I'm not sure I can trust him any more than I can trust Samuel.

'Will you let me know if Samuel contacts you?' I ask.

Hunter nods. 'Piss off back to work,' Angela says, prodding her husband in the arm with her right forefinger. 'I'll see you later.' He hands her the umbrella and then dashes away. I've never seen Hunter move so quickly.

Angela closes the umbrella and leans it against the door frame, stepping forwards as if she's going to push past me into the house, but as much as I love my friend, I need to be alone now. I have to collect my thoughts before doing the school run; practice the fibs I'm going to be telling the children.

'Can we talk at a later date?' I ask, wrapping my arms around myself.

'If you need me to represent you, I'll do it in a jiffy,' Angela says, squeezing my shoulder.

'That seems a bit premature,' I say. I never thought having a divorce lawyer as one of my best friends might prove advantageous.

'Of course, sorry, lovely,' she says, placing both her hands on my shoulders. 'You know you can call me night or day. I'm just so sorry this is happening to you.'

'Did you know?' I ask. 'Or even suspect?'

She shakes her head. 'You know me, Eva. I'd never lie to you. And that's probably why Hunter didn't share his suspicions with me, because he knew I'd tell you the truth.'

'Thanks,' I murmur. She gives me a final squeeze before turning and walking out of our drive.

It isn't until mid-afternoon, by which point I've sobbed and screamed and chucked Samuel's favourite mug onto the floor, shattering it into tiny pieces, that it hits me. All of my husband's belongings are still here. His toothbrush is in the mug on the side of the sink in our en-suite, his wash bag is stashed in the bathroom cupboard. I haven't noticed any clothes that are missing, and even the little bedside clock that he takes with him when he travels, and more importantly, his blood pressure medication, are still on the bedside table. If Samuel is having an affair and has left me, why didn't he take any of his belongings with him? He would have had plenty of opportunity to pack up whilst I was away in Amsterdam. None of this makes any sense whatsoever.

CHAPTER FIVE

THE LOVER

The cottage is small, with just one bedroom and an open-plan kitchen living area. But it's cosy, with wood-lined walls and ceilings, and I've worked so hard to make it homely. I scrubbed the floors and every surface, spending hours in the small bathroom with its antiquated shower and limescale-coated toilet, and the kitchen where mouse droppings lined the insides of the cupboards. Every light bulb was replaced and fitted with a fabric lampshade so there is a gentle glow throughout, and I replaced the moth-eaten curtains with heavy drapes that have blackout linings. But it's in the bedroom where I spent most of my time and money. I put an expensive, down-filled mattress topper on the bed and purchased new linen, a fine cotton with a high thread count.

Samuel loves it. And so he should, considering the effort I've gone to. I found a stack of his favourite thriller books in a second-hand bookshop and they now grace the shelves. The leather-backed gentleman's chair also comes from a second-hand shop, softened with a beautiful sheepskin rug. I want Samuel to be as comfortable as possible. I've piled up his clothes, neatly folding a selection of chinos and polo shirts identical to the ones he normally wears, along with a couple of fine merino sweaters in shades of blue that complement his eyes. It may not look like his grand home, but I've aimed to make it feel like home from home. I've tried to think of everything, even purchasing his toothpaste brand and an electric toothbrush and the delicious woody scent of his ridiculously overpriced aftershave. The transition has to be as smooth as possible.

The kitchen is tiny and simple, but I've bought a few of the recipe books that Eva uses the most often; or at least I assume she does, as her copies are dog-eared and food splattered. Mine on the other hand are pristine. There are three kitchen cupboards. The first houses the crockery and glasses that came with the cottage. The other two are jam-packed full of tins and packets of food; cereals, pasta, long-life milk and everyday provisions to ensure I don't need to go food shopping too often. Unfortunately the fridge is one of those small under-counter types, not big enough really, but it will have to do. I'm following a recipe for chicken carbonara, one of Samuel's favourite meals. As the water is boiling on the two-ring hob, I tiptoe through into the bedroom. The curtains are three-quarters closed, although the light today is grey and murky, so the room is dark. Samuel is fast asleep. I stand there and watch him for a couple of glorious minutes, revelling in the fact that he's here. No. We're here together. He looks so peaceful when he sleeps, his long dark lashes lying against his pale cheeks, the thick beard and moustache which I wish he'd shave off. The duvet has slipped to one side, exposing his hairy chest, but his hands lie relaxed by his sides, the pale band of skin where his wedding ring used to be calling out to be kissed. I restrain myself. Tiptoeing to the side of the bed, I pull up the duvet so his chest is covered and lean over him, placing a gentle kiss on those soft lips, his facial hair tickling my chin.

'Sleep tight, darling,' I murmur. Oh, it would be so easy to tug off my clothes and slip under the bedcovers so I can once again feel his skin on mine. My knees feel weak and a warmth tickles my insides. That's what this man does to me. He melts my body and my heart. I'd happily spend the rest of my life in this bed, wrapped in his arms, making love. But there is more to life, more to relationships than the physical. Samuel murmurs and turns over. For a moment I wonder if his fluttering eyelids will pop open, but no, he settles back into a deep sleep. I turn and tiptoe back to the kitchen, checking the next step in the recipe book. This place may be simple, but it is still our perfect, secret love nest. A place where we can be happy with each other, away from the prying eyes of the world, safe in each other's loving company. I smile as I peel the mushrooms. My dreams really are coming true.

CHAPTER SIX

THE WIFE

It's the day after the text. The moment that may forever define my life into the happy and unhappy, the before and the after. It's as I'm clearing up the breakfast things, having dropped the kids at school, alone again and perhaps for always, that it strikes me. Just because Samuel has left me doesn't mean that he will stop going into work. There's no reason to hide his personal circumstances; no reason not to carry on working. Samuel is proud of Simmons Edge Marketing Agency, and so he should be. He and Jen built up that business into a multi-million-pound agency supporting mid-sized businesses predominantly in the food and wine sectors. Of late, Samuel and I have become competitive about work. Who is working the longest hours? Who is achieving the greatest success? Who is bringing in the most money? Him always, as I'm running a charity. I can see that now, and yet it should never have been that way. Have I pushed him too hard? No. I refuse to become a victim and I refuse to take responsibility for my husband's cowardly behaviour. I pour boiling water from the kettle and miss my cup, the boiling water cascading down the countertop onto my bare foot. I yelp and swear. After dousing the burn with aloe vera gel, it strikes me that Samuel gains his identity from Simmons Edge, so just because he has walked away from me and our family, doesn't mean he'll walk away from the business.

I call the main office number and speak to the new receptionist, a girl called Louise whom I don't know.

'Can I speak to Samuel Simmons,' I say. 'It's his wife speaking.'

There's a pause. 'I'm sorry, Mrs Simmons, but he's off sick.' There's another lengthy pause. 'Oh dear,' she says. 'Have I just put my foot in it? I mean obviously you know he's off sick, don't you?' There's another lengthy pause before she groans, 'Dear God. I'm going to lose this job, aren't I, and I've only been here three weeks. I'm still on probation.'

'It's fine. Of course Samuel is off sick. He's at home right now but I've got so much on my plate, I completely forgot. Your job is safe.'

'Oh, thank goodness. I hope Mr Simmons gets better soon.'

'Just out of interest, did Mr Simmons call in to let you know he was ill?'

'Um, I don't think so. I think Jen said he sent her an email on Monday morning. Something about a sick bug. Must be a nasty one if he's still in bed.' She lowers her voice to a whisper. 'Between you and me, she was livid. She had to do a big presentation by herself. Took it out on the rest of us. Whoops, I'm talking out of turn yet again.'

I'm not sure which of us is more relieved to end that

conversation, but one thing is for sure. Jen needs to fire that loose-talking receptionist.

Simmons Edge Marketing Agency is in a small industrial estate on a farm between Horsham and Billingshurst. A strange location perhaps, but the rent is cheap and it is rare for clients to visit. Samuel, Jen and their senior staff tend to go to their clients, businesses located all over the country. I pull up into the car park, noting Jen's gleaming white Mercedes. At the time I thought it was cute for them to have identical cars in different colours. Now I'm not so sure. I stride up to the glass door and walk into the small reception area. The new receptionist, Louise, has peroxide blonde hair tied up into a topknot and she seems engrossed in something on her phone. I step right up to her and see that she's scrolling through TikTok.

'Excuse me,' I say, and she jolts, slamming her phone screen-down on the desk. 'I'm here to see Jen. I don't have an appointment. Please tell her it's Eva.'

'Um, I'm not sure–'

'I know my way around so I'll head over to her office.' I'm aware that I'm being mean but I'm not in the mood for niceties and this girl doesn't deserve the job.

'Please, just a moment.' She looks at me imploringly before tapping some numbers into her desk phone. I can hear the phone ring and then a muted voice.

'There's an Eva here to see you,' Louise says. 'She doesn't have an appointment.' I can't hear what Jen says but Louise puts the phone down and, with an expression of disappointment, says, 'You can go through.'

I nod and stride towards the double doors behind her. The office space is a square box and Jen and Sam have adjacent offices, smaller square boxes with glass fronts set at the back of the open-plan room. The blinds are down in Sam's office but I stride straight towards Jen's office. She meets me in the doorway.

'Eva,' she says. 'This is a surprise.' She gives me a single kiss on the cheek.

'Can we talk?' I squeeze past her, noting her questioning expression.

'How's Samuel doing?' she asks. 'He must be very sick to be ignoring all of my messages.'

'Mmm,' I say noncommittally. 'How are things going here?'

Jen frowns. She's a tall woman with honey-blonde hair and broad shoulders, the result of her being a champion swimmer in her youth. She's attractive but not beautiful and she has a wardrobe full of crisp white shirts and sharply cut black trousers. I've never seen her dressed in anything else. 'Have a seat.' She gestures towards a red boxy chair. She sits opposite me on the matching sofa. 'Would you like a drink?'

'No, thanks,' I reply. 'I'm worried about Samuel and wanted to have a quick chat with you.'

A look of discomfort passes over her face. 'I hope everything's okay,' she says hurriedly, shifting forwards on the sofa. 'We're re-pitching for the Pellangica account and I really need Samuel's input.'

'Are things a bit stressful around here?' I gaze out of the glass window, looking at the agency's twenty or so staff beavering away at their computers.

She harrumphs. 'If we lose the pitch then there really will be stress. Why? Is Samuel okay? Nothing serious, I hope.'

I wonder if Samuel might have left me for Jen but quickly discount that. They've been colleagues for close on fifteen years and the last I knew, Jen had a long-term girl-friend. It seems disingenuous to ask her anything personal.

'Has he been acting strangely at all? Distracted perhaps?' I don't want to tell Jen about the text message but if anyone is going to know about Samuel's duplicitous life, it would be his business partner.

Jen narrows her eyes at me. 'What's really going on here, Eva? Samuel has gone AWOL and you're here asking questions about him.'

'He's left me,' I say quietly. I chew the edge of a finger-nail. 'I was wondering if you have any inkling as to what's really going on. It's just so unexpected.'

Jen lets out a low whistle and leans back on the sofa. 'Well, that's a shock. I didn't know you had problems,' she says, shaking her head.

'Me neither. It's a complete bolt out of the blue.' Jen throws me a look of pity and it strikes me that from now onwards, that will be the norm. I am someone to be pitied and that sickens me. I wish I hadn't told her; I wish I hadn't come here.

'I was wondering if you knew about this? If you knew who he's leaving me for?'

Jen stands up and starts pacing the room. 'This is as much a surprise to me as it is to you. Yes, he's been a bit distracted the past few weeks, but he's still put in the hours. He hasn't said a word to me. I mean, your photo takes pride of place on his desk.'

I'd like to ask if I can search his office, look for evidence of this other woman, but I know I can't. It appears too desperate.

'He isn't particularly close to a client, is he?' I suggest. 'He's talked a lot about the Pellangica account and the meeting he had in London last week. He seemed positive about that.'

Jen scoffs. 'I'm not sure about a meeting in London but our two contacts at Pellangica are men and no, I'm almost positive he's not having a relationship with anyone from work.' She pauses for a moment and then swivels to face me. 'But why is he off sick and why hasn't he returned any of *my* calls?'

'I think he might be having a bit of a breakdown,' I say.

'What bloody timing,' Jen mutters under her breath, which seems a bit harsh, even to my ears. She must catch my expression of dismay because she quickly says, 'Sorry, Eva. It's just I really need him.'

So do I, I think. 'If you hear from him, will you let me know?' I ask.

'Of course.' She strides across the room and when I stand up she envelopes me in a big hug. 'What a bastard,' she says, releasing me. 'When I see him, I'll knock some sense into the idiot.'

Back at home, I send Samuel another text message.

> Call me urgently. The very least you owe me is an explanation.

That's the eighth message I've sent and, like all the previous ones, it remains unread, with a single little grey tick next to it. Clearly his phone is off and he doesn't have the guts to switch it back on. I always thought Samuel had a backbone. He is many things, but I never thought he would be a coward. I remember when Riley was being bullied at school by the daughter of a friend of mine, Samuel went to meet her parents and resolved everything face to face. When our next-door neighbour in the first house we lived in after getting married threw a punch at his girlfriend, Samuel was around there, restraining the guy, having already rung the police. He's able to deal with difficult situations face-on, so this running away from me just doesn't feel right. On the other hand, if he is under unfathomable pressure from the other woman, whoever the bitch might be, and he's really having some sort of a breakdown, then none of his behaviour will be normal. Perhaps I should be pitying him, worried rather than hurt and angry.

But all I want to know right now is who the hell she is. Whom has he left me for?

I decide to search the house again from top to bottom. I can't believe that Samuel won't have left some breadcrumbs, little mistakes that I might not have noticed before but which now may lay a trail to the truth. Even though I've already looked through his pockets, I start in his wardrobe, literally pulling every single item out and dumping his clothes in a massive pile on our bed. His shoes are in plastic see-through boxes and I chuck them across the floor. It's then that I see it. A silver bag, its handles tied together with a neat white satin bow. I lift the bag up. It's small, about the size of a paperback book, and it's light. I place it on top of the dresser and carefully undo the bow, a sickening feeling in my gut. Inside is a navy velvet box and an envelope. The envelope isn't sealed, so I slide the card out. The words on the front are written in a silver flowery script:

On Our Anniversary.

I gulp as I remember that it is indeed our anniversary in a fortnight's time. Fifteen years. The words on the inside of the card say:

To my love on our anniversary. I love you with all my heart, my body and soul, and with the passing of the years, it's only you who makes me whole.

He hasn't signed it yet. I slip the card back into the envelope and open the little velvet box. Inside lies a stunning diamond necklace. There is one single diamond, circular shaped, attached to a delicate platinum chain. It looks expensive. Very expensive. I grab my phone and search for the symbol of fifteen years of marriage. It's crystal. But knowing Samuel, crystal won't be good enough; he's bought me a diamond instead. I close the lid and put the box and envelope back in the bag.

This doesn't make sense. Why would Samuel buy me such an expensive gift for our anniversary and then promptly leave me? Has this new relationship been a recent thing or has his mistress given him an ultimatum perhaps? Or is this gift meant for her, whoever she might be? No. My gut tells me this is for me; an anniversary present, perhaps an expensive gift to ease his conscience.

My phone rings and my heart leaps. Is this Samuel? I remember wondering whether we would get a sixth sense if anything terrible happened to either of us because our bond was so strong. So much for relying on my gut instinct.

It's not Samuel. It's Kalah. 'Hello,' I say, but even I can hear the disappointment in my voice.

'Is everything alright?' she asks, and just those words uttered by my gentle friend push me over the edge and I start crying.

'Not really,' I say through sniffs.

'Are you at home?' she asks.

'Yes.' My voice sounds strangled.

'I'm coming right over.' She hangs up on me before I can object.

Fifteen minutes later, the kettle is boiling and Kalah is sitting at our kitchen table. The words just tumble out of my mouth.

'Samuel has left me for another woman. He sent me a message and has done a runner. He needs some time to sort out his head apparently,' I say.

Shock passes across Kalah's face. Of the four of us close friends, we all assumed that it would be Kalah's marriage that would disintegrate; I certainly never imagined it would be mine.

'Oh, darling,' she says, reaching across the table to squeeze my hand as I sit down, cups of steaming coffee in front of us. 'Just because he says it's the end of your marriage doesn't mean it really is. I mean, Xavier has had three affairs, and those are only the ones I know about.' She stares ruefully out of the kitchen window. It's windy outside and the trees are visibly swaying, branches heavy with early summer leaves.

'I don't know why you stay with him,' I murmur.

'For Autumn. It would break her heart for us to split up, having to live in two houses, and all that instability. I've just come to accept that Xavier is unable to be faithful, yet I know he truly loves me and despite the affairs he will never leave me. It's not the marriage I dreamed of, but I simply can't imagine my life without him.'

'It seems that I don't get any choice,' I say bitterly.

'I'm sure Samuel will see sense and come back to you soon. He's obviously just having a mid-life crisis. Time is the greatest healer.'

I wish Kalah would stop with her platitudes because I

very much doubt Samuel will come back to me, or more to the point, whether I'll accept him back. I'm not like Kalah. Once someone crosses me I find it hard to forgive, and Samuel knows that. But that is an attitude of such finality and I can't bear the thought of life without my husband. I'm so confused, I can't think straight.

'Would you like me to take Riley and Alfie to their swimming class?' Kalah asks. I shiver. I'd completely forgotten that it's after-school swimming today. Samuel has two non-negotiable parenting tasks: taking the kids swimming and coming with me to parent-teacher meetings.

Over the years, I've tried to overcome my fear of the water, even having a couple of hypnotherapy sessions shortly after Riley was born, but perhaps I haven't tried hard enough. It's not just the water that terrifies me and the knowledge that if I fall in, I'm unlikely to get out again alive, but it's everything that surrounds it. The choking smell of chlorine especially prevalent in indoor pools makes me want to throw up; the loud reverberating noise of kids shouting and splashing, the terror that if Riley or Alfie get into trouble, I won't be able to save them. I think I've been successful in hiding my phobia from the kids. Samuel and I agreed that they should both learn to swim as soon as they could, and Samuel introduced them to the water when they were babies. Ironically, Alfie has just joined the school swimming team and I fear I'm going to have to attend his swimming galas whether I like it or not. Samuel was surprisingly kind to me about my fear; no honeymoon to the Maldives for us. Instead we went on a skiing holiday to Switzerland, staying in a cosy chalet halfway up a mountain. And Samuel always finishes work early on a Wednesday so he can take the kids to their after-school classes. I wonder for a moment whether he'll be at the school gates, ready to collect them as normal, because even though he's hurting me, surely he wouldn't hurt the children?

'Eva?' Kalah nudges me.

'Um, yes?'

'Shall I take your two swimming?'

'Thank you, that would be great.'

'I'll collect them from school and take them straight to the pool.'

'If Samuel is there, will you call me?' I ask.

'Of course,' she promises.

CHAPTER SEVEN

THE LOVER

While the coffee is brewing, I'm squeezing some oranges to make Samuel fresh orange juice. He mentioned that he never has it at home because it's too much of a hassle; the implication being that Eva is too lazy to make it for him. The bacon is sizzling nicely and making my stomach rumble and the eggs are boiling hard. Samuel likes boiled eggs the best, very well done. I've laid out a tray and even picked a rhododendron flower off a bush that's out in full glory further down the lane. The toast pops out of the toaster, startling me, but I hum as I spread butter and thick marmalade over it, placing two slices on a small side plate. When everything is ready, I put all the food, the plastic glass full of sweet orange juice and a steaming mug of coffee on a tray. I fold a paper napkin and place the purple flower on top of it. Other than the lack of starched white linen and gleaming silver cutlery, this could be a breakfast made by a five-star hotel. Smiling, I pick up the tray and carefully walk towards the bedroom.

'Wake up, darling,' I say, as I place the tray on the end of the bed. 'I've made your favourite breakfast.' I walk to the window and pull back the curtains, letting in rays of sunshine that highlight a cloud of dust motes. I'll need to clean in here again.

'Where...' Samuel's voice is croaky and his eyelids flutter as if he's struggling to open his eyes. I hurry to the bedside and kneel down next to him.

'Hey, sweetheart,' I say, stroking his forehead. It's still warm. 'Would you like a sip of freshly squeezed orange juice?'

He turns his head from side to side as if he's confused, groggy. Which he probably is. 'What's going...?'

I interrupt him by placing a gentle kiss on his lips. 'It's alright, darling. You've not been well. You need to stay calm. I've made your favourite breakfast and I'm sure once you've got some food in your belly you'll feel much better.'

'But...'

'Hey, no talking,' I say, running my index finger over his dry lips. 'Everything will be much clearer when you're feeling more yourself.'

He's restless and I have to hold onto the tray to make sure the drinks don't spill over. I stroke his forehead and eyelids gently, placing little kisses on his forehead, around his earlobe, exactly as he likes it. 'You don't need to worry,' I say. I take his right hand and stroke the top of it with my fingers. 'I've taken care of everything. Shall I shift your pillows slightly so that you can eat?'

He nods, his beautiful dark eyes never leaving my face. I support his shoulders with one hand and ease the pillows up with the other, helping him shift upwards in bed. He looks very pale and he yawns, his eyelids flickering closed again.

'Come on, darling. You need to get some food inside you. It was all a bit much, wasn't it? Believe me, you'll feel better with a full stomach.' I reach for the tray and place it on my lap. I'm sitting on the side of the bed, staring at this beautiful man. I pick up the glass of orange juice and hand it to him, but he seems to be lacking any strength and his hand falls away. Instead, I hold the glass up to his lips.

'Drink, sweetheart. Just a few little sips.'

His eyes flicker open as the edge of the glass presses against his lips and he opens his mouth, swallowing a few mouthfuls. But then his face goes even paler and contorts somehow and he turns suddenly, away from me, and vomits the drink all over my side of the bed.

'Shit,' he mumbles, wiping his mouth with the back of his hand. 'Sorry.'

'Oh darling,' I say, placing the tray of food on the floor. I guess I'll be eating it alone. 'Let me get some towels to clean you up, and we'll need to change the linen. Shall I help you to the bathroom?'

He nods, but he looks very grey and for a moment I'm worried. 'Swing your legs out of the bed,' I say, supporting his shoulders. 'Are you dizzy?'

'A bit,' he mutters. I help him to the bathroom, slowly, surely, with love.

Whilst Samuel is in the shower, I strip the sheets, shoving them into a black bin liner, because I don't have a washing machine here and will have to deal with them later. I open the window to let some fresh air in and then remake the bed with fresh linen, plumping the pillows up, taking the tray back to the little kitchen. When the water stops flowing, I knock gently on the bathroom door.

'Are you finished, love?' I ask.

'Yes,' he says. So I open the door and support him as he stumbles slightly back to the freshly made bed. He's wearing a fresh pair of pyjamas, ones that I left out for him on the little stool in the shower room.

'That's better,' I say, as I help him ease his legs under the duvet. 'I've popped a rehydrate tablet into this water. You'll need to drink it so as to settle your stomach.' Samuel's eyes flicker closed. I'll let him sleep a bit but then he really must finish the drink.

'Everything will be okay,' I say, stroking the back of his hand. His breathing settles into a slow, regular pattern and slowly a little colour returns to his cheeks. I sit for what could be minutes or hours. I don't care. This is a dream come true; just the two of us together, me taking care of him, my heart expanding with love in a way that I simply didn't know was possible.

'I love you so much,' I murmur, wondering whether Samuel can hear my words in his sleep. If he was awake, I imagine what he'd be saying to me. 'I love you too, my darling.' And then he'd take me in his arms, lay me down next to him and slowly remove my clothes, making love to me in a way that is both tender and passionate.

CHAPTER EIGHT

THE LOVER

Twelve hours have passed and Samuel is still not well. I'm getting a bit worried. I feel his forehead, which is cooler now, so I doubt he has a fever, but he is still so sleepy. I've made him chicken soup from the carcass of a chicken. It's been boiling away for hours, so it should be full of fine nutrients. I pop a couple of pieces of bread into the toaster. Hopefully he'll be able to keep all of this down because visiting a doctor is most certainly not part of the plan. Pouring some chicken broth into a mug, I take it and the plate of toast back to the bedroom. Samuel's eyes flicker open when he sees me and I think I spot the slightest glimmer of a smile. What a relief! He must be feeling better.

'How's the stomach?' I ask as I sit down on the mattress next to him, but he shuffles his legs and a drop of steaming soup splutters out of the mug, burning the back of my hand. 'Hey,' I say, frowning. 'Please be careful.'

'I'm worried.' His words still sound slightly jumbled and if I didn't know him so well I wonder if I'd be able to make out what he's saying. 'The kids. Riley. Alfie.'

'I know, darling. But you don't need to worry about them. They're with Eva.'

'They'll be wondering where I am,' he whispers. 'Worried.'

'I expect they think you're away on a business trip, so busy, making money, worrying about them unnecessarily. You know what children are like; utterly self-absorbed, I doubt they'll give your absence a moment's thought.' Except they probably will wonder where their dad is. I just hope they will come to realise that they are very much part of this plan and that their futures have been carefully considered too. 'Now try to have a few sips of the chicken soup. It will do you good.'

I hold the mug up to Samuel's lips and he takes a couple of sips.

'Taste good?' I ask. He nods.

'Where's my phone?' he murmurs.

'Oh come on, darling. We've talked about this. You lost your phone when you were out drinking with your friends on Monday night. Have you forgotten already?' He frowns and I can tell that his memory isn't what it should be. I'm rather disheartened that he's even asking, because of course he can't talk to the children; of course he can't use his phone. I'm not a complete idiot. The moment he switches it on, the police will be able to see where he is, and I'm never going to let that happen. A wave of disappointment flows through me. This isn't the Samuel I know and love.

'I need to go home,' he says, after nibbling a few bites of toast.

No. No. No. What's the matter with him? What am I going to do? I stare at him and he looks away from me. I can't let him go there, so I use the oldest trick in the book. Gently,

I take the mug of soup out of his hands and lean forwards to kiss him. His lips yield after a few moments and I'm kissing him properly. My hands are all over his body, caressing, tickling, moving further downwards. When I feel his body begin to acquiesce, I kneel up on the mattress and slowly remove my clothes. We make love. Beautiful love, exactly how I dreamed we would, and I feel such joy as I realise how much Samuel wants me. Needs me. We belong together in body, mind and spirit. When it's over, I can't stop smiling.

'Do you feel better now?' I ask, my fingers playing with the hair on his chest. He doesn't say anything but he does let out a satiated sigh. It feels so good.

'How's your head?' I ask.

'Still sore,' he murmurs.

I lean across him, my skin grazing over his, creating goosebumps and a surge of desire in both of us. I open a packet of pills and drop a couple into his glass of water.

'Drink this, darling,' I say, holding the glass up to his lips. 'It'll make you feel better.'

'Not sure. Need to go home.'

'Drink this,' I say more forcefully this time. That shiver of desire has quickly turned to annoyance. He parts his lips and swallows the liquid in two big gulps.

As his body relaxes back into sleep, I watch him, this beautiful man who is now mine. I wait until I'm sure he is in a deep sleep, and then I slide out of bed. I pull the curtains and switch off the bedroom light before shutting the door behind me. In the living room, I curl up on the small sofa and switch on my phone. I stare at my favourite photo, the one I have digitally manipulated. Samuel is standing there, wearing jeans and a T-shirt, a broad smile on his face, those midnight eyes sparkling. In front of him stand Riley and

Alfie. They're wearing T-shirts and shorts, both of them grinning too as if something hilarious has just happened. And then there's me. I'm standing behind them, smiling as well. If you look very carefully you can see that the background doesn't match one hundred percent, but that's because I had to cut Eva out and superimpose a picture of me. The more I look at this, the more I know that we belong together. Our beautiful family of four. Soon, I won't have to superimpose my photograph. Soon it'll be me standing there for real, my hands gently laying on the children's shoulders, Samuel's arm around my waist, all of us laughing joyfully.

Everything has gone so well this far. The cottage, my handsome, loving Samuel; our cosy love nest. But now I need to put the second part of the plan into action. I unfurl my legs and pad barefoot to the kitchenette. I open the second drawer along, the one that holds the kitchen implements, sliding out the large, sharp carving knife, the razor-edged blade held away from me. The tool that I bought a fortnight ago especially for the next part of the plan.

CHAPTER NINE

THE WIFE

It's 6 a.m. and I've had another sleepless night. Following that initial text from Samuel, I've heard nothing more, despite the numerous messages and voicemails I've left him. And now I'm veering from broken-hearted to angry. How dare he walk away from fifteen years of marriage with a single text. How dare he walk out on our children. He has never gone this long without speaking to them. Even on the nights he went away for business – which wasn't often – or the long weekends he went away with his friends skiing or playing golf. He would always call home and wish the kids goodnight. I thought he loved Riley and Alfie as deeply as I do. But clearly not. If he can walk away from them this easily then he doesn't deserve to be their parent. It's been horrible having to field their questions, having to lie about their dad. I've told them that he's on a business trip in a remote part of Asia where there is no phone signal and where the hour change is such that our day is his night. What a bunch of untruths. It sickens me. And I know Riley doesn't believe me. 'Doesn't Dad's hotel have Wi-Fi?' she asked. 'Why's he not even looked at my WhatsApp messages?'

I'm debating whether to doze for another thirty minutes or so, when my phone pings. I'm alert immediately, and grab it off the bedside table, sitting up in bed. It's a message from a number I don't recognise. I click on it.

Get Snapchat.

What the hell? Who is telling me to get Snapchat and why? It's not an app I've ever used and I've forbidden the kids from having it, at least until Riley is thirteen and at senior school. I reply.

Who is this?

It's about Samuel. Get Snapchat.

My fingers are trembling as I try calling the number the text message has come from. It goes straight to a generic voicemail. What should I do? I know nothing about Snapchat other than it's used predominantly by teenagers and messages disappear as soon as you've read them. I navigate to the app store and download it, following the prompts to input my name, my email and to create my avatar. I don't bother with that and just swipe through the screens as quickly as possible, concerned that I'm allowing access to my photos, my camera and goodness knows what else. But then I reassure myself: I can delete the app at any time. When I've finished, it asks permission to access my contact list. I decline. I'm expecting the ping of an alert but nothing happens. After staring at my phone for a couple of minutes, I get out of bed and go into our ensuite bathroom, bringing the mobile phone with me and placing it on the edge of the sink. Just as I've picked up my toothbrush and squeezed on the toothpaste, the phone pings with an alert, making me drop the toothbrush into the sink. It's a Snapchat message. My first.

The breath catches in my throat as I press the button. Up pops a photo. A photo that takes me a moment to fully understand. It's of Samuel. His eyes are closed and his head is on a pillow, his beard longer than before. He looks peaceful, except there's the jagged point of a knife right up against his throat; a huge, terrifying carving knife. I whimper as I stare at the photograph. It doesn't make sense. Why is Samuel lying there with the blade of a knife up against his throat?

And then the phone rings and the photo of my husband vanishes. I stare at the phone in my hand as if it's a weapon, the ringing sounds too loud in the quiet of the early morning.

'Hello,' I answer, as I clutch the edge of the sink with the fingers of my left hand.

'Listen very carefully.' The voice is deep, weirdly computerised, a bit like a robot, so distorted it takes a moment to understand what the person is saying. 'Are you listening?'

'Yes,' I say. 'Samuel, is it you? Are you being stupid?'

'If you want to see Samuel alive again, do not involve the police, otherwise you'll be putting Samuel and your children at risk. Do you understand?'

'What? Who are you and what do you want?' I ask breathlessly. 'Where is Samuel? Put him on the line.'

My requests are ignored. 'Do exactly what I tell you and complete the bucket list.'

'The bucket list!' I exclaim. *What bucket list?* 'Is this a joke?' If so, it's not funny. Not in the slightest.

'This is not a joke. It is deadly serious. Do what I tell you, otherwise Samuel will die. Do not involve the police. If you do, Samuel will die.'

'Who is this?' I bark, but the call has ended and there's silence. What the hell is going on? I stare at my phone, willing it to yield some answers, but the screen is dark and there is nothing new on Snapchat. I don't understand. Two days ago, I received a message from Samuel, sent from his phone number, telling me he was leaving me. Yet now, I get a message suggesting that he's being held captive. A message telling me not to involve the police. The memory of that photograph of Samuel sleeping so peacefully with that horrific blade at his neck makes me shiver violently. I pull on my dressing gown and tie it tightly around my waist, trying to stop my body from trembling, and then perch on the edge of the bath. I can't make sense of these messages, that horrible, dalek-sounding voice. And what was that about a bucket list?

Did Samuel and I ever talk about bucket lists? Perhaps years ago, prior to having children, but we certainly haven't discussed them of late. What would have been on his? Sailing across the Atlantic, probably; riding a Harley Davidson across Europe; playing golf on some amazing course. And mine? Right now I can't think of anything. All I want is to know that Samuel is safe, whether he's really left me or not. I shiver.

My phone rings again. 'Yes,' I answer, my voice cracking. Is it the same number as before, or another one? Either way, I don't recognise it.

'Bucket list number one. Change your Facebook status to

single.' It's the same computerised male voice as before, monotone and expressionless. 'Then go out on the town with your girlfriends and post photos on Instagram Stories showing you're having a great time. Do not tell anyone about these messages.'

'But why?' I ask, completely bemused.

'If you want Samuel, Riley and Alfie to remain safe, just do it. No questions. No police.' And then the call ends. I feel completely sick that this person knows the names of our children, that he is threatening my family. But why do I have to go out on the town and pretend to have a good time? This ridiculous game doesn't make any sense. And is that photo of Samuel for real? I wish I could look at it again, study it carefully for any telltale signs that it might have been photoshopped or AI generated. I search online to see if you can retrieve pictures sent on Snapchat so that I can screenshot it. The answer is no. The only thing that remains is my memory of the photo and the echo of that horrible voice.

'Mum, where's my school blazer?' I emerge into my bedroom to see Alfie standing there half dressed. I glance at the clock. It's gone 7 a.m., the time when I get the kids up.

'I'm running a bit late,' I say, dropping my phone facedown onto of the bed. 'I'll be with you in a minute.' I pull on yesterday's clothes and hurry downstairs to the kitchen, quickly pulling cereal boxes out of the larder and shoving bread into the toaster. I want to re-listen to the messages, to analyse them, tuning in to any familiar inflections or unusual word choices, but I can't. All I remember are the instructions that I've got to go out with my girlfriends, pretend to have a good time, and post the pictures to my Instagram Stories.

I don't use social media very much. In fact, the only time I regularly post onto Instagram is when we're doing big fundraising initiatives for Leap Ahead, or when we open new premises and invite local bigwigs to cut the ribbon. Very occasionally I post a family photo to Facebook, normally when we're on holiday and I haven't got anything better to do.

Once again, it's difficult to give the children the attention they deserve, and when I've dropped them off at school, I head home to freshen up and to think. My instinct is to go straight to the police, except I can't stop thinking about the photo of Samuel with the knife at his throat. If this was a normal kidnapping – normal, of course, being a ridiculous word to use in these circumstances – then surely the kidnappers would be demanding money as a ransom. And in a sick kind of way, I could understand that. I come from a wealthy family, not that Samuel and I are dripping in wealth; we both work hard for what we have. That privilege belongs to my mother thanks to the extraordinary business acumen of my father, who started life buying and doing up derelict terraced houses and ended life a multi-millionaire, having sold his hugely profitable renewable energy business. On my mother's passing, a large portion of that will come to me. As Dad's success is public knowledge, it would be understandable if the kidnapper was demanding money for Samuel. Perhaps they are toying with me initially and they still will.

Another horrible thought slams into my mind. Has the kidnapper contacted Mum? After all, she's the one with the ready cash. We don't have the easiest of relationships but she adores Samuel and I have no doubt that she'd hand over a million pounds if she had it. The truth is, I've no idea how much money Dad left Mum. She lives a very comfortable life but whenever I asked her whether she needed any assistance with her financial affairs, she shrugged me off, saying her financial advisor is excellent and she knows what she's doing. But what if the kidnapper knows that and is demanding cash from Mum? I take a deep breath and call her.

'To what do I owe the pleasure?' she asks. Mum is an expert in passive aggression and despite knowing that, it still gets to me.

'Just calling to see how you are,' I say.

'That's kind of you. How are Samuel and the children?'

'They're fine, thanks. I was wondering if you've had any strange phone calls recently?' I ask.

'Strange phone call? What sort of phone call?' I hear the confusion in her voice. 'Should I have done?'

'I was worried because there's been a spate of nasty nuisance calls and a friend's mother has been pestered.'

She scoffs. 'I just hang up when those idiots ask me if my computer is broken or pretend to be calling from the bank.' I shouldn't really be worried because Mum's always had a good bullshit detector; she learned that from Dad.

'That's a relief. You'll let me know if anything unusual happens,' I urge.

'Is Stephen alright?' Despite everything, she always asks after my brother.

'Yes, Mum. He's fine.'

She lets out an exhale but it does nothing to dispel my unease.

'Are you still coming for lunch on Sunday?'

'Of course,' I promise, just relieved that Mum, at least, sounds normal.

After taking a quick shower and getting dressed in work clothes, I use my phone to log in to Facebook. Do people even list their relationship status anymore? I navigate to the About section and find the Relationship tab. I see that it's set to Married; something I must have done all those years ago when I first set up a Facebook account. I click edit and choose the Single tab. It creates a hard knot in my stomach. I then go onto WhatsApp and the group chat I have with Kalah, Angela and Nicolette.

I rewrite the message several times before settling on this version:

> *In case you haven't already heard my news, Samuel has left me for another woman. I'd love a night out on the town to forget about it. Subject to babysitters, I can do any evening. Ex*

How I wish I could tell my best friends the truth; that I'm being hounded by some weird kidnapper and Samuel may well be in deadly danger. I'd do anything for their support right now.

My phone rings almost immediately. It's Angela.

'Is Samuel still missing in action?' she asks.

'Yup.' The image of him asleep with that knife flickers through my mind. If I'm going to share my horrible situation with anyone, it would be Angela. As a solicitor, she'll be the friend most likely to know what to do. 'I assume Hunter hasn't heard from him?' I ask.

'No, and believe me, you'd be the first to know if he does. I'm so sorry, Eva. Is there anything I can do?'

'It's kind of you but I'm still in the shock stage. I can't believe I didn't suspect anything, but I really didn't.' I wonder now if the reason I didn't harbour any doubt is because Samuel isn't having an affair after all. But then I recall Hunter's words and how he's been suspicious that Samuel was playing away for some time. Could Hunter be wrong? Could something else be going on in Samuel's life that has led to him being kidnapped? Does Samuel have money problems that I don't know about? A gambling habit perhaps that he's been hiding from me?

'What a bastard,' Angela mutters. 'Look. Are you sure you want to hit the town? It's kind of early days. Samuel's only just told you he was leaving.'

'I'm completely sure,' I say squeezing my eyes tightly shut, relieved that Angela can't see my face. Because no, I'm not sure at all. In fact going out for a meal with my girl-friends is the very last thing I feel like doing. I'd rather march to the police station and demand that they investigate what the hell is going on, and then I'd like to stay at home with Riley and Alfie, the doors bolted and the windows locked, secure and together until Samuel is returned to us safe and sound.

After a flurry of messages, we agree to meet up on Saturday evening. Frankly I'm not sure how I manage to function in the intervening days; on automatic, I suppose. I go to work where I make mistakes and get the strangest looks from Luke. Luke is my right-hand man, who effectively runs the day-to-day operations for Leap Ahead. He's mid-thirties, super-efficient and passionate about giving young people opportunities. At his initial interview, he explained that if it hadn't been for a neighbour offering the then fifteen-year-old Luke a job as a pot washer in a local restaurant, he, like many of his friends, would have ended up in a gang, a drug addict and quite probably an early death. If he'd had a Leap Ahead in his neighbourhood, the lives of many young men he knew would have turned out fundamentally different.

I collect the children from school, make their supper and help them with their homework, all the while fielding off questions as to the whereabouts of their father. Meanwhile, I'm on tenterhooks waiting for another message to arrive on Snapchat, but I hear nothing until Friday at midnight. I've just dozed off to sleep when the ringing of my phone jolts me awake. I grab the phone. It's from another number I don't recognise. With a pounding heart I click answer.

'You've got forty-eight hours to post photos of yourself on Instagram. Get a move on if you want to save Samuel.' Once again, it's that computer-generated male voice.

'Who are you?' I ask. 'And why are you doing this?' I demand but I'm talking to a dead line.

I lie awake for most of the night debating whether or not to go to the police. How will the kidnapper know that I've contacted the police? Are they listening to my phone calls or are there listening devices in my house? Is there a tracker on my car? Surely that's only the stuff of TV and films? But so is this crazy situation I'm in. I make a decision. I'm going to call the police from work. I'm confident that I'm not being tracked there.

The next morning, I shut myself in my office and call the number on the business card that Sherri Sayed handed me. She answers quickly, although I note an edge of impatience to her voice.

'What can I do for you, Mrs Simmons?'

'Since I told you that my husband had left me for another woman, I've received a photograph of him asleep with a knife to his neck and I've received messages demanding that I go out on the town with my friends. Someone has kidnapped my husband and wants me to fulfil a bucket list.'

There's a long silence on the other end of the phone.

'Right,' she says, dragging the word out. 'Is anyone in immediate danger?'

'My husband. The photo showed a knife at his neck.'

'Okay. Can you forward me the photo.'

'Unfortunately not. It was sent via Snapchat.'

'I see.' Her voice is heavy with doubt. 'And you say that the message asked you to go out on the town with your friends. What is so bad about that?'

'Um, nothing per se,' I admit. 'But Samuel has been kidnapped. I know it seems weird.'

'Yes. Not exactly a ransom demand, is it? Look, Mrs Simmons, unless you can prove to me that a crime has been committed or is about to be committed, or that someone is in danger, there's nothing that I can do.'

'I can give you the name of the Snapchat account and the telephone numbers they called me on. The Snapchat account is ISEEU975783.' I start reeling off the numbers but Sherri Sayed cuts me off.

'I'm sorry, Mrs Simmons, but we need to be sure that your husband or yourself are being threatened with harm, otherwise it isn't a police matter. You mentioned that your husband is having an affair. Perhaps this is part of that. Some unpleasant game that your ex is playing.'

A sharp bolt runs through me at the use of her word, ex. Samuel is my husband. Of course, she's right insofar as I have no evidence, but at the same time she's wrong. That photograph of Samuel was horrific. And now I wish I hadn't called her. I feel a complete idiot because it's obvious she thinks I'm demented, a time waster, struggling to cope with my marriage breakdown. And on the surface, that's exactly how it looks, because I have no actual evidence. Except I know something extremely sinister is going on even if it's impossible for me to prove it.

'Sorry to have wasted your time,' I say and quickly end the call.

I've arranged for Mandy, our next-door neighbour's sixteen-year-old daughter, to babysit my two. I'd thought about asking Stephen, but he mentioned he's out tonight and I don't like to take advantage of my brother's generosity, and besides, he deserves to be having some fun. Nevertheless, I'm nervous about leaving Mandy in charge, despite the fact she's babysat for us numerous times previously. The kidnapper might be watching, knowing that I'm out of the house, and I'm terrified I'm putting the kids at risk. But what else can I do?

I wear a simple black dress, one of my staples that has long sleeves and stops just above the knee. I pair it with high suede boots and a chunky gold necklace that I bought at a market stall in Amsterdam. My face looks grey and exhausted, a reflection of my emotions, so I daub on more makeup than usual, lengthening my eyelashes with black mascara and swiping a raspberry-coloured lipstick over my lips. All things considered, I don't look too bad. I take a quick selfie, pouting ever so slightly, but I look ridiculous and delete it. The photos can wait until later.

The über arrives on time and I tell Mandy to lock all the doors and keep them locked, not responding to the doorbell unless it's me. She scowls and I mutter something about some burglaries in the area. I hope I haven't scared her. I've made sure that the Ring doorbells are working correctly so I can check from afar if anyone approaches the house.

We've agreed to meet at a busy bistro in the centre of Horsham, ironically just a few doors down from the pub

Samuel went to with Hunter. Kalah and Angela are already seated at a circular table in the window. I wish we weren't sitting in such an exposed spot, but I can hardly explain why I want us to move. After embracing both of my friends, I sit down with my back to the window and a good view of the door. The noise levels are high from the excited chatter of the clientele, and cheesy Italian love songs play on repeat through the sound system. A server arrives and we order three margaritas for my friends and a gin and tonic for me – the drinks we always choose in this bistro. Nicolette turns up last, slipping into the chair next to me. She's looking exceptionally beautiful this evening in a pale turquoise sweater that drapes just under her bare shoulders and sets off the auburn tones in her hair.

There are a lot of people at the bar and all the tables are full. The bistro is humming but it takes a frustratingly long time for our drinks to arrive. Eventually, a frazzled server arrives with a tray. I take a long sip of my gin and tonic. I need it.

'Bloody hell, Eva,' Nicolette says, grabbing my hand. 'Out of all of us, I would have put my money on you and Samuel staying married until the end of time. What a bolt out of the blue.'

'Um, excuse me!' Angela says, with a twinkle in her eye. 'What about me and Hunter?'

Nicolette laughs and takes a large gulp of wine. 'I'm really sorry, Eva. What a bastard. Do you know who *she* is?'

'Nope, I know nothing,' I say. 'And honestly, I'd rather not think about my marriage or rather its breakdown. I'd just like to have a good time with my besties.' I raise my glass into the air.

'I think you're very brave,' Kalah says, her eyes downcast.

I wish I could tell her the truth; that I don't feel brave at all. I feel like a fraudster. After taking a sip of wine, I delve into my handbag and take out my phone, relieved to see that I haven't received any messages. 'Would you mind taking a pic of me,' I say, handing my phone to Nicolette. 'I want to stick two fingers up into the air.'

'You're a trooper,' Angela says, her eyes large. 'I'm not sure that any of my clients are as brave as you.'

'Cheese!' Nicolette grins brightly, holding my phone high in the air to get a photo of me with my raised glass. It feels so hard to smile, to make it appear real. She takes a couple of photos and hands my phone back to me. Out of the corner of my eye, I can sense Kalah's frown. Of the three of them, it's obvious she's the most concerned about my out-of-character behaviour.

I drink my gin and tonic and when a bottle of wine arrives, I pour myself a large glass of that. Perhaps I can switch off the turmoil of feelings by losing myself in alcohol. We order from the extensive menu but when my bavette steak comes with thin crisps and a small rocket salad, I can barely manage a few mouthfuls.

Kalah puts a hand on my arm. 'You're not okay, are you?' she whispers, giving me her intense, concerned stare.

'Of course she's not okay,' Angela says. 'Her bastard of a husband has just left her, and I am going to get her the best divorce settlement of my career.'

I shiver. 'Maybe it won't come to that,' I say softly. Angela throws me her "don't be so ridiculous" look.

'We always assume that it's women who go through mid-life crises, but men do too,' Kalah announces. 'When we're young, we assume we're going to reach certain goal posts by a particular age. You know, like getting married at 30, having children by the time you're 35.'

'Speak for yourself,' Nicolette mutters.

Kalah ignores her. 'It's like Xavier thought he'd make partner by the time he was thirty, or my brother assumed he was going to run his own business, sell it for a few million and retire at fifty. Angela, I remember you saying that Hunter intended to take early retirement, buy a boat and sail across the Atlantic. It's all pipe dreams, isn't it? Life gets in the way, we become laden down by disappointments. And to compound matters we become increasingly aware of our own mortality. A contemporary dies and it makes us realise that life is short and we've failed to meet our own goals. It's the same for men. They become disappointed in themselves, their lack of achievements, and wonder, is this really it? Do I want to be with the same woman for the rest of my life? Is my life all responsibilities and limited fun? And then we become the squeezed generations, caring for our children and our elderly parents at the same time, leaving no time or disposable income to achieve our personal dreams. It's hardly surprising that men think the grass is greener and walk away from their marriages.' We're all slack-jawed. Is that what she really thinks?

'Wow, you're portraying your life as a barrel of laughs,' Nicolette says.

'Kalah might be right,' Angela mutters. 'It's the classic cause of divorce – men wanting to recapture their youth. But it doesn't excuse what Samuel has done. Ending a marriage by text message is unforgivable. Did you even know he was unhappy, Eva?'

I shake my head and for once I can be truthful. 'I knew he was stressed but I had no idea about anything else. That's why I'm going to drink and be merry, and I'd like you all to join me!' I raise my glass again.

Kalah frowns at me. 'You're burying your head in the sand,' she announces. I bite my lip thinking she's just uttered a classic example of the pot calling the kettle black.

'If this is the way Eva wants to cope with her marriage breakdown, then who are we to stop her?' Nicolette announces. 'Surely it's healthier to be out on the town than sitting at home moping.'

I'm relieved when Nicolette turns the conversation to memories about our Amsterdam trip, which seems like months ago rather than days. Nicolette tells me that the kids and I are welcome to go and stay in her little holiday cottage if I need a break. I'm not sure where it is. Kent, I think. By the time we've finished our meal, I'm feeling tipsy. I ask the server to take some photos of the four of us, me holding my glass high in the air with a wide, albeit forced grin on my face.

Nicolette orders us all a brandy – one for the road. I feel like I've already drunk enough, so I only take a sip. After splitting the bill four ways, the others reach for their coats and bags. I try to stand up but it's as if my legs have lost all their strength and the restaurant swirls around me.

'Are you alright?' Nicolette's face swims in and out.

'I think she's drunk too much,' Kalah says, holding my arm.

I feel so weird, completely drunk but perhaps more so. I haven't felt like this in years, if ever.

'Don't feel so good.' I think the words come out properly, but perhaps they don't because Kalah says something to me, and I can't understand what she's saying; I just see her mouth contorting into weird shapes.

And then I remember nothing.

I wake in my own bed, but my stomach is heaving. I rush to the bathroom on wobbly legs and make it just in time, throwing up violently into the toilet. I'm shivering uncontrollably and everything aches. My first thought is, I've got some horrible virus. My second thought is I drank much too much last night. I call out for Samuel, only a few seconds later realising he's not here, remembering that he is likely being held captive and I've been tasked with doing a ridiculous bucket list. My husband needs me and what did I do? I made a complete fool of myself by getting drunk.

After gulping down a couple of glasses of water, washing my face and brushing my teeth, the panic sets in. How did I get home? Are the kids okay? I pull on my dressing gown and stumble along the corridor, hands pushing against the walls for stability. My head is pounding but my stomach feels a little calmer. I peek inside Riley and Alfie's rooms and am relieved they are both asleep in bed. Then I stagger downstairs into the living room. Angela is asleep on the sofa, cocooned in a blanket that she must have found stashed at the back of my linen cupboard. I groan. How embarrassing that she had to stay to keep an eye on me and the kids.

'Hello,' she says, rolling over to face me. She levers herself into a sitting position and I see she's still dressed in yesterday's clothes.

'I'm so sorry, Angela,' I say. 'I don't know what happened.'

'A little too much alcohol, I think.' She grins at me and then glances at her watch. 'If you're back in the land of the living, I really need to scarper. I've got to get home. Hunter will wonder where I am, and we're off for a walk on the South Downs later.'

'But it's only just gone 5 a.m. Would you like a coffee before you go?'

'Thanks, but I'll get going.'

Ten minutes later, Angela has left and, gingerly, I carry a mug of coffee back upstairs. Back in the comfort of my bed, I think about last night, shame coursing through me. And then my thoughts wander to my husband.

'Oh Samuel, I pray you're okay,' I murmur. I think of the ridiculous bucket list request and decide I might as well post the photographs from the evening onto social media. Perhaps when Samuel's kidnappers see them, they might release him. I open Facebook and to my surprise see I've been tagged by a user I don't recognise. What the hell! There are photos of me collapsed on a pavement, my hair all mussed up, mascara smudged, one shoe off my stockinged foot and what looks like a puddle of vomit next to me. I look a complete mess, a disgrace at any age, let alone for a forty-year-old mother of two who heads up a charity. Who posted these photos and why? Did this really happen? I go onto Instagram and see the same photos. Someone is toying with me and frankly, it's terrifying.

CHAPTER TEN

THE LOVER

I grab my bag and stomp out of the house, checking the chains and double-locking the door behind me. I'm tempted to scream like a little child having a tantrum fit. No one will hear me out here, with the exception of Samuel. And I don't want him to think that I'm losing my nerve or unravelling in any way. Because I'm not. I'm just disappointed with him. When I showed Samuel the photos of Eva looking like a tramp, behaving like an irresponsible teenager, I thought he'd find them funny. I think they are. Throwing up like that on the street; having to be supported home, helped into bed by her friends. Samuel has left her and within a few days she's out on the tiles acting like she hasn't got a care in the world. It's partly hilarious and partly disgusting. She's a mother, for goodness sake!

But Samuel didn't see the funny side and he didn't even seem that revolted. His overriding concern was for his children. He went on and on about, what if Riley or Alfie see the photos of their mother; how damaging it will be for them; how worried they'll be. How out of character that was for

Eva. And all at a time when he's not there to support them all. So what if they see the photos? They'll realise that their mother isn't the person they think she is; that the sensible, responsible persona is just a charade and that underneath she's a selfish, slutty human being.

The cottage is surrounded by trees; tall conifers, beech and oak trees, as well as huge rhododendron bushes and azaleas that have already finished flowering. Over the years, the woodland has become denser, almost impenetrable in places with fallen branches and rotting tree trunks. It keeps the cottage in permanent shadow, which makes the place unduly dark, with the sun rays only entering in the mornings. But that doesn't worry me. It means that we're far away from peeping eyes and even if I did scream, the only living creatures that might hear me would be the scampering squirrels, the small herd of deer that delicately jump through the undergrowth, and the rabbits with their glassy eyes. I have tucked my car behind one of the sprawling rhododendron bushes so even if someone does approach the cottage, they won't easily spot it. My small Honda is filthy, the wheel arches coated in mud, with twigs and leaves scattered on the roof. The weather has been dreadful the past weeks with incessant rain, and at one point I wondered if my trusty car would even make it along the muddy track. As I climb inside, I decide my first stop should be the car wash. I don't want anyone questioning why it's so filthy.

I ease my way through the deep puddles and onto the small country lane. I'd thought I was so clever spiking Eva's drink last night without anyone noticing. And I'd thought Samuel would be disgusted with her. I clearly got that one wrong. I'll leave him for a few hours, let him stew and calm down, let him reflect on who are the responsible adults around here. He'll remember soon enough that it's only me who truly loves him and I would never behave so appallingly.

Unfortunately, money is tight and I need to take on extra work. I'm freelance now so I can pick and choose what I do when, and I do find it rather hilarious that no one knows what I *really* do for a living. The timings for my new job worked out rather well, in fact. The truth is, I'm a cleaner. Some people look down their noses at cleaners; it's the job you have to take when all other options run out, or perhaps they think I'm not clever enough to do anything else. They'd be wrong on every count. Against all the odds, I'm rather enjoying it. I have flexibility, thanks to the contract cleaning firm I'm working for; I can pick and choose the jobs I want, as well as the hours. If Samuel starts to struggle with me being out of the house during the day, then I'll take some night shifts. Mostly I prefer the days, because then I get to clean wealthy people's homes, whereas at night it tends to be office blocks and commercial properties that aren't nearly as interesting. And there's a real sense of achievement, leaving somewhere sparkling and freshly scented, knowing it looks good thanks to my hard graft.

I park my Honda in the narrow driveway outside my three-bedroom semi-detached house and hop out of the car, carrying in the black bin liner full of clothes and linen that need a wash – both my own and Samuel's.

'Hello, love!' I jump. It's Mrs Parker from next door and I can do without talking to her. 'Haven't seen you around for a bit. Just wondering if everything's alright.'

'Absolutely fine, Mrs Parker,' I say jauntily. 'I had to go away for work. I've been assigned a really important project so I'll be away from home quite a bit over the next few weeks.'

'Ooo, that sounds exciting. Not that I understand what you do. Something in retail, isn't it? But I hope you're taking good care of yourself and not working too hard.'

'Thanks for your concern, but I must get a move on. I'm expected back in the office within the hour.'

I hurry to the front door and slip inside before she can say any more. I'm going to have to be careful though. I don't want anyone suspecting I'm living elsewhere. I shove every-thing into the washing machine and set it to run. As I get change into jeans and a T-shirt, I wonder if I should say that my mum is poorly and I'm having to spend a lot of time at her house, making sure she's all right. Yes, that might be a better cover story than going away for work. I have a whole collection of cover stories that I write down in my journal; the journal that I keep in my bag and make sure that no one ever takes a peek at. Every morning I write down my dreams, the things I am determined to manifest. It's amazing how powerful the process is, because the very thing I've been dreaming of for so long is a loving relationship with my perfect man. Samuel Simmons. And against all odds, my manifestation has come true.

CHAPTER ELEVEN

THE WIFE

It isn't until the pale early morning light has started filtering through the gaps in the curtains that I realise something. Those photos on Facebook weren't uploaded by someone else. They were uploaded by me to my account! Except I didn't do it. Did I? I can't actually remember anything between standing up to leave the bistro and waking up in the early hours, hurrying to the loo and throwing up. I scroll to the photos on my phone. There are the two of me holding up my glass that Nicolette took and the photo of the four of us captured by the server. Nothing else. I can't have uploaded photos I didn't take, and I can't have taken photos of me. I go onto WhatsApp, Messenger and Snapchat but there is no new activity on any of the apps and no stray photographs I might have forgotten about due to my drunken stupor.

With a thudding heart I realise that whoever posted those photographs has hacked into both my Facebook and Instagram accounts. Who knows my passwords? I'm pretty sure that Samuel knows them. I gasp. Could his kidnapper have demanded Samuel hand over my passwords and my husband had no choice but to share them? A horrible thought flicks through my mind: could Samuel be behind the bucket list? No, that's ridiculous. Besides, why would he do something like that? It's completely out of character. But even creepier, that means the kidnapper was watching me last night. They were there in the restaurant or hanging around outside, taking photographs of me in my inebriated state. The thing is, I'm not sure I really drank that much to be so drunk. Was something slipped into my gin and tonic to make me so out of it, or has my exhaustion and worry made me unable to hold my alcohol?

I shiver as I look at the dreadful photos again. I suppose it also means that none of my online passwords are safe. I quickly change the passwords to everything important: my email addresses, my social media accounts and even my Amazon account. I come up with a number of passwords unrelated to my family – a random block of numbers, letters and special characters that I write down in a little notebook which I hide under detritus in my bedside table drawer. And then I go onto Facebook and Instagram and remove the horrendous photos. I just hope that no one has seen them, especially my charity colleagues. I try so hard to maintain a professional attitude, and if these photos get out I'll lose credibility immediately.

I lean back against my pillow and wonder who could have taken those pictures. And straight away I think of my three girlfriends, Nicolette, Kalah and Angela. They were with me all evening and Angela got me home, having access to all my devices during my drunken stupor. I groan at the thought of Mandy, our babysitter, seeing me in such a state.

But surely one of my closest friends wouldn't have taken such denigrating photos of me and hacked into my accounts? And then I wonder. Is one of them having an affair with Samuel? Surely it's not going to be Angela? She's married to Hunter, Samuel's best friend, and she's a divorce lawyer. She knows how to manage the ending of a marriage better than anyone, and she wouldn't have the need to play games. And Kalah wouldn't say boo to a goose. She's terrified of Xavier, and I simply don't see her having the confidence to embark on an affair with anyone, let alone my husband. So that leaves Nicolette. She's the one who has openly admitted that she's being having an affair with a married man. She's refused to tell us any details. Is that because it's Samuel? We love each other like sisters, don't we? We've been best friends for years. Surely she wouldn't do that to me? Even if Samuel and Nicolette were together, why send me the photo of Samuel with the knife and why the bucket list?

I pull on my dressing gown and wander downstairs, making myself a strong cup of coffee. And then, on the dot of 6.30 a.m., exactly the same time of day as before, my phone pings. This time it's a Snapchat voice message, once again spoken with that strange, computerised voice.

'Hello, Eva. I want you to set up a profile on the dating app Hinge. Match with people by liking men's profiles and make sure you leave comments. Go on three dates over the next ten days and upload photos of yourself with your dates onto Instagram Stories. Make sure you look like you're enjoying yourself. Remember that if you don't complete this second item on the bucket list, or if you involve the police, Samuel's life is in danger. I know where you live. I know where your children go to school. Enjoy your dates.'

What? I almost snort with laughter, except it isn't funny. It's sick. It's ridiculous. Why does Samuel's kidnapper want me to act as if I'm moving on from him? As crazy as it sounds, I'd rather they were demanding money, because then I'd know where I stood. But what is the purpose of me going on dates, pretending to the world that I'm over my relationship with Samuel? Who would come up with such absurd tasks? And why? I just want to know why.

Is this the sort of game that Nicolette might invent? Was she laughing at me last night, knowing that she was controlling me in some crazy game that only she knows the rules to? It's depressing thinking of my friend in this way, but she has to be the main suspect.

Nicolette owns a dress shop in town. She's had it for over five years and she sources little-known brands from France and Italy, clothes in natural flowing fabrics that you would imagine might be expensive, except they're not. Nicolette has an eye for designs that suit women regardless of their shape and size. As a result, she's built up a thriving business selling to ladies who visit from across Sussex as well as online further afield. At least I assume it's a thriving business; perhaps it isn't. I have two of her dresses, although they're a little bohemian for my taste. I try calling her a couple of times during the day, but she doesn't pick up. Somehow, I get through an uneventful Sunday with the kids, and eventually call her from the car on my way to work on Monday morning, after dropping the kids. She doesn't open the shop until 10 a.m. so she's normally available to talk at this time of the day.

'Recovered from your hangover?' She laughs.

'Just about. I'm sure I didn't drink that much,' I say.

'You must be out of practice. Anyway, what can I do for

you this bright and early in the day? Sorry I didn't return your calls yesterday. It was all a bit hectic.'

'I want to start internet dating and thought I could enlist your help.'

There's silence on the end of the line. For a moment I wonder if we've been cut off but then Nicolette coughs. 'Sorry, Eva, but did you just say you want to start dating?'

'Yes. I know it seems soon but it's my way of moving on.'

'But Samuel's only been gone a few days.'

'Indeed, but he's made his decision and I've made mine.' I try to imagine if the shoe was on the other foot. I'd be horrified, but I'm not sure if Nicolette's reaction is genuine or if she's acting. I wish I could see her face; it would be easier to assess if she's lying or not.

'But what if he comes back? I mean, this could just be a blip. Have the two of you actually discussed this; talked about counselling?'

'I appreciate your concern,' I say, feeling briefly guilty about the abruptness to my tone. 'But with respect, you're the one having an affair with a married man. Has your lover had counselling with his wife?'

'Touché,' she mutters.

'Can't you tell me about him? I mean, you haven't shared a single detail. Where he lives, what he does, whether he has children. Is he going to leave his wife for you?'

'Have you rung me to have a go, because I'm not in the mood, Eva. I've got work to do and no doubt you do too.'

'No, sorry. I'm on edge at the moment. I just wanted your help writing my profile for Hinge.'

'Truthfully, I think it's a terrible idea.'

'So that's a no?'

'Let's touch base next weekend and if you still want to do

it then, I'll help you. But seriously, Eva, I'm worried about you. This is so out of character.'

'Yes, well, that's what a cheating husband does to you.'

She grunts. 'Take care and we'll talk soon.' She hangs up on me.

I regret that conversation. Of course Nicolette is right; it's ludicrous that I am dating. Yet what choice do I have? I moot going to the police again, but the crazy thing is, even if the kidnapper doesn't find out I've snitched to the cops, I still have no evidence. No photos, voice mails or anything to suggest that I'm telling the truth, except a couple of phone numbers that probably belong to burner phones and a Snapchat account that is likely untraceable. I think about contacting Snapchat directly, telling them that I'm being threatened, but I recall the media reports about poor young-sters who have taken their lives due to online bullying, and I'm in no doubt that they wouldn't pay the slightest attention to the unsubstantiated complaints of a grown woman. Whoever the person is pulling the strings, they've been clever, leaving no trace of their instructions. I think of that horrible computerised voice and I research voice-changing apps. There are loads of them. Some change your voice in real time and others you have to record yourself. And as I feared, they can change a woman's voice into a man's or vice versa, so I have no idea if the kidnapper is male or female.

I'm at my desk in the office, trying to write up my profile for Hinge. I wish I could discuss it with members of my team. A number of them are young and regularly talk about their online dating experiences but they all know I'm married with kids and they'd look at me as if I was crazy.

After downloading the app and creating a free email account I'll use just for this ridiculous dating experience, I click through the various screens, skipping quite a few of the questions. I have no desire to share where I work or the highest level of education that I attained. I select the "prefer not to say" option for my religious and political beliefs. I admit to drinking from time to time and select no to smoking and drug taking. Does anyone actually click yes for the latter? And then I have to choose six photos or videos. This is hard because the vast majority of my photographs include the kids and Samuel. I do a little bit of photo editing and eventually find five passable photos where I've managed to crop out everyone except me. The sixth photo is the one of me raising my glass on my night out with the girls. And now it gets more difficult. I have to record a video of myself. I barely utter three words before deleting my first attempt. I write down what I want to say and then hold my phone up in front of my face.

'Hi, I'm looking for someone who is reliable and kind. Someone who will respect me and my kids and bring fun and stability into our lives.'

'Eva, can you –' I start and drop my phone onto the desk.

'Sorry, I didn't realise you were on a call.' Luke raises an eyebrow.

'It's fine. I wasn't,' I mumble. 'What's up?'

'We've been approached by Felix Lockenhardt about writing a recipe book and using it to promote Leap Ahead. He's suggesting writing recipes that cost no more than a couple of quid to make and are easy to follow. His agent is supportive and they've potentially got a publisher on board. Fifty percent of the money raised will come to us and we'll be featured heavily in the recipe book. What do you think?'

Felix Lockenhardt is a local celebrity chef. He won

MasterChef and went on to set up his own Michelin-starred restaurant.

'Quite the coup. Do you want to invite him in to discuss in further detail?'

'Actually, I've already pencilled a date in your diary.'

I chuckle. Sometimes I think Luke could run this place without me. 'Excellent. Let's hope he invites us for a meal.'

Luke leaves my office and I listen back to my video recording. It's cringeworthy but frankly I don't care. Next up on the Hinge app are the prompts. I have to choose three and write my answers. This proves hard. After much deliberation the prompts I decide to go for are, "All I ask is that you tell me the truth at all times. I'll fall for you if you're kind to my children. A life goal of mine is to visit the Northern Lights and write a book." I click on next and then I'm done. Pictures of middle-aged men appear on my screen along with their prompts. I've done my research online and know that I need to click the heart button of the profile pictures and prompts that I like and the x button on those that I don't like. And then, bingo, I get my first match. Then my second. And third. The first looks creepy. The second is young enough to be my son and the third, mmm – boring? But I remind myself that this is all make-believe and then I feel bad because whomever I really match with, I'll be conning. I'm not in the dating market. Yet I need to set up a date, and quickly.

I choose Anthony. He lives in Worthing and we start chatting via the app. He's divorced with a five-year-old son and runs a computer-fixing store, or at least that's what he tells me. I'm not sure we have anything in common but at least he seems vaguely normal. And so we message each other, my comments becoming increasingly flirtatious because I need to hurry this along so we can meet in real life.

Then I wonder whether I can digitally manipulate our photos together and post that on social media, obviating the need for an actual date. I quickly dismiss the idea because I'd be using Anthony's photo fraudulently. But our conversation progresses well and by the end of the day, Anthony has asked to meet up for dinner. To my disgust, I agree. What the hell am I doing? Am I being weak, giving in to the requests of the kidnapper? Should I tell him to take a running jump? Yet, each time I consider ignoring him, the image of Samuel with the knife at his neck sears my mind, and the thinly veiled threat to our children sends shivers down my spine. It's not like the kidnapper is asking me to do anything illegal. It's only a date with a stranger, and I'll happily do that if it means Samuel remains safe and is released. I'd just like to know why I'm being toyed with like this.

I'm embarrassed to ask Mandy to babysit again so I contact Stephen. My older brother was married to a woman called Kylie. One day Kylie was there, the next she was gone. I see her around town occasionally; she's got a new husband and twin toddlers. I'm sure that must hurt Stephen but every time I bring up Kylie's name, he shuts me down. I worry about my brother, although he tells me I shouldn't, that he's perfectly happy with his life.

He has plenty of friends and seems to have a better social life than me. Every evening there's some activity, ranging from martial arts to a theatre class, cinema outings and rambling. Quite how he manages to fit it all in with his early start at work, I really don't know. I suspect that Stephen might have a new woman, but if so, he hasn't shared that with me.

Stephen's semi-detached Victorian house is in a street behind the station about ten minutes' drive from us. I was surprised he chose it, imagining he'd prefer the sterility of a new build, like the house he had with Kylie. He moved there after their divorce, and I was happy that he chose to be so near us. He's always been good with Riley and Alfie, despite having no children of his own, but I try not to make him my first choice of babysitter because I don't like to impose on his busy life.

I change my clothes several times, deciding on a silk blouse and a pair of black trousers, an outfit that looks more work-like than suitable for a date. But I don't want Anthony to like me; all I need is a photo of the two of us and then we can never see each other again. When I leave, the kids are both in their rooms, Alfie on his play station and Riley scribbling something in a notebook which she proceeds to hide from me. The questions about Samuel come every morning and evening. Why hasn't Dad called us? When's he coming home? And I know that I'm going to have to come up with another excuse, or worse, lie to them and tell them that their dad has left me. I kiss them both goodnight and when the doorbell rings, I hurry downstairs.

Stephen gives me a peck on the cheek and follows me into the kitchen.

'Are you alright?' He peers at me.

'Not really,' I admit, shutting the kitchen door. 'Do you want a drink?'

'I'll help myself to a cuppa later,' he says, placing his brown leather messenger bag on the kitchen table and sitting down. 'What's up?'

For a moment I'm tempted to tell him the truth. Stephen is my brother and is probably the only person in the world whom I can truly trust. We've had our ups and downs, but we're family. But why should I put him at risk too? I simply can't do that.

'I haven't told the kids yet, but Samuel has left me for another woman.'

Stephen stares at me and for a moment I wonder if he's understood what I just said.

'Samuel?' he exclaims at last. 'But he loves you.'

'Apparently he doesn't,' I say. 'He's taking some time out to evaluate things. It's blindsided me.'

He opens his mouth as if he's going to say something and then changes his mind. 'I'm stunned. And so sorry. I know what it's like.'

That's another reason I feel bad for lying to him, because Kylie left him and I know that it broke his heart, despite him trying to make light of it, despite him saying they were thoroughly unsuited to each other.

'So where are you going tonight?' he asks.

'Just a work do. I won't be back late.'

'I think you're very brave for carrying on as normal.'

I smile tightly before blowing him a kiss and leaving the room.

'Be good for Uncle Stephen,' I shout up the stairs to the kids and get no response.

The restaurant is on a shopping street one row back from the seafront, serving Italian food. The signs on the outside proclaim that the business has been in the same family for eighty years. Unfortunately the interior looks as if the decor hasn't been touched in decades and to my dismay, only three tables are occupied. I was hoping the place would be thrumming with people as if that might somehow minimise the awkwardness of the date. I'm early, so the server leads me to a table for two near the back of the restaurant. I choose the seat against the wall so that I can spot Anthony as he walks in. In the meantime I study the menu but my stomach is roiling and I'm not sure I'm going to be able to eat anything. A shadow passes over the table and I glance up.

'Eva?' he asks, peering through thick glasses.

'Yes.' I stand up. He looks absolutely nothing like his photos, which must have been taken twenty years earlier. Balding, he is overweight, his pregnant-like stomach and man boobs accentuated by a too-tight olive green polo shirt, a colour which does nothing for his complexion. I put out my hand to shake his, but he moves straight in for a kiss on the cheek, leaving a stomach-curdling wetness which I try to subtly wipe off.

'Such a pleasure to meet you,' he says effusively, sitting down with a thud. 'You're even more beautiful than your photos suggest.'

I smile awkwardly. We sit in silence for a moment, both of us staring at the menus, until a server arrives and asks us what we'd like to drink.

'A beer for me,' Anthony says without asking what I'd like. There's a faint shine of sweat on his upper lip.

'A small glass of white wine,' I say. 'Thank you.'

'What do you do for a living?' he asks, with no preamble.

'I work in admin,' I reply, and then realise that if he Googles me he'll see that I'm in fact the trustee and managing director of Leap Ahead. I wish I'd been able to use a false name when setting up my Hinge account, but I'm sure the kidnapper wouldn't have agreed to that. 'I work for a charity,' I add.

'Right.'

'And you? You're into computers?'

'Yes. Love the things.'

'I think my Facebook and Instagram accounts were hacked. I've changed the passwords now but how does someone even do that?'

And then he's off. It's like he doesn't take a breath for the next ten minutes, talking about firewalls and VPNs and regaling me with sentences that I don't understand. The server takes our food orders and then Anthony carries on talking about hacking and the dark web and coding. I feel like closing my eyes and going to sleep. He only stops when our starters arrive: soup of the day for me and bruschetta for Anthony, at which point he takes a breath and starts eating.

I'm going to have to get a photo of us, but how? He's going to think I'm really keen on him if I ask the server to take a picture of us together. I'm racking my brain for a plausible excuse when I realise he's asked me a question and I've no idea what he said.

'Sorry,' I say. 'One of my girlfriends doesn't believe I'm doing online dating. Do you mind if I get a photo of the two of us so I can prove to her I've taken the plunge?'

'Is this your first date?' He edges closer to the table so his chest is almost in his plate of food.

'Yes.' I feel my face redden, goodness knows why.

'You're just the cutest,' Anthony says, leaning even further across the table and placing his clammy hand over mine. I'm sure my smile is a grimace but he doesn't seem to notice. He waves at the server, who hurries to our table.

'Can you take a photo of us?' he asks, removing his phone from his back trouser pocket.

'On my phone, please,' I say, handing my phone to the server first.

'Pinky promise you'll send me the photo?' he asks. What grown man uses language like that?

The server stands back and I hold my wine glass in the air and pretend to smile. She then hands the phone back to me and I put it straight into my handbag without looking at the photo.

'You're really lush,' Anthony says, licking his lips. I don't know where to look because this man sickens me. It's not his fault; I'm sure he'll make a nice enough partner to someone, just not for me.

'My apartment is on Western Road. I've got some prosecco in the fridge. Do you like prosecco?'

'Actually I'm not drinking more than this glass. I'm driving home.'

'Well that's a shame, but it won't stop us, will it?' He leans even further forwards causing the table to teeter, before glancing around rapidly so his double chin wobbles and then he lowers his voice. 'I'm going to make you squeal and beg for more.' He winks at me. This disgusting man actually winks at me.

'I'm sorry, but–'

He interrupts, putting his hand up. 'No buts, Eva. We're two consenting adults and I think there's going to be fireworks. You feel it too, don't you?'

I'm not sure where he's got all of these lines from; watching porn, perhaps. But all I know is that I have to get out of here. When the plates for our starters have been removed, I pick up my bag. 'Could you excuse me, please, whilst I freshen up?'

'You're already fresh, darling. But yes, if you need to take a piss, go for it. Think of me whilst you're doing it.'

My goodness, he really is gross. I edge between the tables and wonder if I can bolt straight out of the front door, but Anthony has turned around in his seat and is watching me, his tongue lolling out of his mouth. I shudder and head towards the ladies' toilets. I need to get out of here, and quickly. Rather than going into the ladies, I follow the corridor towards the bustle of the commercial kitchen. And then I see our server.

'Excuse me,' I say. 'My date is going terribly and I need to leave. Is it possible for you to find my coat and let me out via a back entrance?'

The young woman, who probably isn't much older than twenty, stares at me. 'Are you doing a runner and actually telling me about it?'

'No, I'm only running out on my date. I'll give you cash for my food. Please help me on this,' I implore, taking my wallet out of my handbag and counting out some notes. 'Would you mind fetching my coat?'

'Alright then,' she says, a cheeky grin crossing her pretty face. 'What does your coat look like?'

I give her a description and wait in the corridor. She returns with it a couple of minutes later.

'How much is our bill?'

'You know you could just tell him that it's not working out rather than ghosting him.'

'You're right, I could. But honestly I just want to go home. I know it makes me a bitch, but so be it.'

She rolls her eyes at me. I hand her fifty pounds, which more than covers my half of the meal I won't be eating, and then I hand the girl a ten-pound note. 'For you,' I say.

'This way then,' she says. I follow her to the fire exit. 'Shall I tell him that you're ill and have gone home?'

'Thank you,' I say, briefly touching her arm. 'That's very kind of you.'

Out on the street, I tug my coat on and walk briskly

towards the multi-storey car park. It's only when I'm in my car, with the doors locked, that I relax back into the seat. I open my phone and send Anthony a message on Hinge.

Very sorry I had to leave. Not feeling well. Best, Eva.

And then I post the photo onto my Instagram Stories and add the caption, *Great first date*. What a lie that was. I just hope Anthony doesn't see it.

CHAPTER TWELVE

THE LOVER

I'm in a Tesco supermarket, two streets away from my morning job where I was cleaning the offices of an insurance brokerage. I won't be cleaning for them again. If I'm going to do offices, they need to be an interesting business, not dull insurance. I'm a quick worker, vacuuming, tidying, emptying bins so it leaves me time for snooping. I've got a curious mind and I like to learn something new, whether that be reading a non-disclosure agreement left carelessly on a desk or rifling through boxes of samples, ready for the taking, skin care or trinkets.

Anyway, I need to do a shop both for food and bits and pieces for Samuel. I wander down the toiletries aisle and pick up some shaving foam. It's time for Samuel to shave his beard off. I've never liked it, the way it prickles my face and makes him look older than he really is. I'm sure I can persuade him to get rid of it. A new start, a new look and all that. I pick up a man's razor and some shower gel. I hope he likes the scent.

I find some lobster tails in the Finest section and despite

the price, add them to my basket. I hope I don't run into someone I know. How would I explain the extravagance? But Samuel deserves it. The poor man has cabin fever. He's desperate to go out; to take me for a lovely meal at a cosy country pub, or to a fine dining restaurant prior to a theatre visit in London's West End, but of course he can't. It's hard for him, being confined to the cottage for so long, and I understand that, I really do. But it's for the best. It's much too soon for the two of us to be seen together, even though that's what I want more than anything in the world. We need to be patient. At least I'm able to get out of the cottage, live an almost normal life. It's much harder for Samuel, and that's why I need to ease his stay, making everything as comfortable as possible, preparing his favourite foods, spoiling him in any way I can.

I choose a bottle of expensive red wine and add some other grocery items to my basket. Later, when we've eaten well and perhaps made love again, I'll show him the photo of Eva on her date. If truth be told, I am disappointed. Firstly, there was only the one photo, and her date was so very unattractive and ordinary. He's not at all the type I assumed Eva would go for. Not a patch on handsome, debonair Samuel, so I wonder if she just went with the first man who approached her. It will be interesting to see what Samuel thinks.

It's 8 p.m., we've eaten and I showed Samuel the photograph of Eva on her date. I thought he'd laugh, say what dreadful taste she's got, but no. He went very quiet, said she looked lovely, particularly her gorgeous hair. I've always been envious of her hair. These days there's a reddish tint to it and she has luscious thick curls that sit on her shoulders. It's definitely her best feature, hair that could feature in a shampoo advert and glistens even in low light. But Samuel saying that Eva looks lovely is like he's taken a dagger to my stomach. Doesn't he realise how much he's hurting me by saying nice things about his ex? It's as if even though he doesn't want Eva for himself, he doesn't want anyone else to have her. And he's going on and on about Riley and Alfie; how they must be missing him, worried as to why he hasn't called them in days; concerned that Eva is being negligent towards them, going out and partying; worrying about how they might react if they see her social media posts. We had an argument and I could feel the anger boiling up and up and I knew that if I wasn't going to say or do something I regret, I had to get out of the cottage. In silence, I fixed the chains, refusing to meet Samuel's eyes, ignoring his complaints. I have a plan and I need to stick to it. And now I'm outside in the woodland, the sun has disappeared and the air is heavy with damp. I walk and walk, letting the anger ease out of my body, focusing upon the plan and the future. The wonderful future that is so nearly within my reach.

CHAPTER THIRTEEN

THE WIFE

Even though he was a sleazy bore, I feel bad about running out on Anthony. I got him there on false pretences and rather wish I'd paid for both of our meals to ease my guilt. And I'm furious with the kidnapper. It's complete nonsense that I need to go through that charade with two more people. I'll post the picture on Instagram Stories as the kidnapper requested, but that's that. I'm not going out on a date with any more people.

When I got home, Stephen was with the kids in the living room watching some game show on the television. I'm pleased, even if it's past Alfie's bedtime. I love that they have such a good relationship with their uncle.

'You're home early,' Stephen says, looking at me with an expression of surprise.

'I thought we were meeting for dinner but it was only drinks.' The lies are tumbling out of my mouth much too easily at the moment.

'Did you clinch the deal?' Stephen asks.

For a moment I wonder what he means but then realise

he's referring to the business event he thought I was attending. 'It wasn't that kind of meeting. Would you like a beer or glass of wine before you go?' I ask.

He stands up. 'No, thanks. I've got lots to do this evening. Don't hesitate to call me if you need any help or just a shoulder to cry on,' he says, placing a kiss on my cheek, before picking up his bag and doing high fives with the children.

'Why do you need a shoulder to cry on?' Alfie asks.

Stephen throws me an anguished look and mouths sorry.

'It's just a figure of speech,' I explain. 'I've been having some problems at work and Uncle Stephen is offering to help.'

Riley scrunches her forehead as if she doesn't believe me.

'Upstairs, both of you, please.'

Later, when the kids are in bed, I post the photograph of Anthony and me on Instagram Stories. I don't add any text or hashtags because I don't want it to be found. I lie on my bed trying to work out what I can do, racking my brain if there's any way I can discover if Samuel really was having an affair. My assumption is that he wasn't; that the initial text from him was sent under duress or someone else got hold of his phone. I have to hang on to that because the thought of Samuel lying to me for weeks or months is too much to bear. So that means someone is holding him captive and that person is toying with me, sending me off on some weird wild goose chase, demanding I complete crazy bucket-list items that seem to prove I've somehow moved on from my marital relationship. Do they want the world to think I've abandoned my marriage? But why? Why go to all of these lengths? As much as it pains me, my number one suspect is still Nicolette, but would my friend really do something like this? It doesn't make any sense. I clench my fists and rub them into my eyes. A sudden exhaustion settles on me and I can barely force myself to stumble to the bathroom to get ready for bed.

Sunday is a hellish day. I feel like I should be out looking for Samuel, except I have no idea where to start. Every day I miss him more and the panic curdles in my stomach whenever I think of him. We are booked in to go to Mum's for Sunday lunch and I would like nothing more than to cancel, except I know I'd never be forgiven. I have a precarious relationship with Mum, who veers between suffocating love and indifference. Although she pretends she's coping with being a widow, I know she misses Dad and is fundamentally lonely. These past few days have given me a taster of that.

Mum is a serial charity worker. It gives her a sense of purpose and I admire her for that. Except she's never wanted anything to do with Leap Ahead, which I've found weird. Perhaps it's because in her roles there isn't any great sense of responsibility. She helps out three times a week in the Oxfam shop, she runs a second-hand stall for the local church (not that she ever attends any services) and is the first to volunteer to help in local fetes or charity runs. When she's not doing something for charity, she's playing golf or bridge with her army of widowed friends, hobbies she only took up after Dad's death, but in which apparently she excels. She adores Samuel, probably because he's a golf player, and sometimes I wonder whether she loves him more than me. Once a month, she gives us Sunday lunch, making a big deal as to how much work it is to prepare, how expensive joints of meat are these days. I offer to help, to bring a starter or dessert, but she always declines, inferring that my cookery skills aren't up to hers.

To be fair, they're not, but then I don't have all week to prepare a meal.

Mum lives in the big house that Dad built her two decades ago. It's her pride and joy; shoes have to be removed, cushions plumped up when you get up from chairs, and sinks wiped down after use. Riley and Alfie have to be on best behaviour and we only manage to cajole them to attend because Mum has a present cupboard and the children are allowed to select one gift on each visit. I'm pretty sure the presents come from the charity shop, not that the kids seem to mind. She's really good at gifts, choosing Alfie computer games (someone must be helping her select them) and Riley cute little sweaters or sparkly skirts.

Mum wasn't always like this. Dad's money changed her. She was a milkman's daughter and trained as a nurse. After pregnancy issues, she quit work and was a stay-at-home mum and she gave Stephen and me a happy childhood. I often wonder where that down-to-earth wife and mother has gone, and although I admire how she keeps herself busy, truth be told, I prefer the old Mum to this imposter.

'Darling,' she says, air-kissing me as I stand at the front door holding a bouquet of flowers that I bought yesterday. 'Lovely lilies, thank you.' She tilts her head and narrows her eyes at me. Her fair hair is streaked with grey, but there's still enough colour to make her look younger than her years. 'You look exhausted. What's going on?'

'Samuel's away on a business trip in Malaysia and I'm inundated at work.' I ease past her into the dark hallway. Mum can read me like a book and she'll know I'm lying. Her yapping white fluffy little dog, Pudding (she would never have gotten away with that name if Dad had been alive), nips at my ankles.

'Alfie, can you take Pudding into the garden,' Mum asks. The dog adores Alfie and surprisingly, it's mutual. 'Riley, you can help me in the kitchen.'

Riley rolls her eyes behind Mum's back but she'll do as she's asked because of that present cupboard. I wonder how many years the bribery will work for. I follow them through the house, into the farmhouse kitchen.

The cupboards are made from oak and there's an old butcher's block that acts as an island unit, smooth and curved with age.

'Can I do anything to help?' I ask.

'You need to sit down and have a cuppa,' Mum instructs. 'Have you been sleeping?'

'Not very well,' I admit.

'You're a bit young for the peri-menopause but you might want to get checked out.'

I groan inwardly. Mum is such a fixer, and no, I'm not going through an early menopause. 'You tell that husband of yours to hurry home and look after you.'

I turn away from her and squeeze my eyes shut.

Somehow, we get through lunch but the strain of pretending to Mum that I'm okay when I'm clearly not weighs on me like thick treacle, dampening the speed of my thinking and making me desperate to escape from her saccharine concern.

As always, when we're about to leave, Mum pulls me to one side and whispers, 'Have you spoken to Stephen? What's he been saying?'

'Absolutely nothing, and he's fine, Mum,' I assure her. 'Absolutely fine.' I know she's worried that Stephen might pull me away from her, corrupt my thinking in some way, but my relationship with Mum is fundamentally different to

Stephen's. Mum is our only parent and despite everything, I love her. How I wish I could bash their heads together, but it seems that stubbornness runs in our family. Stephen can't forgive Mum and Mum can't forgive Stephen.

For a few hours on Monday, I can almost forget that life is far from normal. The kids go to school, I go to work and absorb myself in the minutiae of running Leap Ahead. Jen calls me to ask if I know when Samuel will be back in the office. I'm telling her the truth when I say I don't know.

I've collected the children from school and we're in the car on the way home when Riley says, 'Where's Dad really? Autumn said that Dad has left us. Is that true?'

I swallow hard. How does Autumn know that? Kalah must have said something to her daughter and that infuriates me. That was totally inappropriate. I'm at a loss how to answer the question and am quiet for too long.

'Mum. What's going on? I'm scared,' Riley says, and Riley is never scared.

'Yes, it's sort of true. Dad has left me but he hasn't left you. He still loves you very much.'

Alfie bursts into tears, so I pull the car over and switch the engine off. Riley stares at me with big eyes, tears welling.

'I'm so sorry, darlings. I should have told you but the circumstances are complicated.'

'Are you getting divorced?' Alfie asks through hiccups.

'Come here, sweetheart,' I say, holding out my arms. He slides from the backseat towards the central console and I hug him. Riley also joins us, although it's awkward holding them both in the car.

'Dad needs a little time out but he'll be back in contact very soon. Sometimes adults need to go away to clear their heads.'

'But why hasn't he called us?' Riley sniffs. 'Has he got another family now?'

'No,' I say, horrified that she would even think that. 'He hasn't been in touch because he's somewhere without mobile reception. I'm sure he'll call you both very soon. He loves you so much, as do I.'

Lie after lie after lie slips out of my mouth and I hate myself for it. When both children have wiped their eyes and their sobs have stopped, I say, 'Shall we go out for pizza to cheer ourselves up?' It doesn't do the trick.

'Ralph's parents are divorced,' Alfie says, as he wipes his eyes with the back of his hand. 'He's got two bedrooms and two console players. Will we get two of everything?'

'No. Nothing has been decided yet and I'm hopeful that your dad and I will stay together, so I really don't want either of you to worry. Okay?'

The children nod warily. 'Don't say anything to Miss Smith or anyone at school,' Riley says. 'I don't want anyone to know.'

'I won't, darling, I promise.' That at least is a pledge I can keep.

Later that evening when the children are in bed, I send a Snapchat message to user ISEEU975783.

When are you going to release Samuel? What do I need to do?

Long minutes slip into hours as I wait for a response. The message remains unread.

It's Tuesday morning and I'm awoken by the ping of a Snapchat message, once again on the dot of 6.30 a.m.

When I swallow, it feels like something hard has caught

in my throat. My hand is trembling as I press the listen button. 'Cut your hair off,' the computerised voice says. 'Don't leave more than one inch all over.'

What! No, this is crazy. Beyond crazy. As I stare at my phone screen, the message vanishes. I groan. No, I'm not doing anything that stupid. It's ridiculous and I'm fed up of being this invisible person's puppet. I send a message back.

> *I'm not going to do anything more until you tell me what you want from me. And when are you going to release Samuel?*

Another Snapchat message arrives, almost instantly.

> *Samuel will die if you don't cut off your hair.*

The message disappears.
I type:

> *But why?*

> *Do as I say.*

I'm quicker this time and I manage to take a screen shot, not that the words, 'Do as I say,' are particularly threatening out of context, and certainly not sufficient for me to take to the police. As I stare at the screen it tells me that the other person is speaking, and then a few seconds later there's another ping announcing the arrival of a voice note from user ISEEU975783.

The computerised voice says, 'Delete that screenshot otherwise Riley and Alfie are in danger. Snapchat notifies me when you take a screenshot. Understood? And cut off your hair today otherwise your whole family will suffer. Do not go to the police. I'll know if you do.'

This is horrible, menacing, and now I'm truly terrified. If I shared that voice message with the police, then without a doubt they'd swing into action but this damned app deletes everything immediately. I need to act faster.

Of course I'll cut off my hair if it's going to keep my children safe. I get out of bed and pull back the curtains. It's light outside now and I peer into the garden wondering if someone is there, hiding between the trees watching me. I shiver, close the curtains and walk into the bathroom where I pull the blind down just in case there's someone in the garden. I stare at myself in the mirror. My hair is my best feature. It's thick and wavy and it has different hues of gold with hints of copper, framing my face without requiring much styling. Samuel has always loved my hair. I'm going to look horrible without it. My face is long and I definitely won't suit a pixie cut. I wonder if I could pretend I'm ill, going through chemo and that's why I've cut my hair off. But no, I can't do that. It's horrible. Or perhaps I could go to another hairdresser and pretend she cut off more hair than I'd wanted. I run my fingers through the locks and they feel silken, but it's only hair and hair grows back. And then I have a great idea. I can hide my hair underneath a wig. Hurriedly, I get dressed and do a search for wig shops. There are quite a few in neighbouring towns, so I select the nearest, sending Luke a message, once again letting him know I'll be late into the office.

The children are subdued at breakfast and it breaks my heart that they think Samuel and I are splitting up.

'I know you don't want me to say anything at school,' I

tell Riley. 'But if either of you are feeling sad or worried, I want you to tell your form teachers so they can call me. Anyway,' I say, brightening my voice, 'I thought I'd go for a haircut today, choose a completely different style. What do you think?'

Alfie shrugs his shoulders. Riley says in a small voice, 'But I like your hair.'

I like it too.

The wig shop is overwhelming. There are so many different types of wigs in every conceivable colour and style. I stand in the middle of the shop, with no idea where to look.

'How can I help you?' A woman steps forwards, similar in age to me, with very pale skin and shocking pink hair; a wig, I assume.

'I'd like a wig so I can change my hairstyle. I want a pixie look.'

She eyes me with a slight frown and picks up some locks of my hair. 'You'll need to braid your hair, ideally into four braids starting at the nape of your neck, then secure them around the crown of your head. You'll need to wear a wig cap and then you can pop the wig on top. A pixie cut, you said?'

'Yes, an urchin or pixie cut.'

'Alright.' She speaks slowly, and I'm pretty sure she's thinking my choice is a bad idea but she's being polite because the customer is always right. 'Let's try some on you, shall we? What colour are you after?'

'As close to my own as possible,' I say.

'And are we going for synthetic or natural hair?'

'What's the difference?'

'The texture and price.'

She talks me through the options, and the prices for

natural hair are eye watering. It would certainly be much cheaper to have a haircut. An hour later and I've decided not to buy a wig. I'm not adept at styling my own hair and I find the wig cap and wig hot and itchy. In addition, I'm not convinced that it looks natural, possibly because I was trying the cheaper ranges, but I'm not going to spend close on a thousand pounds just because some stranger has ordered me to chop off my hair. I thank the manager effusively and tell her that I'll think about it. Another lie.

Except Samuel's kidnapper said I have to get my hair chopped off today, so I don't have time to think about it. Five shops down, there's a hairdressers, one I know nothing about but frankly I don't care. The door jingles as I step inside and walk up to the counter, an overwhelming scent of peroxide catching the back of my throat.

'Do you have any free appointments?' I ask the young man at the till.

'For when?'

'Right now.' He peers at his computer screen. 'Actually we do. Amber can see you.' He leads me to a chair in front of a tall mirror. 'Can I get you a tea or coffee?' he asks.

'A strong black coffee, please.'

A few minutes later, I've explained to Amber that I want a pixie cut, not more than an inch left all over.

'Are you sure?' she asks, letting my curls tumble through her fingers.

'Yes. I'm doing it for charity.'

'That's very brave of you,' she says. 'I'll try to make it look as lovely as possible.' The implication is that it will look awful despite her skill.

Fifteen minutes later, I've had a wash and a condition

and I'm back staring at my reflection in the mirror. Even wet, my hair is thick and healthy looking.

'Are you sure about this?' Amber asks, holding a large pair of scissors.

I nod.

And then she starts cutting. I close my eyes, listening to the horrible *chop, chop* noise of her scissors that sounds so loud even over the Radio Two music being piped through the sound system.

'Are you alright?'

I open my eyes and gasp at my reflection. My hair is all gone and I look terrible. Tears well up in my eyes and I try to wipe them away except all of the stress of the past few days seems to bubble up inside me, and to my embarrassment I can't stop crying.

Poor Amber, she looks horrified. She places a hand on my shoulder. 'I'm not finished yet. Honestly, it'll look lovely by the time I've finished cutting it and we've given you a blow dry.'

'It's just the shock.' I gulp. 'I've never had short hair, even when I was a child.'

'The good thing about hair is, it always grows back.'

The poor girl looks really worried and for a horrible moment I wonder if she's going to start crying too. 'You're doing a great job,' I say, trying to reassure her. 'It's just it'll take me some time to get used to it.'

'And it's for a good cause,' Amber adds, smiling weakly. For a moment I wonder what she means and then remember I told her I was doing this for charity.

'Exactly,' I reply, with a watery smile.

I don't suit a pixie cut. To be fair to Amber she did a good job, it's just the style looks awful on me. It accentuates my already rectangular face and somehow I appear gaunt and about a decade older. Or perhaps that's just the effect of the past week. Either way, I need to buy a hat and I hurry into Monsoon Accessorize and buy a baseball cap, a straw sun hat and a wide-brimmed navy felt hat for cooler days.

When I'm in the car, I take a selfie and post it onto Instagram Stories with the caption #newhairstyle. Once again, I hope that no one except the kidnapper sees it. I wouldn't describe myself as vain; I visit the hairdressers typically once every couple of months and indulge in a facial once a year. I paint my own nails when I can remember to do them and my beauty routine consists of a cleanser and a moisturiser. Except today I feel embarrassed by my new look, ashamed that I've been bullied into cutting my hair when it was the last thing I wanted to do.

I put the baseball cap on before leaving the car and walk up the path towards the children's school, standing on the fringe of the group of mums in the hope I don't have to talk to anyone, the air feeling strangely cold on the back of my neck.

'Eva?' I turn to see Kalah. 'What...' Her hand flies up to cover her mouth. 'What's happened to your hair? I don't mean to be rude, it's just... When did you have it cut off?'

'This afternoon. I'm doing it for charity.' Yet another lie.

'For Leap Ahead? That's amazing, Eva. Are you getting sponsorship?'

'Yes. No. Haven't decided yet.' I should have thought through my response beforehand.

Kalah puts her hand on my arm and steps closer to me. 'You're not alright, are you?' she says in a low, knowing voice.

'It's very difficult at the moment,' I reply.

'Of course it is, darling. And you know we're all here for

you. But it was quite drastic cutting your hair off.' She pauses for a moment, as if she's plucking up the courage to say something else to me. 'Don't take this the wrong way, but it might be a good idea to speak to someone. I've got a very good therapist if you need a recommendation.'

'You talk to a therapist?' I ask. I'm surprised Xavier lets her.

Kalah flushes slightly. 'No, not me. She's a friend of a friend and comes very highly recommended.'

'Thanks, but I don't need a therapist.' What I really need is for the police to believe in me and investigate the disappearance of my husband.

The children emerge from the gates in a swarm. As always, Alfie is out first. He doesn't notice my hair but chatters about the swimming team and the races they've got coming up. Riley arrives with Autumn. She takes one look at me and tears well up just as they did this morning. 'What have you done to your hair, Mum?' She sounds horrified. Autumn stares at me, her mouth open.

'It's not that bad,' I say, trying to sound cheerful.

'Yes, it is.' Riley swabs at her eyes with the back of her hands. 'You look terrible. It's embarrassing.'

I'm exhausted by 9 p.m. so I lock up the house carefully and climb the stairs. By 10 p.m., I've switched the lights out and despite everything I fall into a deep sleep.

I have the nightmare again. I'm drowning, being pushed down under dark, viscous water, unable to breathe. My lungs are bursting and I watch little bubbles rise out of me, popping as they disappear into the murkiness. I am drowning. I am going to die.

But then I awake with a pounding heart. I gasp and sit up in bed. What was that? I'm sure something woke me, pulled me from my nightmare. I grab my phone but the screen is dark and there are no messages or missed calls. Then I hear it. The sound of breaking glass. My God. Someone is breaking in.

For a moment, I freeze. What should I do? I don't have anything in the bedroom to defend myself with, and without Samuel it's up to me to look after the kids. I strain to listen, terrified that I'm going to hear footsteps, the creak on the third step from the bottom of the stairs.

My stomach clenches. I should have set the burglar alarm. We only set it when we go out, but I'm furious with myself for not using it. The kidnappers have threatened me, and despite fulfilling all the stupid tasks, they're still coming to get us. I needn't have bothered to fulfil the stupid bucket-list items. Using my mobile, I dial 999, my heart thumping so loudly it sounds like a drum beating in my ears.

'What service do you need?' the operator asks.

'Police,' I whisper. 'Someone is breaking into my home.'

'Please hold.' I'm transferred to another operator.

'Police. What's your emergency?'

I repeat myself and give my address. 'I'm home alone with my children.' My voice wobbles.

'Can you hear anyone now?' the operator asks. I hold my breath as I listen out, straining my ears, but all there is is silence. Did I imagine it?

'I can't hear anything now, but I did hear breaking glass earlier.' I climb out of bed and tiptoe to the bedroom door, opening it and expecting to see lights on downstairs or at least the bouncing light of a torch. The house is pitch black and very still.

'We'll send a patrol car around. Do you have a room you can lock yourself and your children in?'

'The bathroom,' I say.

'Please stay on the line whilst you collect your children.'

I pull on a jumper and tiptoe out of the bedroom, using my phone as a torch, putting the emergency services operator on loudspeaker, but all I hear is my ragged breath and the creaks of my footsteps. Riley's room is the nearest. I open the door and creep inside, tiptoeing to her bed. She's asleep, her back to me.

'Darling, you need to wake up.' I shake her gently.

'What is it?' she turns towards me, rubbing her eyes.

'I think someone might be in the house. I've called the police and I want you to come with me and we'll lock ourselves in the bathroom.' She stares at me with horror and fear, and then sits up, her face ghostly pale in the low light. I grab her dressing gown and hold it out for her. Quickly, she puts it on, wedging her feet into her pink furry slippers. I grasp her hand and we tiptoe together to Alfie's room. He's lying on his bed in the shape of a star fish and he's harder to wake up. But eventually, with arms around both my children, the phone wedged under my ear, we hurry to my bathroom where I lock the door and lean back against it.

'We're in the bathroom and I've locked the door,' I tell the operator. 'And I can't hear anything. Perhaps I disturbed them.'

'The patrol car will be with you in three minutes. I'll need you to let them in.'

'I'm scared, Mum,' Alfie says, gripping my arm tightly.

'Don't be, darlings. The police will be here in a moment and I think we've scared the burglars away. I haven't heard anything else.' It's at a time like this I wish we had a dog.

And then I hear a siren, distant at first but it rapidly gets louder and louder, and relief courses through me, making my legs weak.

Two police officers jump out of their patrol car and stride up to the front door. I open it before they can ring the bell. I explain I heard the sound of breaking glass, and so together we switch all the lights on and walk around the whole house. Firstly in the living room, then into the kitchen, the study and the utility room. Everything is as I left it last night. The final door I open is into the downstairs toilet, and I gasp. The small window is shattered, shards of glass all over the cistern and on the floor. But why this window? I can't imagine anyone except a child would be small enough to wriggle through the narrow opening so it's strange that this window has been broken. I have to step back into the hallway to let the police officers in. One of them bends down and, after pulling on a pair of latex gloves, picks up a rock.

'Probably kids,' he says. 'No one can climb through that.'

He's right about no one climbing through the window, but he's not right about it being kids. I have absolutely no doubt that the window was broken by Samuel's kidnapper, almost like a warning sign to show he knows where we live and that we are vulnerable. And now I'm completely unsure what to do. I want to tell the officers everything, except I still have no proof.

'I've been receiving some threatening messages on Snapchat,' I say.

'What sort of messages?' the older of the two uniformed officers asks, standing up straight, pressing something on a gadget that is making a beeping noise. And now I regret saying anything. Images of Samuel, his throat cut open, fill my mind.

'As you say, probably kids,' I mumble. 'I'm too old to be using Snapchat anyway.' I try to laugh but it sounds strained.

The officer raises an eyebrow.

'Will you be able to keep an eye on our house in case the burglar returns?' I ask.

'Our resources are very overstretched but I'll see what we can do. Maybe a patrol car can come along your road a couple of times over the next twenty-four hours.'

I'm not sure what good that will do, but I thank him anyway.

CHAPTER FOURTEEN

THE LOVER

I love it! Eva looks dreadful. That pixie cut probably cost her a fortune but she looks a fright. Short-cropped hair is so unflattering on her long, drawn face. And her expression of disappointment is simply priceless. I got this one right. It's amazing how vain people are, and Eva's always been just a little bit too pleased with herself. I feel a personal victory, as if I've pricked her exactly where it hurts the most. She won't be feeling so pleased with herself now, looking like that. But the more I stare at Eva's picture, the more I realise I've only been tinkering at the edges. The hair was a great idea because it's hurt Eva personally but it's not going to get me what I really want. Next I'm going to have to attack the very people Eva loves the most – her children.

She doesn't deserve those children and I'm going to make sure that she loses the right to motherhood, something she's taken so much for granted.

Today I'm cleaning a private home. It's on a small estate of five luxurious houses and as I drive up to the electric gates, my heart does a little flip. Samuel and I will be living somewhere like this before too long. I plug in the numbers that the agency has given me and the gates slide open silently. I edge my Honda forwards and turn to the left where Number Two, The Close, sits proudly, with a little white picket fence around the front garden and a circular gravelled driveway. All of these houses are different in style, and Number Two looks rather American to me, with white plaster render and pillars either side of the double-width royal blue front door. But then again, what would I know? I've only been to the United States of America once. Perhaps next year we can take the children to Florida, visit Disneyland and have a lovely, relaxing holiday. I climb out of the car and carry my basket of cleaning materials in one hand and the vacuum cleaner in the other. I've been given another code for the front door. It swings open into a vast hallway with a floating staircase on the right.

'Hello!' I shout out. The agency said no one would be here, but I don't want to risk walking in on the owners and giving them the fright of their lives. 'Hello!' I shout again. There's no answer.

I wander around the whole house to assess what needs cleaning. Honestly, it's immaculate, so perfect I wonder if anyone actually lives here. The beds are neatly made and the bathrooms are sparkling. It'll make my work very easy. I go into the kitchen last, and find a mug, bowl and spoon in the sink. So I was wrong then; someone must have had breakfast here this morning.

Upstairs, after vacuuming the master bedroom and wiping down all the surfaces in the already immaculate en-suite, I wander into the dressing room. The men's clothes are on the left and the women's on the right. I head for the rack of men's shirts, all in shades of blue with button-down collars, so perfectly ironed they've probably been cleaned at the dry cleaner's, or perhaps some of them are completely new. Why does a man need twenty shirts, all practically identical? I lift one of the hangers off the rail and notice that it's Samuel's size. This baby blue colour will look gorgeous on him. Is the owner of this house really going to miss one shirt when he has so many of them? I very much doubt it. I ease it off the hanger and fold it neatly, carrying it downstairs and burying the shirt in my large handbag.

Once I've finished vacuuming and dusting downstairs, I notice a staircase that must lead to a basement. Switching on the light in the hall, which throws a lovely white hue on the stairs at foot level, I go downwards. There are three doors in the downstairs corridor. The first one opens onto a cinema room, a huge screen across the far wall and nine plump armchairs with leg extenders facing it. How the other half live. The next door opens onto a triple garage. There's a car at the far end covered in a cloth. I'm not interested in cars. On opening the final door, I gasp. Here there is a massive wine cellar, bottles lining the walls, all in temperature-controlled cupboards and fridges. The wall at the end holds champagne bottles. There must be tens of thousands of pounds' worth of booze in here. I don't know much about wines, but unless the owners of this house employ someone to maintain an inventory of their bottles, I'm sure they won't miss one or two. I open a fridge door and take out a champagne bottle from the lowest shelf, hopefully one that won't be missed. Samuel will be thrilled with this, I've no doubt. And he knows plenty about wines so I'm hoping he'll be impressed.

I wander back upstairs and put the bottle into my bag. People who live in houses like this are so rich and self-absorbed they don't notice when inconsequential things disappear. I know that for a fact, because I've taken things from other houses I've cleaned and nothing has ever been reported missing. I'd never steal from someone who couldn't afford to lose stuff; that would be just mean.

As I'm doing a final check on the house, I notice a pile of estate agents' glossy brochures on the coffee table in the living room. I flick through them. They're all the same. This house, Number Two, is on the market. So that's why it looks so immaculate. I skim through the brochure, admiring the photos. The price is printed on a separate white piece of paper tucked into the back page. Two million five hundred thousand. I could see myself living here, and the children would love it, with the cinema room downstairs and an outside heated swimming pool. Perhaps we can negotiate to buy the wines too; Samuel would love that. I take one of the brochures, wondering whether this place will still be on the market when we come into money. It really would be perfect; still within the school's catchment area so not too much upheaval for Riley and Alfie, and near enough to Samuel's work. Although perhaps he'll quit working for Simmons Edge. It's not like he's going to need the salary.

As I switch the alarm back on and gently close the front door behind me, I turn around and whisper to the house. 'Maybe see you again soon.'

CHAPTER FIFTEEN

THE WIFE

I let the kids sleep in my bed when the police have left. Eventually they both drift off, but I don't. I'm on hyper alert. If only the police would dust for prints, perhaps we'd make some progress as to who is playing with me. But as nothing was stolen or vandalised other than the smallest window in the house, they weren't interested. They didn't even check for footprints outside in the flower beds.

The fear for Samuel has ramped up. I'm terrified that he's being held somewhere, treated badly, and all for what? I just can't make sense of it.

This time the beep of the phone on the dot of 6.30 a.m. doesn't wake me. And that's because I'm expecting it. I'm also ready to record the message. Unable to sleep, I've been up for a while, spurred into action when I remembered that we have an old iPhone in the desk in our study. It's Samuel's phone, one he promised to give to Riley when she goes to secondary school. I've been charging it for the past hour and now it's ready.

Just before 6.30 a.m., I take both phones and hurry to the

spare bathroom, locking the door behind me. I press record on the old phone and then hold it up to my phone before pressing play. That all too familiar dalek voice starts speaking.

'Riley and Alfie need to go and live elsewhere. Organise that today. I don't want to see you with them.'

What? There is no way that I'm sending my children anywhere. They're scared, as I am. They need their mother, especially as they think their parents are splitting up, and the frightening break-in has only compounded matters. I want to keep them close and with everything that's going on, I was considering not sending them to school, wondering if perhaps we should go and stay with Mum for a few days. The kidnapper has gone too far with this request. But at least I've recorded this message.

At last I have some evidence.

I send a message back via Snapchat.

I will not be sending my kids away. They need their mum. What do you really want? I'll give you whatever you want. Money in exchange for releasing Samuel unharmed.

But I get no response.

Nevertheless, I've made up my mind. I'm going back to the police.

I suggest to the kids that they stay at home for the day, but both of them want to go to school. Alfie is in a football match and Riley wants to audition for the end of year gala, playing the piano and singing a Taylor Swift song. I'm super vigilant, looking out for any suspicious cars or vehicles that might be following me. But I see nothing. Immediately after dropping them at school, I drive to the police station and park up on the street outside. I pray I'm doing the right thing but there's no way that I cannot involve the police. Not now that the kidnapper is threatening our children. I'm about to get out of the car when my phone pings with an incoming message. My heart sinks. I hate all messages now. I wonder what would happen if I delete the Snapchat app.

It's Snapchat again. This time there's a photo of Samuel, chains attaching his wrists to metal bed posts, his eyes closed, his face covered in blood. I think I might throw up. I shove open the door, gasping for air. By the time I look at my phone again, the photo has vanished and there's a voicemail message.

'You might want to reconsider. Do not go to the police. I know where you live. I decided not to break in last night but won't hesitate to do so next time. I know where your children are. I know everything about you. I reiterate. If you want to see Samuel alive and for Riley and Alfie to remain unharmed, do not go to the police.'

This is the longest message so far. How does this person know where I am? Are they looking at me right now? There are prickles at the back of my neck, and I'm not sure if it's because someone is actually watching me, or I'm just consumed with fear. I climb out of the car, my knees weak, and glance all around me. I'm parked up on the side of a busy road, with vans and cars cruising past, office buildings sat behind pavements, and the big, sprawling red brick police station up ahead. I glance around, looking maniacally for someone loitering under a lamppost or behind a tree, or a person sitting in a nearby car. And then I wonder if I'm being tracked. That would explain a lot. Has someone put a tracker on my car? Swallowing down a wave of nausea, I walk all around the car but what am I looking for? If a tracker is under the bonnet stashed in the engine, I wouldn't have a clue what it looks like, but then I think of the movies and how small trackers are stashed inside wheel hubs. I crouch down and run my hand underneath the wheel hub of the rear passenger side, my hand coming away filthy, covered in old mud and grease. Perhaps I need to lie down under the car to see properly, but I can't do that here on the pavement. I walk slowly around the car, bending my knees, peering at the bottom of the vehicle, but I can't spot anything out of the ordinary. Perhaps, when I'm back home, I can lie on the garage floor and shine a torch up at the car's belly.

'Excuse me, ma'am, but is there a problem with your car?' I jolt at the sight of the uniformed police officer.

I glance all around. This is my chance to tell a police officer what's really going on and it's not as if I've gone to him; he's approached me. But then I think of the latest message and the implication that the sender knows I'm parked outside the police station and I bottle out. I cannot risk Samuel's life.

'Um, no. I was worried whether one of my tires might be flat.'

He cocks his head at me and strides around the car. 'They look fine to me, but there's a petrol station three hundred metres up the road. I suggest you check your pressure there.' He eyes me as if I'm a criminal and stands with his arms crossed whilst I get in the car and carefully drive away, indicating, glancing in the mirror, doing everything I'm meant to do.

I don't go to the petrol station and instead head for work. I'm behind on my emails and I've been fobbing Luke off, so much so, I haven't even approved the minutes from our board meeting. As soon as he sees me, he's up out of his chair and follows me into my office.

'Do you mind, Luke, if you give me half an hour?' I say. 'I've got a few things to deal with straight away.'

He holds his hands up in an expression of surrender and backs away. 'We've got a lot to go through though,' he adds.

'I'm know, and I'll be with you shortly.' I shut my office door behind me and sit down at my desk.

Thinking about it, could the tracker be on my phone rather than on the car? It's more likely, especially if the kidnapper is Nicolette. She's had access to my phone. But then I discount it. None of my friends are tech savvy. I mean, Nicolette runs a dress shop and she's forever complaining about her website and payment systems and how the technology drives her insane. And then it hits me. Anthony, my dreadful date – he runs a computer repair shop. He didn't shut up about hacking and I've no doubt he's a pro on tracking too. But I didn't leave my phone unattended; in fact we were only together for half an hour and during that time, other than when the server took that photo, my phone was in my bag, wasn't it? I groan. And besides, the messages arrived well before I met Anthony on Hinge. But maybe he's working in collaboration with someone else and he fixed things in such a way that it was an inevitability for us to 'meet' on the dating site. But no. That's crazy. This whole damn situation is crazy. I groan, running my fingers through my hair, shocked all over again that it's so short. The trouble is, I've no idea what I'm looking for.

I do a search on my laptop for what to do in a kidnap situation. I'm blown away and shocked by how many kidnappings happen around the world every single day. And there are so many different types; ones I've never heard of, such as

Tiger Kidnapping, which is where a person is coerced into performing an action for the kidnapper and the kidnapper has abducted someone highly valued by that person as leverage. And then there's Express Kidnapping, where people are forced to withdraw the maximum amount from an ATM, which of course I've heard about but didn't know it had its own name. Yet, despite there being so many different types of kidnapping, fulfilling a bucket list doesn't feature anywhere. Shockingly one figure suggests that up to 80% of ransom demands are paid out but conversely the majority of people kidnapped are then released. What I can't establish is whether these people involve the police or not.

I am not going to take a chance with Samuel's life, and I'm not going to put the children at any greater risk than they're already facing. It looks like I have no choice but to fulfil this kidnapper's demands. Although it pains me to even think it, perhaps they'll be safer away from me. When I finish in the office, I'll nip home and pack up a small suitcase for each of the kids, filling it with enough clean clothes and school uniform for the next few days, along with toiletries, their favourite toys and a few books. The question is, where will they be the safest? I'm sure Riley would like to stay with Autumn, but I'm not sure I trust any of my friends. If they go to Kalah's, am I sending them into the lion's den? I could send them to Mum, but the reality is, Mum is too busy with her daily activities. Also, she doesn't live in the school catchment area so I'd be spending hours of the day picking them up and dropping them back off, which is completely impractical.

The best solution is to ask my brother, Stephen. He lives in the same catchment area and I've no doubt that he'll help out. I message him and ask if he's got time to meet me for lunch. I suggest the coffee shop adjacent to John Lewis. With a plan in place for the rest of the day, I settle down to work. Luke and I go through the minutes of the board meeting and then update our huge spreadsheet with who needs to do what and by when. For a couple of hours I lose myself in work, and it's almost a relief. Just before 1 p.m., I leave the office and head for John Lewis. Stephen is already there, seated at a table for two near the food counter.

'You look exhausted,' he says, as I slide into the chair opposite him. He's already bought both of us a flat white coffee and he's sipping his despite it still being steaming hot.

'I was wondering if you'd have the children for a couple of nights.'

His face lights up. 'Of course I will, but what's going on, Eva?'

'I'm just under a lot of stress with Samuel leaving me and could do with a little time for myself.'

He narrows his eyes at me. 'That's not like you.' He takes another sip. 'I mean, you're the mother who has steadfastly refused to let her children stay with me except that one time when I had Alfie because you thought Riley had meningitis.'

I look at the floor, ashamed, because Stephen is right. I've been happy to let him babysit but have never felt at ease with him having the kids overnight. Is it because he's a single bloke? Surely not; I know my brother would never do anything to harm my kids.

'How long do you want them to stay with me?'

'Two, three nights maybe. I'm not sure exactly.'

'Eva, look at me.'

I hear the big brother tone that Stephen used to speak to me with and glance up at him. 'What's really going on? Are you sick?'

'No, I'm fine.'

He leans closer towards me. 'Except you're not. You're acting really weirdly and I think the time has come to tell me the truth.'

I stare at him. This is Stephen. Steadfast, solid Stephen. The person who has known me the whole of my life. Should I tell him the truth about the kidnapping? He'll be so shocked, and knowing him he'll try to fix things. I can't take the risk.

'I'm not coping well with Samuel's behaviour, the way he's just walked out and is refusing to talk to me.' I lean forwards and place my hand over his. 'You know, I feel really bad that I didn't give you enough support when your marriage broke down.'

He scoffs. 'That was a lifetime ago and my marriage wasn't like yours. It should never have happened. You don't need to feel bad.' He peers at me. 'I know you think I'm prying, but I really am worried about you. If you won't talk to me, have you shared how you're feeling with any of your friends?'

I shake my head, not wanting to admit that I don't trust them. Well, that's not completely true. I do trust Angela, except with her being a lawyer, I fear she'll go to the police.

'Just know that I'm here for you, day or night.'

I wait until the children are installed in the car and hand them both a treat; a KitKat instead of the piece of fruit they normally get.

'I've got something I need to tell you,' I say, swivelling around to talk to them both. 'You're going to be staying with Uncle Stephen for two or three nights. I've got to go away for work.'

'I want to stay with Dad,' Alfie says plaintively.

'I know you do, darling. But Dad is still away.'

'So the KitKat is bribery because you know we don't want to stay at Uncle Stephen's?' Riley says, holding up the wrapper. There's a bitterness to her voice that takes me aback.

'I'm sorry, darlings. I thought you loved your uncle. Stephen will look after you really well and it's only the evenings and nights. You're at school during the days.'

'So we'll be home for the weekend?' Riley asks.

'Yes,' I say, hoping I can keep that promise.

'Will Uncle Stephen take us swimming?'

'He will. And unlike me, he's a good swimmer.'

I turn on the engine and head for Stephen's house, only belatedly realising that we didn't agree a time for me to drop the children off. If he's not there, we'll go out for tea.

As we pull up in front of Stephen's small redbrick semi, I see that his car is parked in front of the house. That's a relief: he's home. The children get out reluctantly, while I open the boot and drag out their two suitcases. I'm sure their lack of enthusiasm is because of all the unsettling things happening at home. The front door swings open.

'Welcome, Riley and Alfie,' Stephen says with a big grin on his face. He gives Alfie a high five. 'We're going to have such fun together.'

I just hope he's right.

CHAPTER SIXTEEN

THE LOVER

Samuel is up and dressed when I get back, sitting on the edge of the bed, obviously waiting for me.

'I'm sorry I've been away for so long,' I say. 'But it's all for a good cause.' I step towards him and place a quick kiss on the top of his head. I'm sure he flinches slightly and it makes me stiffen. I sit down next to him.

'So, the good news. Riley and Alfie are living with me now. It's happened so smoothly. I'm taking Eva's place as their principal carer, and thank goodness I am. Eva is behaving so erratically, it's extremely worrying. Half the time she isn't making any sense, and then there's her appearance. That hairstyle makes her look positively crazy. Really, it just proves Eva isn't the woman you think she is. I'm so relieved she's brought the kids to me, as I'd be genuinely worried that she might harm them in her current state of mind. She'll probably leave the gas hob on and burn the house down, or because she's so distracted all the time, she'll drive the car off the road.'

'I want to see them,' Samuel says.

'That's not possible. Not yet,' I reply, reaching for his hand but to my dismay, he jerks it away from me.

'Come on, Samuel. Don't be like that.'

'You can't possibly understand,' he says. 'When you're a parent and you haven't seen your children for a fortnight, it's as if a part of your soul has been wrenched away.'

'Don't be so melodramatic. We've talked about this. You'll see them soon enough.'

'What do they think has happened to me? They won't understand why I haven't been in touch. They'll be so worried.'

'Alfie and Riley are kids,' I say sharply. 'They only think about themselves. The universe centres around them and their needs. And they don't have a sense of time in the way that adults do. A day, a week, a month; they're social constructs that they don't fully understand.' I haven't got a clue if that's the case because having no children of my own, I have no idea how kids' brains work. But I'm looking forward to finding out. It's a relief that I'll be stepping into their lives at this age and stage because I can't bear little children. The messiness of them, the noise, their irrationality. Alfie and Riley are old enough to look after themselves. No disturbing Samuel and me in the night, no need to supervise them at weekends, but they'll still be sufficiently malleable to forget their birth mother and allow me to step into her shoes.

'Come on, darling,' I say, throwing my arms around Samuel. 'You're such a worry guts. Everyone and everything is going to be just fine.'

Except I do have a little niggle at the base of my spine. A little prickling sensation that Samuel is pulling away from me, and that is a worry. A very big worry indeed.

CHAPTER SEVENTEEN

THE WIFE

The house feels so empty without Samuel or the kids. I've never been frightened to stay alone in our home before but right now I'd rather be anywhere else except here. I can't help wondering if the kidnapper will try to break in during the night, this time smashing down the back door or forcing out one of the panes of glass in the sliding doors in the living room. I set the alarm before I went to bed, so if anyone tries to break in downstairs, the alarm will sound and the monitoring station will be notified. Even so, when the clock hits 1 a.m. I'm still wide awake.

Earlier, I rang Stephen's mobile to wish the children good night, but he didn't pick up. Then I sent him a message asking him to call me so I could speak to the kids. He did, eventually. It was nearly 10 p.m. and he apologised profusely, explaining that he'd helped them complete their homework, then they all watched a film, followed by quick baths and bed. It's not his fault that he doesn't know how much I need to talk to them before they go to sleep. He promised me that the kids were fine and shattered after a long but fulfilling day, both fast asleep in bed.

'I'd really like to speak to them in the morning, before they go to school,' I said.

'Of course,' he reassured me. 'Concentrate upon yourself,' he said. 'The kids are in safe hands with me.'

After tossing and turning for a further hour, I succumb to taking another sleeping pill. So when my phone pings at 6.30 a.m., I awake with a start, annoyed I've overslept. I fumble for my phone and press the play button before remembering to record it on my other phone. That all too familiar voice speaks again.

'File for divorce from Samuel and get engaged to someone else. Post evidence of this on Facebook and Instagram. I want to see a ring on your finger within three weeks.'

The voicemail is deleted. I laugh. I actually laugh out loud because that is the most ludicrous thing I've ever heard. For a moment I wonder if I'm being toyed with by a kid because surely only someone utterly naive would think I could get divorced and engaged within such a short time period. But then I think of the photo of Samuel and the fact that he is still missing, and my next thought is, three weeks. This nightmare is still going to be going on for at least another three weeks. I can't bear it. What is the kidnapper trying to achieve? It's as if they're wanting to prove that Samuel doesn't love me anymore, and they're using me to tell the world that our relationship has ended and that I'm happily involved with someone else. But why? Why do they care and what is their end game? I'm being toyed with, like I'm a puppet in a game to which I don't know the rules. I don't know anything about the mechanics of divorce, but I'm pretty sure it requires two parties and it's certainly not something that can happen overnight. I do a quick online search to double-check.

It's as I thought. The fastest time to complete a divorce in the UK is 26 weeks, and that's when it's a no-fault divorce and both parties agree. Does Samuel agree? Is he being forced to sign divorce papers? And if I do go through this farcical charade, then where do I send the divorce papers? I assume Samuel will have to sign them and I can't imagine the kidnapper being so stupid as to share an address with me. Or will they forge Samuel's signature?

And then there's the second half of this demand. Get engaged to someone else within three weeks. How ridiculous is that! I can't make someone fall head over heels in love with me and even if I could, that timescale is impossible. Then it hits me. The kidnapper doesn't care about me finding love. They want the world to think I've moved on; for all our friends and family to presume that I'm the one at fault in my failed marriage. Why can't I just put a statement out on social media apologising for being unfaithful to Samuel and saying we're going our separate ways? Would that satisfy the kidnapper? Would that bring an end to this charade?

I send them a message on Snapchat, suggesting that. And then I stare at the screen as it tells me that they're typing. I sink back onto my pillows at the answer.

No. Do as I say.

I think through our male friends, but they're all married, mainly to my girlfriends, so that isn't going to work. I need to recruit a single friend. I think of George, the divorced dad of one of Riley's school friends, but I only know him to say hello to, and it would be super awkward. It isn't until I'm sitting at the kitchen table cradling a mug of coffee that my mind wanders to Ian. Ian is not only one of my oldest friends, he's a trustee for Leap Ahead and we briefly went out together two decades ago. In fact we were each other's plus-ones when we weren't going out with other people for several years in our late teens and early twenties. I see him more for work these days than socially, and that's because I'm slightly awkward around him. I'm aware that he's held a torch for me for a very long time.

It was shortly after Samuel and I got engaged and we attended the wedding of a school friend. Ian accosted me when Samuel was at the bar collecting drinks.

'Eva,' he said, clasping his arms around my waist and squeezing me tightly. 'Darling Eva. You're so beautiful.'

'And you're drunk.' I tried to wriggle out of his grasp.

'Maybe. But are you sure?' He grabbed my hand and brought the back of it up to his lips.

'Sure about what?'

'Marrying that very boring man, Samuel.'

'That's rude, Ian,' I said. 'I love Samuel.'

'And I love you. Always have done. You're the one that got away, Eva. Broke my heart. Condemned me to a life of solitude.'

'You're being ridiculous. You and I would never work together. You're a free spirit and I want to settle down. How many women have you slept with in the past year alone?'

'None of them live up to you.'

'You like to play the field. I want children. Samuel and I are going to start a family soon.'

'I would have a family for you, my little Eva.'

'I don't want anyone to have a family for me, I want my partner to want to have children, to dream of being a dad.'

And then Samuel appeared holding two glasses of wine and I introduced him to Ian, explaining we went to sixth form college together. Ian slipped away then, quickly starting a conversation with a beautiful blonde wearing a skirt that barely covered her backside, and I chose to forget what Ian told me. He was inebriated, as careless with his words as he was with his roving eye. Except Ian has never married. Instead, he's a tech millionaire with a string of relationships with girls much too young for him. He has spent the past decade working all hours, lining his and his associates' pockets while committed relationships just aren't on his agenda. Ian was one of the first people I approached to become a trustee of Leap Ahead. His business black book has proven invaluable to raising more funds, and his associates have helped hundreds of young people gain computer skills, so very vital to their future success. I'm sure Ian will be shocked when I tell him what's happened to me, and I'm equally sure he'll be willing to help.

I send him a message and ask to meet up, as soon as possible.

He replies by return, suggesting a wine bar in central London. It's not at all convenient, but beggars can't be choosers.

I take the train to London Victoria, fortunately going in the opposite direction to the majority of commuters, and then walk the short distance to Eccleston Yards, a trendy development with a bunch of new eateries. All the restaurants and wine bars are busy, many with customers spilling out onto the pedestrianised squares, music pumping out, loud, excited voices mingling in a cacophony of sound. I ease past the revellers into the Asian-styled restaurant Ian has chosen. In here, it's quiet, almost serene, the tables mostly empty. Ian is sitting at the bar, nursing a cocktail.

'This is a surprise,' he says, sliding down from his stool and giving me a kiss on both cheeks. 'What would you like to drink?'

'Whatever you're having,' I say, not in the mood for being decisive.

When the server has finished mixing what looks to be a very complicated concoction of unusual spirits, he pushes the glass towards me and walks to the other end of the bar.

'Is everything alright?' Ian asks, peering at me with a concerned face, his thin wire glasses giving him an owlish appearance. 'What's with the hair?'

I run my fingers through it self-consciously.

'I know it looks crap but it's part of what I want to tell you.'

'It doesn't look crap exactly.'

I laugh. 'Yes, it does. You don't need to be polite.' I glance at his hair, noticing that it's peppering slightly at the sides. It lends him gravitas, a contrast to his torn, baggy jeans and sweatshirt, the uniform of someone twenty years younger. 'What I'm about to tell you, ask of you, is going to sound crazy. And I'm begging you not to tell anyone else. Do you promise?'

'Alright,' he says, tilting his head to one side. 'You know you can trust me.'

And that's the thing. I do trust Ian, so I tell him everything; all about the messages, the bucket list, the sense that I'm being followed, that I can't go to the police and how I'm terrified for Samuel's wellbeing, as well as the children. Finally, I ask him if he'll pretend to get engaged to me.

'Jeez, Eva. I always said I'd do anything for you, but this?' There's an unreadable expression on his face and I wonder if he's a bit hurt. But surely he doesn't still like me, not after all of these years, not when he can have whichever young woman takes his fancy.

'If it's too much, I totally understand. It's crazy, I know, and I haven't even got any proof to show you. You do believe me, don't you?'

'You've always had a great imagination, but even you couldn't come up with a story as preposterous as this. And I'm sure if you really wanted to dump your husband for me, you could come up with a simpler way to go about it.'

'So you'll do it? Pretend to be engaged to me.'

'Of course I'll do it,' Ian says, squeezing my hand. 'The question is, do I need to buy you a ring?'

'A fake will do just fine.'

'Only the best for you, my darling. Can your fiancé kiss his wife to be?' There's a twinkle in his eye now and the cheeky Ian has returned.

'Nope.'

He doesn't even try and we both sip our drinks.

'We need to find out who is behind all of this,' Ian says. 'As much as I'd really like to be engaged to you, we're playing a very dangerous game here. We don't know what the kidnapper wants or why. We've no idea if he wants to hurt you or your family or how long this is going to go on for. I think you should go to the police.'

'No,' I say abruptly. 'If the kidnapper is tracking me, they'll know I've gone to the police. And they must be tracking me because how did they know I was about to walk into the police station the other day? I'm not going to risk Samuel's life.'

Ian's shoulders drop. 'Alright, so if you don't want to go yourself, I can go to the police for you.'

'No. Please don't. It's too risky.'

'Mmm,' he says, reluctance in his voice. 'But let me do some digging. I've got ways and means to track people online. Can I look at your phone for a few minutes?'

I pull it out of my bag and hand it to Ian. He navigates to Snapchat, his fingers racing across the screen. Then he leans down and removes a sleek laptop from his brown leather messenger bag. 'Do you mind if I back up your phone onto my laptop? There's nothing there that you don't want me to see, is there?'

'If you mean nude photos or a history of me visiting dodgy websites, then no. I'm afraid I'm as boring as ever.'

'Shame.' Ian elbows me and I elbow him back.

'What are you going to do?' I ask.

'Not sure yet, but I'll be able to see if there's any tracking software on your phone and hopefully I might be able to work out who Snapchat user ISEEU975783 really is. At the very least, I'll be able to put some software on your phone so we can copy any future messages from Snapchat without them knowing.'

I feel such a relief having Ian on my side. For the first time, I am hopeful that this nightmare can be brought to a successful conclusion.

'I'll also do some general digging,' Ian continues. 'Find out whether Samuel has been seeing anyone else.'

'He hasn't,' I interrupt. 'I think that was all a red herring.'

Ian looks at me doubtfully. 'At least let me rule it out.'

'You will be careful though, won't you? If this person gets wind that you're looking into them, they might hurt Samuel or the kids, or even worse.'

'Eva, I specialise in online security, commercial espionage and all of that. It's what I and my team do day in and day out. You really don't need to worry.'

I lean over and place a kiss on his cheek. 'Thank you,' I murmur. 'Can I tell the world that we're engaged?'

He snorts. 'We'd better take a selfie then.'

CHAPTER EIGHTEEN

THE LOVER

I didn't think she'd pull this off but not only has she done what I've asked, she's done it in record time. My sister has posted online that she's engaged to Ian Oakley. This is gold dust!

I've just finished cleaning a four-bedroom house that has been let out to holiday guests and it was a complete mess. Shameful really, how people have so little respect for others' belongings. I'm shattered but I need to hurry home for a shower before nipping back to see Samuel. My days are hectic now because I have to be home for 4 p.m., give Eva's spoiled children tea and pretend to enjoy their company until bedtime. For the past two nights, I've sacrificed myself and stayed at home, but goodness, how I miss Samuel. I can't wait until the time when the four of us will be together. Tonight, I'm going to hang on until Riley and Alfie are asleep and then I'll lock them in my home whilst I go and spend a few hours with my love. I'll be back before the kids wake up and they'll be perfectly safe.

Ian Oakley. Well, well, well. I telephone Eva and she answers on the third ring.

'What's going on, Eva?' I ask.

'What do you mean?'

'You know exactly what I mean,' I say in my big brother authoritarian voice. 'You've posted on social media that you're engaged to Ian Oakley. What the hell are you playing at? I saw your story on Instagram, Eva. On bloody social media. Didn't you think that it might be nice to let me, your only sibling, know what's going on?'

'I'm sorry,' she says quietly. 'It's been a very difficult couple of weeks, and of course I should have told you.'

'Have you been seeing Ian behind Samuel's back? Is that why he's left home and why you're chucking out your own kids, so you can carry on a sordid affair without the responsibility of your family?'

'No,' she protests. 'It's nothing like that. There have been some really bad things happening. Not just the break-in and Samuel's disappearance. Stuff I can't tell you about. As soon as the divorce comes through, I'm marrying Ian,' she says. I wonder if I didn't know the truth whether I'd believe her.

'Are you saying that Samuel left you because you were having an affair? God, Eva. You've made out that it was Samuel's fault.' There's a long pause before I speak again. 'I'm really worried about you, Eva,' I say. 'Would you like me to come to the doctor with you?'

'What doctor? There's nothing wrong with me,' she replies tightly.

'Clearly there is. You've pushed Samuel away and now you're destroying your marriage, sharing all of your dirty linen in public. And what are Riley and Alfie going to say when they find out?'

'I'm sorry, Stephen, but I can't be having this conversation right now.'

'I remember how you two were an item all those years ago. I suppose if you're going to be with anyone else, Ian Oakley is as good a choice as any. At least you have history. But you've only just broken up with Samuel and this is obviously a rebound situation.'

'Look, Stephen, I don't want to have this conversation. I'll collect the kids from school and bring them over to yours later.'

And then she's gone. The ungrateful bitch.

It's ironic how Eva has slid straight back into the arms of Ian. She used him terribly in the years before she met Samuel, stringing him along with promises that they'd be together one day; it was all lies. She just needed someone to take to posh events or a bed partner when she couldn't find anyone else. And then when Samuel came along, she dropped Ian like a hot poker. Everyone could see that she should have stuck with Ian, but no, she chose Samuel. And what Eva wants, Eva gets.

I start the car engine and head towards home. But the more I think about Eva with Ian, the more I realise my initial delight that they're together is in fact a mistake. No, not just a mistake; it would be a disaster. What if she genuinely falls in love with Ian and really divorces Samuel? That would completely destroy my plan.

Back at home, Eva drops her sulky children with me and she seems relieved that I'm not inclined to have a further conversation with her. I let the kids do their own thing, because frankly it's not my problem if they complete their homework or not. And half an hour after saying goodnight to them, I slip out of my house and head back to my love.

I'm quietly reading a book while Samuel is snoring gently, asleep again. What was that? I start and let the book slide to the floor. There's a *crunch, crunch* noise, much like footsteps. I freeze. The curtains are pulled and it's dark outside. I stand up and edge towards the window. A beam of light bounces along outside.

Shit. There's someone here.

And then there's a loud rapping on the front door, so much so that Samuel stirs in his sleep. I tiptoe to the door, my heart thudding. Surely they haven't found me? I've been so careful. Have I been stupid to think that these woods are deserted? I should never have left the lights on, or lit the fire to warm the cottage, because now there's smoke coming out of the small chimney.

'Hello!' It's a man's voice, gruff and vaguely familiar.

I open the door just a couple of inches.

'Hello,' I say. 'How can I help you?'

The man is in his sixties, stocky with a thick greying beard and wearing a dark green wax jacket and brown boots. His eyes widen, his thick eyebrows dancing upwards. 'Stephen? Is that you? Good heavens! I haven't seen you since you were a wee little boy.'

I stare at him blankly.

'It's Fred Teather. I live at Purnell Farm, the next farm over. I was out lamping and saw lights on. Thought there might be squatters here because this old place has lain empty for years. Never seen anyone here before.'

'Oh, that's nice of you to check,' I say. 'But no, it's just me.' We stand there in an awkward silence for a few beats.

'How's your mother? I heard that your father passed away some years ago. My condolences.'

The last thing I need is for this busybody to make contact with Mum.

'Unfortunately my mother is dying and I'm sorting out her affairs. I have power of attorney, so thought I'd tidy this place up a bit before putting it on the market to sell it.'

'I'm sorry to hear that. And how is young Eva? We were so fond of that lassie. Such a lovely girl who has no doubt grown up to be a beautiful woman.'

That peeves me. Why is it that everyone loves Eva? What has she got that I haven't?

'Eva's out of the country,' I say. 'Upped and left years ago without so much as a goodbye. We've lost contact.'

'Well, blow me down. I never thought she'd do something like that. But then again, there's nothing so queer as folk, as they say. Please pass on my best wishes to your mother.'

'It's kind of you but she has dementia and barely recognises me, let alone anyone else.' There's another awkward pause. 'Anyway, thank you for checking out the cottage but all's fine.'

'Fair enough. Please let me know when you put the land and cottage on the market. I might be interested.'

'Will do,' I say, and move to shut the door. Fred Teather looks as if he's going to say something else, but then he nods his head and steps backwards into the dark night.

CHAPTER NINETEEN

THE WIFE

The water is pressing me downwards, as if someone with the strength of an iron man is pushing down on my head, squeezing all the air from my lungs and then burning every cell in my body. My chest is screaming with pain, as if everything inside it is about to burst out, yet all I want is blackness, the nothingness of death. And then I see Samuel, floating up above me, his face so calm I'm terrified he's dead. I reach up to grab his foot but it's forever just a few metres in front of me, and I can't grab him however much I try. There's panic, knowing he's out of my reach and that we both might die if I let him drift away. I hurl myself forwards but then there's a bright light that beams into my eyes, forcing them wide open. I gasp and sit bolt upright in bed. I'm covered in sweat, the sound of blood swishing in my ears, and my heart is racing so fast, for a brief moment I wonder if I'm having a heart attack. It's that nightmare, again. I'm having it almost nightly now. Rationally, I know it's because I'm under unimaginable stress, that I'm petrified about what has happened to Samuel, but it does nothing to ease the terrifying sense that my life is spiralling out of control. At least I've slept longer this morning. It's nearly 8 a.m. and to my relief, I haven't received another message.

I'm in the bathroom when the doorbell rings. I hurry downstairs, my mind in turmoil as to who it could be this early in the morning. Except by the time I've unlocked the door and opened it, there's no one there. Instead there's a bouquet of flowers on the doorstep and a small white card wedged between several stems of brightly coloured Gerbera. I pull it out. The words are typewritten:

> *Congratulations on your engagement.*
> *Samuel is very pleased that you've*
> *moved on.*

I run barefoot down our short drive and onto the road in the hope that I'm going to catch sight of a flower delivery van, or any vehicle for that matter. But I know I'm too late. Whoever put these flowers on my doorstep is long gone. I walk dejectedly back to the house, the soles of my feet sore from the gravel.

I pick up the bouquet from the floor of the hallway where I dropped it. It's gaudy, full of bright orange and shocking pink Gerbera, a bunch of flowers that I would never choose for myself. I take it outside to the bins and shove it inside the green wheelie bin. The house seems so empty without the normal morning freneticism of getting the children ready for school, and my heart aches with loneliness. I call Stephen but once again he doesn't pick up. No doubt it's hectic at his house in these few minutes before they have to leave for school. I hope Alfie and Riley aren't missing me too much. I also wish we'd given in to Riley's demands and let her have her own phone. At least then I could be in direct touch with them. I have the television on and am drinking my second strong cup of coffee of the morning when the doorbell rings once again. This time I don't hurry towards it, but I open the Ring app on my phone. I'm terrified of who might be on the doorstep at 8.30 a.m. But I needn't have worried.

'What are you doing here?' I ask, as I swing the door open and Kalah and Angela step inside.

'We've brought coffee and croissants,' Angela says, holding up a paper bag with the name of a local coffee shop printed on the front.

'Why aren't you doing the school run?' I ask Kalah. She flushes slightly.

'Xavier has taken Autumn to school this morning. Angela and I wanted to catch you before you head off to work.'

'Alright.' I eye them both suspiciously. Angela looks relaxed; Kalah the opposite. We're close friends but it's rare that any of us turn up on each other's doorsteps without checking in advance that it's convenient. They follow me into the kitchen and Angela places the bag on the table. I fish out plates.

'So what's going on?' I ask, as we settle in our chairs.

'That's what we wanted to ask you,' Angela says. She holds my gaze. Kalah seems more interested in the dark depths of her disposable coffee cup. 'Riley told Autumn that she and Alfie are living with Stephen for a few days. And then there was that post on Instagram stating that you're engaged to Ian Oakley. We're worried about you, Eva.'

'And we're worried about the kids,' Kalah adds, still

without meeting my gaze. 'Riley says she hates living with Stephen and Alfie is crying himself to sleep.'

I flinch. The thought of my kids suffering is too much to bear. I stare out of the window at a small finch pecking at the nuts that hang off the bird bath on the patio and wish I could push back time to the days before I went to Amsterdam.

'Are you telling me I'm a bad mother?' I ask through gritted teeth.

'Goodness, no,' Kalah replies rapidly.

'We're worried about you,' Angela interjects. 'This is all so out of character.' She waves her hands around. 'Is there more to Samuel leaving you than you're telling us? Have you actually sat down together and discussed everything? And how long have you and Ian been together?'

'I'm sorry, but there's a lot of stuff I'm not at liberty to tell you.'

Angela nudges her chair closer towards me. 'We're really concerned about you, Eva. We think you're having some sort of a breakdown. All of this is so out of character.' She points towards my hair. 'The dates, the engagement, changing the way you look, palming the kids off onto your brother whom you don't even really like. It's not you. Have you and Samuel actually discussed divorcing, because you need proper legal advice if that's the route you're going down? Normally I'd recommend mediation first.'

I don't say anything because what can I say?

'I mentioned a therapist to you the other day,' Kalah adds. 'We'd really like you to go and see her. I'll come with you if you like.'

'Kalah is right,' Angela continues. 'If you want to get a good divorce settlement and keep custody of the children,

you need to be in the right headspace and not share everything publicly.'

I jump up from the table, knocking my chair over in the
process. I'm normally level headed but the last thing I need
right now is the interference of my friends. I stride across to
the kettle and angrily press the switch.

'I am not having a breakdown,' I say, realising that my
heightened tone and actions are in direct opposition to my
words. 'And I will come to you for legal advice in due
course,' I promise Angela. For a moment I'd love to tell them
the truth, watch the expressions of horror cross their faces
before they dissolve into sympathy. Except I can't. Angela is
much too officious, and she'd be dialling the police before
stepping out of my front door. On the positive side, the fact
they're here means – unless they're playing a game of double
bluff – I'm pretty sure neither of them is holding my
husband. But where is Nicolette? She's not in my kitchen
supporting my friends. In fact, I haven't heard from her since
our awkward conversation the other morning. I swivel
around to face them, clicking off the noisy kettle.

'Where's Nicolette? How come she's not here to berate
me? When did either of you last speak to her?'

'I spoke to her briefly yesterday,' Angela says.

'Really?' Kalah asks, appearing slighted.

'She's not in a great space herself,' Angela adds.

'And why's that?' I ask spikily.

Angela frowns. 'She's split up with her man.'

'You mean her married lover? Has he decided to go back
to his wife? Oh, poor Nicolette,' I say, my voice heavy with
sarcasm.

Angela stands up. 'Why are you being such a bitch?' she
asks. 'I know it's tough that Samuel has left you and that he

seems to have done a disappearing act, but you don't need to take it out on us. We're your friends, Eva. We want to support you.'

I turn away from them and place my palms flat on the smooth marble countertop. Are they? Is Angela protesting too much? Is Nicolette my friend or has she kidnapped Samuel? Did my husband end the affair with my friend and in response, she's tied him up and hidden him away somewhere? Is that why she hasn't been present for the rest of us this last week or so? Is she consumed with jealousy?

I sigh before turning around to face them, keeping my voice steady. 'Look, I know you mean well and I'm grateful for that. But rest assured, I'm not having a breakdown. There's a lot of stuff going on that I can't share with you, but when the time is right I'll explain it all.'

'And Ian? First of all it's weird for you to get engaged so quickly when you're not even divorced from Samuel, and secondly, isn't that the sort of thing you'd share with us before posting about it on social media?' Angela asks. 'And Nicolette said you asked her to help you set up a profile for online dating. What was all that about?'

She's completely right. It doesn't make sense and we all know it.

'It's more like a promise to Ian. Obviously I can't get engaged properly until I'm divorced.' I hide my fingers behind my back realising that I'm still wearing the engagement ring and wedding band that Samuel gave me.

'How long have you been together?' Kalah asks.

'A very short time. As you know, we've been friends forever, and we went out together back in the day. He's here for me, and perhaps it has moved too quickly but he's a good man. I haven't cheated on Samuel. My husband left me.'

Kalah can't hide her expression of doubt. She never much liked Ian, found him too flighty.

'Look,' I say, clasping my right hand over my left to hide the rings. 'I love you both and really appreciate your concern, but I need you to go. I've got to get to work. With everything that's been going on, I've been neglecting the charity.'

My friends leave reluctantly, reassuring me that they're there for me, day or night, and if I change my mind about visiting a therapist, I should let Kalah know. That is never going to happen. The very last thing I need is someone probing my mind, uncovering the layer upon layer of lies that I've been forced to tell.

Work is a good distraction, helping me ignore the misery in my chest; the longing for not only my husband but my children too. I'm devastated that Riley and Alfie are suffering and decide to collect them from school and take them out somewhere as a treat. At lunchtime I call Ian.

'I haven't got any news for you yet,' he says, butting in before I can speak.

'Actually, I was calling to share my suspicions. Do you remember Nicolette? She went out with Stephen briefly and was the year above us at college. She's one of my besties now... at least I thought she was. She openly admitted she was having an affair with a married man, but now Angela has told me that she's split up with him. I'm wondering if it might have been Samuel, and now he's dumped her, she's keeping him kidnapped somewhere. She would have had access to my phone and she was with me the day those awful photos were taken of me throwing up outside the restaurant.'

'Okay,' Ian says slowly. 'I'll look into her, try and find out who she's been having an affair with. Might be tricky though. I'm a computer geek, not a private detective.'

'I know, Ian, and I'm so grateful for your help. You're the only person who knows what's really going on and it's such a relief to be able to share it with you.'

'No problem, fiancée,' he says. 'I've got one of my best techies looking through your phone and I'm hopeful we'll able to trace down the location from which the messages have been sent to you. I'm expecting his feedback in the morning. We should meet up for dinner. How about tomorrow?'

'Um.' I hesitate.

'Look, I'll call you in the morning. I'm sure I'll have plenty to tell you by then.'

I thank him effusively and then send Stephen a message, telling him I'll be collecting the kids from school and taking them out for tea. We'll aim to be at his house around 6 p.m. Finally, I send a Snapchat message to user ISEEU975783.

Do whatever you want to me but don't punish my kids. They're scared and unhappy and need to come home. Please let's end these games by you telling me what you really want.

I wait and wait but get no reply.

Both the kids' faces light up when they see me waiting in the throng of parents at the school gate. Even Riley throws her arms around me and doesn't wriggle away when I squeeze her tightly and walk back to the car with my arm around her shoulder. Alfie holds my left hand, something he hasn't done in a very long time.

'Are we coming home?' he asks, eyes bright.

'No, I'm sorry. Not yet. But I thought I'd take you out for tea before returning to Uncle Stephen's. Where would you like to go?'

Alfie's shoulders sag. 'I want to be at home.'

'I know you do, darling, and hopefully you can come back very soon.'

'I don't understand why we can't be there now,' Riley says.

And another lie trips off my lips. 'The police think it's safer for you to be at Uncle Stephen's, just until they catch whoever broke the downstairs toilet window.' I pray I'm not making them scared of their home in the longer term. I see Kalah and Autumn up ahead, but I don't want to talk to them, so we walk slower than normal and I hang back until I see Kalah's car pull out onto the road.

'So what's it going to be? Pizza or burgers?'

'Pizza,' they chime together.

A couple of hours later and we've had a lovely tea, filling up the children's bellies with all the food I normally wouldn't give them. They're both a little hyper on sugary ice cream and I'm still not ready to take them back to my brother's. Instead, we go to the bowling alley, somewhere we've never been. But I want to create new memories, not yearn for Samuel. Even so, I wish he was with us. I'm lousy at bowling. Even Alfie is better than me. But at least we laugh, and that's something I haven't done in what seems like a long time.

We arrive back at Stephen's just before 7 p.m. He swings open the door with a scowl on his face.

'I thought you'd be back ages ago,' he says, standing to one side so the kids can go past him. I jolt when I see my children's jackets hanging on the pegs on the wall and their wellington boots neatly lined up underneath. 'Riley, Alfie, can you go upstairs and get ready for bed,' Stephen commands. 'I need a word with your mum.'

'It's too early,' Riley says, her lower lip jutting out.

'Alfie, you go and have a bath,' I say, feeling awkward that my brother is telling my kids what to do. 'Riley, you can finish your homework.'

I follow Stephen into the small kitchen. There's just enough space for a table and three chairs wedged into the corner.

'Is everything alright?' I ask, noting the tension in his jaw.

He gestures to the table and I sit down. Stephen stands, leaning his back against the countertop near the sink, his arms crossed over his chest.

'It's me who should be asking you that question,' he says. 'What the hell is going on between you and Ian?'

'As I already told you, we're engaged,' I say quietly. 'Well, not properly engaged, obviously, because I'm not divorced from Samuel.'

Stephen rolls his eyes at me. 'I think you're losing it. Your behaviour has been completely irrational the past fortnight. You've been rolling around drunk, cut your hair off, farmed your kids out to me, gotten engaged just a fortnight after your marriage broke down. None of this is rational, Eva. I think you should go and see your doctor, get your mental health checked out, and pronto. If not for yourself, you need to do if for your kids.'

Wow. Stephen has really let rip, just like Angela and Kalah did. And I can see my situation from their perspective, and from the outside it does look like I'm cracking up, on the edge of a nervous breakdown. Except I'm not. For a split second, I wonder if they're right. After all, I have no proof of everything that's been happening, so maybe it's all a figment of my imagination. But then I dispel that notion. I'm not having a breakdown. In fact I'm being strong. Stronger than I've ever been before, carrying everything alone, siphoning strength from a depth I didn't know I had in order to save Samuel. I don't deny it's taking its toll, but I am not going crazy. And then, against my better judgement, I get up, shut the door to the kitchen and sit back down again.

'Firstly you've got to promise you won't tell anyone what I'm about to share with you.'

He eyes me suspiciously but nods his accord, sliding into the chair opposite me.

I recount everything that has happened, describing the messages, the bucket-list tasks, the horrific photos and the threats. Stephen's jaw falls open and his eyes widen, the more I tell him until finally we sit in silence.

'Are you saying you don't actually have any messages, no proof whatsoever?'

'The only thing I have is a recording of the message they sent me saying, "Riley and Alfie need to go and live elsewhere. Organise that today. I don't want to see you with them." I used another phone to record it. But with all the other messages, they delete the instant I've read or listened to them.'

'You haven't taken screenshots?'

'I tried, but the person on the other end of Snapchat could see when I've done that and they were furious. I wasn't fast enough to take a photo with another phone.'

'I can't believe this,' Stephen says, shaking his head.

'Well, it's true. I'm terrified, Stevie,' I say, using the nickname from our childhood. For once he doesn't complain.

'You've got to go to the police,' he says. 'You've got to, Eva. You can't put your family's lives at risk.'

'But the extortionist knew when I'd driven to the police station. I think they're listening to my conversations, following me wherever I go.' We both glance out of the window into Stephen's small, unkempt garden.

'I don't know what to say,' he murmurs. 'I'll look after the children, of course I will. But I'm worried for you too and I really think you should tell the police.'

I disagree with him. I've got no concrete evidence to show them, and besides, I'm not prepared to take the risk.

'Don't take this the wrong way,' Stephen says after a lengthy pause, 'but you're not having a breakdown, are you? Sometimes the mind plays horrible tricks and if Samuel has left you for another woman, then perhaps...' His voice tapers off.

And this is exactly why I won't be involving the police and why I didn't want to tell my brother. I'm not going crazy. Those instructions were all too real. I'm going to play the long game here because eventually the kidnapper will make a mistake, or better still, if I complete all of their ridiculous tasks, then I have to hold out hope that they'll release Samuel unharmed.

'Does that mean you're not really engaged to Ian?'

I bark out a short laugh. 'Of course not. I just need it to look like I am.'

'I can't believe Ian is going along with this.'

'He's a good friend,' I say.

Stephen nods slowly. 'But he's only a friend. I'm your brother, and remember what Dad always used to say? The only people you can truly rely upon is your closest family.'

'I'm sorry I haven't told you before.' I grimace. 'But I need to protect you too.'

'You know I'm a grown man. I can look after myself. And Mum? Have you told her?'

'Of course not!' I exclaim.

'Where does she think Samuel is?'

'In Malaysia. We had lunch with Mum on Sunday. She asked after you.'

'But you'll have to tell her the truth soon, or at least that Samuel has left you.'

'I suppose I will,' I say, dreading the prospect of that conversation.

A strange look passes over Stephen's face and I reckon I know what he's thinking. Does that mean I'm no longer the prodigal child?

CHAPTER TWENTY

THE LOVER

I'm at home clearing up the mess left behind by Riley and Alfie. When they're living with me permanently there is no way they will be allowed to dump dirty cereal bowls in the sink or leave their laundry on the floor of their bedrooms for me to trip over. But for now, I have to bite my tongue and pretend that I love having them around. A bit of discipline is going to do them the world of good, and I'm sure that Samuel will agree.

The doorbell rings just as I'm taking out a load of washing. It's probably the postman, hopefully not with a registered letter final demand. I hurry to the door and stupidly swing it open without glancing through the peephole. A mistake.

'What are you doing here?' I ask coldly.

Ian Oakley has barely changed. He's still wearing those silly wire-framed glasses and is dressed in oversized clothes that are more suitable for a teenage boy than a forty-year-old man.

'Hello, Stephen,' he says. 'Long time no see. How are you?'

'Fine,' I reply curtly. 'Why are you here?'

'As your future brother-in-law I thought I might get a warmer welcome. Can I come in? I've got a couple of things I wanted to run by you.'

'If you're talking about the ridiculous engagement between you and Eva, then I know it's not real. Eva has told me everything so there's nothing for us to discuss.'

'Actually, it's not that.' He takes a step towards me and I instinctively step backwards. I could slam the door in his face but I'm not sure that's going to serve me, so reluctantly I wave him through the door.

He stands awkwardly in my small hallway so I point for him to walk through into the living room.

'Take a seat, then,' I say. He perches on the sofa but I carry on standing, my hands on my hips.

'I turned up at your work, at the builder's merchant's, but I understand you're no longer employed there. I think Eva might be surprised, because she was convinced that was your place of work, and has been for the past few years.'

I cross my arms. 'I moved on.'

He chuckles. 'Is that what you call it?'

I bristle. It's none of Ian Oakley's business and I'm livid that he's intimating he knows I was fired. I haven't told a soul about that, not even Samuel, or perhaps especially Samuel. Yes, I lost my job and now I'm working as a cleaner. So what?

'Have you had any contact with Nicolette recently?'

'Nicolette? Eva's friend?' I'm surprised he's mentioning her.

'Yes, although she was your friend too, wasn't she? You

went out with her for a while if my memory serves me correctly.'

'Why are you asking me about her? She's Eva's friend now, not mine.'

'Except you follow her on social media.'

'What's the crime in that?' And why all of this questioning?

'No crime, except you've only started following her recently.'

I'm getting prickles up the back of my neck now. What does Ian Oakley know and why is he tracking my social media?

'I'm afraid I need to get on,' I say. 'I'm freelancing at the moment and have a job I need to get to.'

Ian raises an eyebrow. 'This won't take long. You and Samuel were friends back in high school, weren't you? But then something happened, and you fell out.'

'Fell out?' I scowl. 'Samuel and I barely knew each other. I met Samuel when Eva got together with him after Angela and Hunter's wedding.'

Ian looks at me dubiously. He's right, but I'm relying on the passage of time to blur everyone's recollections.

'Were you upset that he started dating Eva, and if so, why?'

'Your memory must be playing tricks on you, Ian. I've always been supportive of Eva's relationship, and I have a good friendship with my brother-in-law.'

'Is that what you call it?'

My hackles are raised and the little hairs are standing up on my arms. How does Ian know this? I try to suppress the panic and keep my voice calm. 'Look, I don't know what you're insinuating, but you're barking up the wrong tree.'

He chortles. 'It must have been hard for you with Eva marrying Samuel.'

'Not at all. I was happy for her, just as I'm happy that she's pretend-engaged to you.'

He holds the palms of his hands up as if in a peace offering. 'Look, we both know the reason I'm here is I want to help Eva. From what you're saying, I assume she's told you that she's in a bit of a pickle.'

I would like to laugh out aloud at how Ian is downplaying Eva's situation. 'The truth is, I think my sister is having a breakdown. She's all over the place, behaving irrationally.'

'Mmm,' he says, letting his gaze wander to my mantlepiece where I have two photos in silver frames on display. The first is of me, Eva, Mum and Dad before everything went so wrong, and the other is of Riley and Alfie, taken when they were toddlers. As Ian's eyes travel across all of my belongings, that sense of unease returns. Ian is here because he's suspicious of me. I don't think he's completely sure why yet, but he's like a dog with a bone and I'm suddenly very scared. I remember how Eva told me he's a tech millionaire, and with his skillset I'm not at all confident I've sufficiently covered my tracks. I have a horrible realisation. If anyone is going to uncover the truth, it'll be Ian. And that means I'm going to have to take action to eliminate him now, otherwise he might totally destroy all of my plans. Do I have it in me to kill someone? I'm not sure that I have any choice.

'Stephen?' Ian asks, breaking into my thoughts.

'Sorry. I'm miles away. Would you like a beer? I'm parched.'

'I'd rather have a coffee. Instant is fine.'

'No problem,' I say.

I stand up and walk to the kitchen, filling up the kettle and switching it on. Then I immediately race up the stairs to my bathroom. I've got just the thing I need in my bathroom cupboard; an innocuous-looking box with two strips of little white pills. I push out six and hold them tightly in the palm of my right hand, pushing the boxes back into the cupboard. For good measure, I flush the toilet and run the taps, then quickly hurry back to the kitchen. When the kettle boils, I spoon two full teaspoons of instant coffee into a mug and drop in the pills, stirring the mug until I'm sure everything is completely dissolved. A few moments later, I'm back in the living room. I hand Ian the mug and offer him a digestive biscuit straight from the packet.

All I need to do now is steer the conversation towards my devastating concern for Eva and wait whilst the pills take effect.

CHAPTER TWENTY-ONE

THE WIFE

Ian seemed so eager to help me. He promised to call me yesterday morning, and he'd talked about us meeting for supper. Except two days have passed and I haven't heard a word from him. It's strange and not at all like Ian. I call his mobile but it's switched off, so I ring his office and speak to his PA. She tells me that Ian is away on business, but there's something in her tone of voice that suggests she might be withholding information from me. That's fair enough because as far as she knows, I'm just a work colleague. I'm desperate to know what Ian has uncovered and decide that if he's still ghosting me by tomorrow, I'll go to London and track him down.

I'm at my desk when an email pings into my inbox. It's from Ian, so I open it eagerly.

Dear Eva,

I've been giving your situation a lot of thought and on consideration I think that you have some serious mental health issues. I wish you well but I'm afraid I'm not in a position to get involved. I'm away on business for a couple of months but I'll be in touch when I'm back. In the meantime, good luck and get better soon.

Yours, Ian.

What! This doesn't sound like Ian one little bit. For starters, he's never serious with me. Even during our board meetings for Leap Ahead, Ian's always the joker. He just doesn't communicate this way. And since when does he go away for a couple of months? I'm sure he goes away on business for days, but months? He'd tell me, wouldn't he? And then signing the email, Yours, Ian? He always signs off with 'Love, Ian'. This email doesn't feel right. If Ian had really thought I'd lost it and was making everything up, he'd pick up the phone or come over and tell it to my face. Everything about this email is wrong: the content, the delivery, the sentiment.

But then again, I have asked him to do something completely outrageous. To get engaged to me.

It takes a few moments for the additional consequences of the email to hit me. If Ian has genuinely disappeared, I don't have anyone to be engaged to. What will happen if I don't follow the orders? It's not like I can magic up another engagement, especially as I've already posted about Ian online. I'm just going to have to bluff it out and pretend I'm still with him. Perhaps if I fulfil the second part of the request – filing for divorce – then that might be good enough. I would rather go to a divorce lawyer I don't know, someone who won't pass judgement and knows nothing about me, but if that gets back to Angela, she'll be so deeply offended I wonder if our friendship will survive. On the other hand, could I tell her the truth? Explain everything, tell her it's all a charade. I dispel the thought. Angela upholds the law; I simply don't trust her not to go to the police, and that's a risk I can't take. It feels like once again, I'm stuck between a rock and a hard place. After vacillating for a few minutes, I call Angela and ask whether she could squeeze me in to discuss my divorce; an official client meeting, not her helping out a friend.

Angela set up her own solicitor's practice with two other lawyers a couple of years ago. Their office suite is above an outdoor clothing shop in the centre of Horsham and although I've passed it hundreds of times, I've never been inside. I ring the bell and am buzzed inside. The hallway is narrow and I climb a steep staircase that rises directly in front of me. Angela is standing at the top of the stairs wearing navy linen trousers and a white blouse with a pussycat bow.

'Welcome,' she says, kissing me on both cheeks. I follow her along a short hallway, glancing into a couple of offices on my left where people I don't recognise are staring at screens.

'This is me,' she says, pushing open a door. It's a small room with a bookcase spanning the wall behind Angela's desk, and a window that looks down onto the pedestrianised street below. There are numerous piles of papers stacked up on her desk, with just enough space for a desktop computer and keyboard.

'I'm so sorry it has come to this,' Angela says. 'Have you spoken to Samuel?'

'No.' That's the first honest thing I've been able to say in ages. 'He did a vanishing act after sending me that email. Has Hunter heard from him?'

'Not a word since their night out together. It's so out of character.'

'I want to file for divorce,' I say, trying to keep my gaze level.

'Don't you think you should talk first, try mediation?'

'No. This is my final decision, Angela, and I'd really like you to represent me.'

She places her arms on her desk. 'In all my years of practice, I've never seen a marriage unravel like this, Eva. I understand you might want to be with Ian, but this has all happened so fast.'

I cut her off. 'This has nothing to do with Ian. That may have been a rebound reaction, stupidity on my behalf. The fact is, Samuel has betrayed me and I want to file for divorce. Can you help me or is there a conflict of interest with Hunter being Samuel's best friend?'

'Absolutely not. You are my number one priority and as your lawyer, I would never discuss your circumstances with Hunter. If you're sure this is what you want, then of course I'll help you.'

'Thank you,' I mutter. 'So how can I divorce him when I don't know where he is?'

'We'll need to submit a sole application, on the basis we don't know where Samuel is or whether he'll agree. Obviously it would be so much better if we could all sit down together and discuss your financial split, child custody and the like.'

And suddenly I remember. 'We have a prenup.' Dad insisted on it, even though I was mortified. Samuel didn't seem to mind though and frankly, I'd forgotten all about it.

'I'll need to see a copy of it. Can you send me that along with all your official documents, birth and marriage certificates?'

'Sure,' I say. 'And how quickly can I get the divorce papers?'

'What do you mean?' Angela frowns.

'Just whatever documents there are to visibly show I'm applying for a divorce?'

'This isn't going to be a quick process, Eva, and these days most forms are filed online. If we can't find Samuel, then we'll need to complete a form D13B, which is a statement requesting to dispense with service of the divorce. We'll need evidence that you've tried to find Samuel, and that means getting confirmation from his employers, friends, etc. that he can't be found. We'd have to ask the court for an order that makes a government agency such as HMRC hand over the latest address for him that they have on file. And then the court may still withhold permission for divorce. Honestly, the first thing we need to do is find Samuel. Until then, I don't think we should take any action.'

If only Angela knew how badly I want to find Samuel. But how?

'I understand how difficult this must be for you, Eva. Have you thought about hiring a private detective to track him down?'

I sigh, because that was the role I'd hoped Ian would fulfil. I would like to employ a private detective, but how different is that from telling the police? Would the kidnapper find out, and if he or she did, what then?

'I've got someone I can recommend, if that would help.' Angela pulls open a drawer in her desk and removes a business card, which she slides across the desk towards me. I place it in my handbag without glancing at it.

The phone call from the children's school comes a few minutes after I've left Angela's office.

'Mrs Simmons, we have a problem with Riley. The head teacher would like you to come in to see her.'

'What sort of problem?' I ask.

'Mrs Granger will explain everything. How soon can you come in?'

'Is Riley alright?'

'She's fine. Could you get here in the next thirty minutes?'

I swallow hard. I've never been summoned into the kids' school before.

'Yes, of course,' I say. 'But what's happened?'

'Mrs Granger will tell you.'

I message Luke and then hurry to the car, driving quickly towards school. When I walk up the path, I feel like I'm about to be chastised by the head teacher, and all those conflicting feelings about school rumble inside me. I press the intercom and am let in.

Mrs Granger is mid-forties and very officious. She terrifies me so I can't imagine how the kids feel about her. I'm ushered into her office, where she affixes me with her green eyes and gestures for me to sit on a chair that is too small and too low to the ground.

'I'll get straight to the point. Riley hit another child this morning. It is completely unacceptable behaviour.'

'That's not like Riley,' I say, immediately coming to her defence. 'She must have been provoked. Who was the other child?'

Mrs Granger sighs. 'It's Autumn. Fortunately, her mother has decided not to press charges.'

'Press charges!' I exclaim. 'We're talking about two eleven-year-olds having a playground bust-up.'

'Autumn has a big bump on the side of her head and cuts on her knees.'

'But Riley and Autumn are best friends; they've been inseparable since they were babies.'

'Yes, I'm aware of that.'

'So Autumn must have provoked Riley.'

'Is there anything going on at home that I need to know about?' Mrs Granger asks.

I sigh. 'Yes, we're going through a tricky period. My husband and I might be splitting up and Riley and Alfie are spending a few nights with my brother. It's a stressful period for us all.'

'I assumed there might be issues at home. As you say, this is out of character for Riley. We will need her to apologise to Autumn and she will be suspended for twenty-four hours.'

'Thank you,' I say, relieved that Riley isn't being expelled. But on the other hand, Autumn must have provoked Riley into hitting her. There is no way that my daughter would turn on her best friend unprovoked. 'Shall I take her home now?'

'Yes, she's waiting for you next door.' Mrs Granger stands up and opens a door to the left of her desk.

'Your mother is here to get you,' she says, beckoning at Riley.

My daughter emerges, her face red and tear streaked, her eyes swollen. Her shoulders are slumped and she refuses to look at me.

'Come on, darling,' I say, holding out my hand. Riley

walks past both Mrs Granger and me and mutters audibly, 'But it wasn't my fault.'

We walk in silence out of the school building and down the path. 'This is very out of character,' I say. 'I'm not angry, darling. I just want to know what happened.'

Suddenly, the gate swings open and there's a woman rushing towards us. It takes me a moment to realise that it's Kalah. Her hair is wet, her face makeup free, a raincoat flapping wildly.

'How could you?' she screeches at me and jabs her finger at Riley. I grab my daughter because Kalah looks almost feral. But then she pushes past us and runs up the path into the school. Riley bursts into tears. I put my arm around her shoulders, tugging her closely to me, and we stride to the car.

'I didn't start it,' Riley sobs. I find a tissue in my bag and hand it to her.

'I know you didn't,' I say, squeezing her hand. 'Can you tell me exactly what happened?'

'Autumn said that Dad has done something really bad, which is why he's gone away. I told her that he's having some time out because that's what you said, isn't it?' She sniffs.

'Yes.'

'And Autumn said that Dad is in love with another woman and that he's going to have another family, and he's done some really bad stuff. I told her she was lying but she said she'd overheard her parents talking about you and Dad and that she wasn't lying. I got really upset and tried to walk away but I nudged her with my shoulder by mistake and she tripped. I didn't mean to do it, Mum, I really didn't. But there were lots of other kids around us and they started shouting, "Fight, fight." Autumn got to her feet and swung her fist at me, but she missed and then she fell again and banged her head. I didn't want her to get hurt, I just wanted her to stop saying horrible things about Dad.'

'Oh sweetheart,' I say, tugging her towards me and kissing the top of her head.

'Is it true, what Autumn said?' She pulls away from me and rubs her eyes.

'No, it isn't. Dad has done nothing wrong and he'll be back home soon.' I wish I meant what I'm saying.

'Autumn also said that you're sick in the head and that's why we're having to stay with Uncle Stephen.'

I feel a surge of anger towards Kalah, because the only person who will have told Autumn this is her mother. Why is Kalah talking like this? And then I wonder. Does she know more than she's letting on? Is Kalah just being a gossip or is she involved with Samuel? What's the saying? Those who protest too much? I know she's unhappy in her marriage, and suddenly wonder whether she has been plotting to leave Xavier for Samuel.

CHAPTER TWENTY-TWO

THE LOVER

I telephone Eva.

'I'm sorry, but the kids are going to have to go home. I can't have them here any longer.'

There's a long pause before she speaks.

'That's fine,' she says. 'Something happened at school today and Riley has to stay at home for twenty-four hours.'

Now that annoys me. I want Eva to be dependent on me, not willingly scooping her kids back up and taking them home. And what has spoiled Riley done now?

'But thank you for having them,' Eva continues. 'I'd never palm the kids off unless it was really necessary. Believe me, it's like a part of me has been ripped out, not having them at home.'

'Will they be safe with you?' I try to laden my voice with suspicion. Let Eva be fearful as to whether her children will be at risk in their own home.

'God, I hope so. Otherwise Riley will have to stay with Mum for a couple of days.'

Here we go again; even as an adult, Eva is still running to Mummy.

'That might be a good idea,' I suggest. 'After all, you're not in the best of head spaces, are you? And didn't you say the kidnapper ordered you not to have the children at home? Look, I'll have the kids again later in the week if you want, it's just tonight I need to go out.'

'Thank you, Stephen,' Eva says. 'I don't know what I'd do without you.'

I suppress a chuckle. I know exactly what I'd do without Eva.

WHEN I BOUGHT MY SEMI-DETACHED, it never crossed my mind that a basement might be useful for anything other than wine, suitcases and general detritus that I can't be bothered to take to the tip or the second-hand shops. But how relieved I am to have it today.

Ian is comatose on the sofa, his jaw open and drool trickling down his chin. Somehow, I have to drag him across the living room, into the narrow hall and shove him down to the basement. I start by locking and bolting all the external doors and pulling the curtains downstairs. I can't have any peeping toms peer in during this exercise. Then I pull him via his feet, tugging and wrenching him until he flops off the sofa, his head bouncing against the wooden floor with a sharp crack. He's like a dead weight and it's just as well that I'm fit, thanks in part to my cleaning job and also because I know how much Samuel likes a six-pack. I don't have to drag Ian far, but honestly it feels like a marathon. I catch the side of his head on the doorframe as I tug him around the corner into the hall, leaving a smudge of blood on the skirting board. I'll wipe it down with bleach later. Eventually, I position him at the top of the stone steps, and with all my might, push him. He tumbles down the stairs like a rag doll, landing in a heap of limbs at the bottom. If I'm lucky, the fall will have killed him. For now, he's sufficiently drugged up to be out of it for hours. I switch the light off, close the door, lock it and shove the key into my jeans pocket.

At best, he's dead. At worst, Ian is drugged and concussed, but either way I can't have the children staying here any longer. The risk is too great that they might smell his rotting corpse or go snooping around the house, somehow finding the key and going down to the basement. Besides, having them here is limiting the time I can spend with Samuel, and he is the most important thing in my life. He is the reason for all of this.

And then I get nervous. What if the drugs haven't done their thing, or if the fall actually woke Ian rather than hurt him? I stride back to the basement door, take the key out of my pocket and turn the handle. After turning the light on, I run down the stone steps. Ian is lying at the bottom, his limbs contorted at strange angles, his eyes shut. I lean over him, but I don't touch him. He's not going anywhere anytime soon. And if he comes to, then I'll kill him. A bash over the head with a hammer is all it'll take.

CHAPTER TWENTY-THREE

THE WIFE

It's wonderful having Riley and Alfie back at home. They've only been gone for three nights but it's seemed interminable. It's not just Riley who appears different, they both seem as if they've been forced to grow up in the space of a few days.

We're eating supper together when Alfie asks, 'Is Dad dead?'

'What!' I exclaim. 'Where have you got that idea from?'

He shrugs and drops his fork. 'It's just he's never not contacted us. Why hasn't he written or sent an email if he can't get to the phone?'

I sigh loudly. 'I'm not sure, darling. But no, Dad isn't dead.' I pray I'm right. 'He's gone away for a few weeks for a complete change of scene. Sometimes if grownups are completely exhausted, they need to do that, to step away from their lives. But he still loves you very, very much.'

Riley looks dubious and I don't blame her. The only reassurances she has are from me and even to my ears, they sound pretty pathetic. And Autumn's gossip has clearly increased her suspicion.

'Why did we have to go and stay with Uncle Stephen?' Alfie asks. 'Is it because you don't love us anymore?'

'What!' I exclaim. 'Absolutely not. I love you with all my heart. You both are the most important people in my life, in Dad and my lives. Where did you get that crazy idea from?'

'Harry said that people get sent away if their parents don't love them any longer. It's why kids get sent to boarding school,' Alfie pronounces. Harry is a friend of his from school.

'Well, Harry is speaking a complete load of nonsense,' I exclaim. 'My cousins went to boarding school because they lived far away from a decent local school. Their parents thought it would be good for them, having new experiences and a great education.'

'I don't want to go to boarding school,' Alfie says.

'I wouldn't mind. If it's like Harry Potter, I think it'd be cool.' Riley toys with her lasagne.

'Well, sorry to disappoint you, but you're both going to Farlands. If, when you reach the sixth form, you want to go somewhere else, then we can discuss that when you're older.' Farlands is our local secondary school and it has an excellent reputation, with students getting outstanding results.

'Autumn says you're not well,' Alfie mutters. 'That's why Riley hit her, isn't it, Riley?'

'I don't want to talk about it,' Riley mutters. She's scraping her fork on the plate, and under normal circumstances I'd tell her off for making an unpleasant scratching sound. But today, I hold my tongue, desperate not to alienate the children or scare them in any way.

'That's not true. I'm perfectly well.'

'I had a tummy ache at Uncle Stephen's,' Alfie says.

'Not that sort of ill,' Riley steamrollers over her

brother, and all the while I'm feeling terrible for not knowing that Alfie had been under the weather. 'Ill in the head. Autumn said you're on the edge of a nervous breakdown.'

'What's a nervous breakdown?' Alfie asks.

I lay my cutlery down on my plate. 'First of all, there is absolutely nothing wrong with me. My head is perfectly okay.'

'Except your haircut,' Alfie says, tugging at the side of his lip.

I chuckle. 'I agree that the haircut perhaps wasn't such a good idea. But what Riley is suggesting is that my feelings are out of control, that I'm feeling sad all the time, or I'm really anxious and crying a lot.'

'Have you been crying?' Alfie peers at me with concern.

'No, because I'm not sad. Well, I was when you weren't here, because I missed you so much, and of course I miss Dad, but that's just normal sadness. I'm not ill, in the head or body.' What I am feeling is intense frustration. No, it's more than that – anger – towards Kalah. How dare she discuss my situation in front of Autumn. Or, to give Kalah the benefit of the doubt, perhaps Autumn overheard her parents talking, but if so what the hell was Kalah really saying? I genuinely thought she was one of my closest friends but now I'm not sure that I can trust her. She and I are going to have to have a very difficult conversation.

We finish our meal, and rather than sending them up to their rooms to complete homework, I suggest that we find a film on Netflix to watch together. I know I'm overcompensating, that I shouldn't be rewarding Riley for what happened with Autumn, but I can't have the children worrying about me.

After the film, Alfie doesn't want to go to sleep. 'Can I sleep in your bed?' he asks, for the first time in years.

'Why, darling?'

'I'm scared the burglar is going to come back.'

'There was no burglar. Some naughty teenagers threw a stone up against the window.' Yet another lie trips off my tongue. 'No one has been back.' At least that is the truth.

'How do you know they won't climb up a ladder and try to break into my bedroom window?'

'Because what burglar would be stupid enough to do that when there are much easier windows to access? Besides, I'm putting the alarm on at night so if anyone breaks in, they'll be scared off by the loud noise. I promise you, you don't need to worry.'

'Will you check on me in the night?'

I hug Alfie and stroke his back reassuringly. 'Of course I will.'

I hate how much this situation is affecting the children.

I may not be having a breakdown, but all the lies and the uncertainty are both physically and emotionally demanding, so by 9.30 p.m. I switch on the burglar alarm and go to bed. I'm reading *The Times* on my iPad when my phone vibrates with an incoming message. My heart sinks as I reach for it. As I feared, it's another Snapchat message.

I've heard about your broken engagement. Poor you. It must be so hard for you to be unable to keep a relationship going. Are you heartbroken? Have you really got anything left to live for? Perhaps it would be best if you kill yourself. Final item on the bucket list. Give your life for Samuel's, and Riley and Alfie will be safe and happy for the rest of their lives.

I let the phone slip onto the duvet. Did I just read that correctly? The words, 'kill yourself' flicker and then disappear. My stomach roils and I have to breathe hard to halt the nausea. So this is what all the threats have been leading to. The kidnapper wants me to die in order to save Samuel. With trembling fingers, I type out a message.

Are you threatening my children?

I don't get an answer.

I think back through the message. 'I've heard about your broken engagement.' But how? I haven't posted anything on social media about Ian walking away. In fact I haven't told anyone: not my friends, my family, literally no one. The only people who know about it are Ian and me. Unless of course Ian has told someone, perhaps inadvertently notifying the kidnapper? And then I wonder, is Ian the kidnapper? He knows a great deal about me, professionally and personally, and all those years ago, he intimated he loved me. But that was a lifetime ago. If he was holding Samuel, why go through the farce of the engagement? Why was he willing to let me tell people about it? He seemed so genuinely eager to help me. Or could the person who hacked into my social media a couple of weeks ago still have access to my email? But I changed my passwords, except I did give Ian access to everything. He has a clone of my phone, so if someone has access to his laptop, they would have my details too. On the other hand, Ian is a cyber security expert, so it's very unlikely someone would hack him. I groan. I'm going around and around in circles, my mind a complete mess. And then, as I lean back against my pillow and squeeze my eyes shut, it hits me. Is Ian in danger? By involving him, have I inadvertently dragged him into my nightmare, putting him in as much risk as my family?

Despite the exhaustion, the night is long and torturous. I can't settle, desperate to know who is threatening me. Who wants me to die? It's beyond crazy to think I'm going to harm myself just because of a message. Yet, if it really came down to it, of course I would give up my life for my children's. Even if he doesn't want to talk to me, I need to talk to Ian.

The next morning, I call Ian's mobile. It goes straight to voicemail. I call his work and I'm told he's not available. I don't know any of his colleagues, so I ask to speak to the head of human resources. The phone is answered by a brusque woman called Nicola Parsons.

'I'm sorry to disturb you. However, I'm calling about Ian Oakley. I'm an old friend and I'm concerned that something might have happened to him.'

'Right,' she says, hesitation in her voice.

'He sent me an email which was very out of character and I haven't been able to get hold of him. I was wondering whether anyone at work had seen him in the past couple of days?'

'I'm afraid I'm not at liberty to discuss any of our employees.'

I sigh. 'I realise that, and I'm not asking you to divulge anything to me. However, if he has gone AWOL from work, I urge you to contact the police. I'm worried for his safety.'

'Could I take your details, please.'

'Um, sure.' And then I realise giving my name probably isn't a very good idea. I hang up.

Now I'm terrified I've put everyone in danger. What about Stephen? Will they threaten him too? Does the kidnapper know that the kids are back at home with me?

And what will they do next? I can hardly fake my own death. I realise that the time has come where I have no choice. I have to go to the police. But first I have to deal with the children.

I call Mum. 'I have a bit of an emergency and was wondering if you could have Riley for the day?'

'Riley? Isn't she at school?'

I realise I'm going to have to tell her a version of the truth.

'She got into trouble at school and has been suspended today, although I think she's being made a scapegoat when it really wasn't her fault. I have some important work meetings to attend.'

Mum harrumphs. 'She takes after her uncle Stephen then.'

'That's not fair,' I say, forever coming to Stephen's defence. 'Don't you remember, it was me who got into trouble at school, not Stephen?'

My fear of water was so overwhelming after the accident, I point-blank refused to attend swimming lessons. When my teachers discovered I'd been forging sick notes, I got a detention. When I bunked off my lessons, hiding in a store cupboard, I was suspended. Eventually, someone – I'm not sure if it was Mum or an insightful teacher – realised I had developed a terror of the water, and I was sent to see a doctor. Although no one had the foresight to address my phobia, at least I was excused from swimming thereafter.

'Is it okay if I drop her off after I've taken Alfie to school?'

'Of course it is. I'll bash some sense into her young head.'

That's the last thing Riley or I need, and I debate telling Mum to back off, except I'm indebted to her for agreeing to look after my daughter at such short notice. And Mum is clever. If she gets wind that something is seriously wrong with my marriage, she'll start digging. I shudder at the thought of Mum knowing what's really going on. She'd likely hunt down our local chief inspector of police, march me into his office, and demand immediate action. No. It's me who needs to take control of this situation.

CHAPTER TWENTY-FOUR

THE WIFE

This time I drive straight to the police station, locking my car and striding across the road, not allowing myself any opportunity to doubt whether I'm doing the right thing. I walk in through the glass double doors and stride up to the counter, where two plain-clothed officers are seated behind plexiglass.

'Good morning,' the young male officer says.

I try – and fail – to smile. 'Is it possible to speak to someone about my husband?' I lower my voice and glance around me. 'It's about a kidnapping.'

The officer raises his eyebrows. 'Please take a seat whilst I find someone to talk to you.'

The plastic chairs are uncomfortable, so I pace around the lobby, ignoring a woman who is clearly high on some drugs muttering to herself in the corner. Perhaps ten minutes later, a man appears from behind a door.

'Mrs Simmons?'

I start at my name and stride towards him.

'Good morning. I'm Detective Sergeant Will Nguyen. If you'd like to follow me.' We walk along a wide corridor, our shoes vibrating on the vinyl floor, passing various closed doors on both sides, all with blue-painted door frames. There are cameras in the corners of the corridor and an institutional smell that makes my stomach curdle. He opens the door to a small room.

'Please have a seat.' He gestures to a blue plastic chair on the far side of a fake-wood-topped table. He sits on the other side, adjacent to a computer screen that is attached to the wall. There are no windows, and the bright florescent ceiling light makes me blink. He's holding a large pad of paper which he places on the table, and removes a biro from his pocket.

'How can I help you, Mrs Simmons?'

'I reported my husband missing a couple of weeks ago, but then I received an email saying he'd gone off with another woman. Shortly thereafter, I was contacted by someone who demanded that I fulfil actions on a bucket list, otherwise my husband would be killed. This kidnapper forbade me from contacting the police, threatening to hurt my children and my husband. They've been clever and have sent me messages via Snapchat, which means I've got very little evidence as to what has been happening.'

'Right. So are you saying your husband is being held against his will?'

'I believe so. At first I thought he'd left me, but now I'm convinced that someone is taunting me, playing with me, and that Samuel is in serious danger. They sent me photos of him with a knife to his neck, blood on his face, and now they've said that I need to kill myself otherwise Samuel and our children might be harmed. I'm terrified they'll know that I've come to you, especially as they said Samuel would be hurt if I tell the police, but this has got completely out of control and I don't know what else to do.'

'Can you show me details of these bucket list demands?'

I open Snapchat and navigate to the dialogue with user ISEEU975783. As all the messages have been deleted there's nothing to see. 'I managed to record the person talking using another phone, but I couldn't take screenshots or record via Snapchat because the other person was notified when I was doing that.' I play the only message that I managed to record:

'Riley and Alfie need to go and live elsewhere. Organise that today. I don't want to see you with them.'

Detective Sergeant Will Nguyen leans back in his chair. It squeaks. 'This sounds rather like a disgruntled husband.'

'This isn't Samuel,' I say. Samuel would never be that cruel.

I talk the detective through all of the demands and show him my social media accounts, except that everything I posted on Instagram Stories has now vanished, so I have to show him the photos I took of myself: my hair newly cut off; me holding a glass up in the air with my girlfriends; the horrendous date with Anthony.

'I know this doesn't amount to much and effectively you've only got my word for everything, but please will you help me? I'm terrified for the safety of my family.'

Will Nguyen stares at me, unblinking, for a long time. He has a kindly face, his large eyes bright in his dark face, black hair cut very short.

'And then there's my friend Ian Oakley. When the kidnapper demanded that I get engaged to someone else and put evidence of that on social media, I turned to Ian. He's an old friend and runs a tech company. He promised to help me and started to investigate, except then I got this weird email from him saying he couldn't help me, and now he's disappeared.' I realise the words are tumbling from my mouth and with every sentence, Will Nguyen is eyeing me with greater suspicion. 'At least I think he has disappeared. I'm wondering if the kidnapper has him too.'

'Alright, Mrs Simmons. I'll need to go and talk to some colleagues, follow up on some of the names you've given me here.' He glances down at his notepad and then turns it over so I can't try to read his scribbles.

I feel a rush of hope as well as regret that I didn't come to the police any sooner.

He stands up. 'Would you like me to get you a drink whilst you wait?'

'A water would be great,' I say.

A minute later, he returns with a plastic cup filled to the brim with lukewarm water.

'Thank you,' I say, smiling at him. He doesn't return the smile.

I wait and I wait. Ten minutes pass, then twenty minutes, and when I've been in that small, suffocating space for half an hour, I stand up and start pacing. Can I leave this room? Is it the done thing to be wandering around a police station unaccompanied? I'm beginning to feel really uncomfortable, almost as if I've done something wrong. And just when I'm plucking up the courage to open the door and peek into the corridor, there are heavy footsteps outside. The door swings open and I step back rapidly, to avoid being hit in the face.

'Sorry to keep you waiting so long,' Will Nguyen says as he strides to the chair he vacated earlier. He's followed by a stocky woman with short mousy-coloured hair, wearing black trousers and a creased blue blouse. 'This is my colleague, Detective Sergeant Suraya Braemore.'

The female detective puts her hand out and squeezes mine tightly before pulling out another chair and sitting next to Will Nguyen.

'So, Mrs Simmons.' Suraya Braemore leans her forearms on the table and peers at me. 'We've been following up some of the things you told my colleague, DS Nguyen. We spoke to our colleagues who visited your house and we've carried out a quick check of your social media. It looks like you've been having a rough time recently.'

I'm about to retort, but she carries on speaking.

'You mentioned Ian Oakley. We had a missing person's report filed on him yesterday.'

'Oh God,' I say, my hand rushing to cover my mouth. 'I had a bad feeling about him and I reported him missing to the head of HR at his company. Did she report him missing?'

'This report was filed by his brother, an Adrian Oakley. Do you know him?'

'Not really. He was a few years above me at school. I might have met him once or twice. I'm really worried that the kidnapper might have harmed Ian. He was helping me investigate Samuel's disappearance and then he sent me this email.' I pick up my phone which I'd lain on the table between us and scroll to Ian's email. I push my phone across the table, towards Suraya Braemore.

She reads it quickly before passing it to Will Nguyen.

'It seems perfectly reasonable,' she says.

'Except it isn't,' I interject. 'It's out of character. For starters, it's not the language he typically uses when writing to me, and Ian would never just dump me in it. We go back a long way.'

'Mmm,' she says, drumming her fingers on the table. 'You say that your husband is also missing. Have his phone or bank cards been used?'

'Not as far as I'm aware. I can't get access to his sole bank account. As I told your colleagues, his passport is still at home, as is his medication.'

'So it's possible that he has a bank account that is being used.'

'It's possible, I suppose, but I'm worried he doesn't have his blood pressure medication.'

'That's easy enough to get hold of, isn't it?' Detective Nguyen says.

The two police officers glance at each other and a cold shiver passes through me. It strikes me that they don't believe me, that they think everything I've said is the ravings of some lunatic. The walls seem to move inwards and the stale air that I was able to breathe before, now is heavy with dust mites and stale sweat. I start coughing as I'm hit with a wave of claustrophobia. It reminds me of my dream, where dark water is pushing me downwards, forcing the air out of my lungs.

'I'm sorry,' I splutter, standing up. 'Is it okay if I leave now?'

There's a heavy silence before Suraya Braemore speaks. 'I'm sorry, Mrs Simmons, but we'd like you to stay put to help us further with our investigations. Of course, we can't force you to stay, but it would be extremely useful.'

I sink back down into the chair and take a big gulp of the tepid plastic-tasting water.

'How was your marriage before Samuel disappeared?'

'It was fine, normal, nothing out of the ordinary. Why?'

'Because it seems rather unusual for you to fall straight

into the arms of Ian Oakley within a few days of your husband disappearing.'

'I told you that my engagement to him was a sham. I only told people about it because it was one of the bucket-list demands of the kidnapper. I wasn't really with Ian.'

'And yet your social media posts suggest that you have had a long-term relationship with him.'

'As a friend and colleague, but that's all. I've never been unfaithful to my husband.'

Will Nguyen taps his fingers on the table and purses his lips together. 'So we have two missing men and the one connection between the two of them is you. You must admit that it seems suspicious. And then you spin us this wild story about bucket lists and kidnapping demands yet you present us with no evidence. From a cursory look at your social media, it seems that you've been acting somewhat – how shall put it? With abandon, out on the town, having a good time. It's not exactly the actions of a desperately worried wife, is it?'

I gawp at the officers as I realise the implications of what Nguyen has said. They don't think I'm a victim. They think I'm a perpetrator.

There's a very long pause during which time I don't know where to look or what to do with my trembling hands. I squeeze them between my knees.

'We would like to formally interview you with regard to the disappearance of Ian Oakley and Samuel Simmons.'

'What, this wasn't a formal interview?' I ask.

'No. This was just a chat where you have been helping us with our enquiries.' Nguyen replies.

'Do I need a solicitor?'

'You are entitled to have a solicitor present if that is what you wish.'

'I do. I wish to have one,' I garble. 'Can I use my phone and call one?'

Suraya Braemore sighs loudly and then scrapes her chair back. 'Yes. We'll take a break and will return when your solicitor gets here.'

I telephone Angela's office, but the receptionist tells me she's in a client meeting and can't be disturbed.

'I'm at the police station and need a solicitor to support me.' My words tumble out in a panic. 'I desperately need help.' There's the sound of papers being shuffled before she speaks again.

'Have you, or are you likely to be charged with a criminal offence?' I wonder if she's reading off a crib sheet.

'I don't know. Maybe. They want to formally interview me.'

'In which case Mrs Hunter wouldn't be able to assist you as she's a family lawyer. Her colleague, Damien Caulder, is a criminal lawyer; let me see if he's available.' She puts me on hold and I have to listen to some frustrating hotel foyer type music.

A long minute later, a man with a deep bass voice answers the phone. I tell him briefly what has happened and where I am and he promises to be with me as soon as possible, hopefully within the hour.

The minutes pass so slowly. The battery is dying on my phone so I daren't use it for inconsequential scrolling. Instead, I go over and over the events of the past three weeks, thinking of opportunities I've missed for proving that I'm not the perpetrator, that I'm perfectly sane. In my mind, I flick through every person I know, considering their relationship to Samuel. I've spoken to everyone in my address book, but I've been limited as to what I've told them. And what about Samuel himself and our relationship? I've got no benchmark but I think we're tight. At least I used to think that. And then there was that first day after Samuel had gone missing and Hunter intimated he thought Samuel might have been having an affair. I should have interrogated him more, pushed him to disclose everything about my husband. That's what I'll do when I'm out of here. And I'll confront Kalah.

It's nearly two hours before Damien Caulder arrives, during which time I've used the remaining percentage of my phone battery firing off a message to Stephen, apologising profusely and asking him to collect Alfie from school and to take him to swimming. I also message Luke to let him know I won't be in the office. Finally, I message Mum and tell her Riley might need to stay the night at her house. My daughter won't be thrilled. Time seems to bulge and slow down in this place and I'm literally watching the seconds pass by, all the while a deep unease spreading through every cell of my body.

It's a relief when Damien Caulder arrives. Despite his deep voice, he is a short man with piercing blue eyes and an abrupt manner. Briefly, I fill him in on everything that has happened and if he's surprised, his face gives away nothing. And then the police officers return, sitting down opposite us.

Will Nguyen speaks first. 'Thank you for attending, Mrs Simmons, Mr Caulder. This is a formal but voluntary interview where we want to ask you questions about the disappearance of Ian Oakley and Samuel Simmons. You do not have to say anything. But it may harm your defence if you do not mention when questioned something which you later rely on in court. Anything you do say may be given in evidence. Do you understand what that means?'

I nod, a wave of icy cold spearing through my body.

'This interview will be recorded, so for the sake of the tape, please can you say your names.'

We both do as we're told. And then the police officers ask me to repeat everything I have already told them. By the time I've finished, my voice feels raw and my shoulders ache. There's a nauseous burning in my stomach, a fear that the police have got it all wrong. And then Damien Caulder speaks.

'My client is the victim here, not the perpetrator. In addition, you don't have any concrete evidence against my client, or indeed any proof that crimes have been committed. On that basis, unless you are going to charge her, you need to let her go.'

There's another long silence during which the officers look at each other, as if they are telepathic, and eventually Suraya Braemore nods.

'Mrs Simmons, you are free to go, but we will want you to assist us further in our enquiries and as such, please do not leave the country.'

'I'm hardly going to jet off on holiday when my husband is missing, being held kidnapped,' I snap and then immediately regret my sarcasm.

CHAPTER TWENTY-FIVE

THE WIFE

I have a parking ticket on my car. How ironic it is that the police held me for so many hours and then another arm of the law gave me a ticket. I'm tempted to complain but considering they seem to think I've committed some hideous crimes, I decide to pay up without a fuss. It seems like the least of my worries. I climb into the car and let out a loud sigh. What a mess. As I'm attaching my phone to the car charger, I see I've got a missed call and a message from Kalah as well as a missed call from the kids' school. My heart judders. I play back Kalah's message first.

'Hi, Eva. Is everything okay? No one turned up to collect Alfie from school, so I've got him. Look, I've forgiven Riley and I've told Autumn she needs to forgive her too. I know you guys are under a lot of pressure at the moment. I've taken Alfie to his swimming lesson but I've got to get Autumn to a dentist appointment for 4.30 p.m. so can you collect him from the pool? Let me know when you get this message.'

A knot of panic grabs my neck. As if my nerves aren't

already frazzled. This I can do without. Why didn't Stephen collect Alfie, or more to the point, why didn't he let me know that he couldn't make it? I realise I've been imposing on him a lot but he's normally reliable. I call his number but it goes straight to voicemail. For a horrible moment, I wonder whether he's also gone missing. It's as if everyone who is close to me has disappeared. And then a cold brush of fear runs down my spine. Is Alfie safe? Is he really at his swimming lesson? Did Kalah stay with him or has she left and taken Autumn to the dentist? I glance at my watch. Kalah can't be there if she's got to get Autumn to the dentist for 4.30 p.m. There are fifteen minutes to go until the lesson finishes. I'm terrified of going to the pool but I'm even more terrified that someone might abduct Alfie before I get there.

I drive like a maniac, swerving past slow cars and screeching through traffic lights just as they're turning from amber to red. I'm flashed by a speed camera as I race along the dual carriageway and then career along the residential streets towards the leisure centre but even with the speeding, I'm still late. It's a while since I've been here and the car park is full. Drumming my fingers on the steering wheel as I search for a space, I eventually find one tucked at the back of the building. Racing out of the car I sprint to the main entrance, weaving between parents leaving with their children, ignoring the strange looks and mutterings as people stare at me, the crazy woman. I halt at the reception desk. There are turnstiles operated with electronic passes and I have nothing to get through. Samuel always collected the kids.

My voice is panicked as I turn to the young man at the desk wearing a navy blue T-shirt with the leisure centre's logo emblazoned on the front. 'I need to go through to the swimming pool to collect my son. Alfie Simmons.'

'One moment,' he says as he inputs Alfie's name into a computer. 'Let's see.' He's being painfully slow and I feel physically sick.

'It looks like Alfie Simmons has already left.'

'What? Who did he leave with?'

He frowns at me as if I've asked the most ridiculous question. 'I'm sorry, I've no idea.'

'And did he actually attend his lesson?'

He glances at the screen again. 'Yes. He was checked in and checked out. Is everything alright?'

I don't hang around to answer. Back at the car, I try to quell my panic. Be logical. Alfie is either with Stephen or Kalah, or Mum. Perhaps Riley asked Mum to take her to her swimming lesson and she collected Alfie at the same time. I jab Mum's number.

'Is Riley still with you?' I ask without a preamble.

'Yes,' Mum says quizzically. 'We're baking a cake. She's standing right next to me.'

'And Alfie?'

'No. You didn't ask me to collect Alfie. What's going on, Eva?'

'Nothing. Don't worry. I was held up longer than expected. I'll call you back shortly.' I hang up before Mum can ask any further questions. My kids are sensible and would never go off with someone they didn't know. Yes, Alfie is young, but he's sensible, isn't he? I call Stephen and to my utter relief he answers.

'Have you got Alfie?' I ask.

'No. Should I?'

'I left a message on your phone asking if you could

collect him from school and take him to his swimming lesson.'

'Hold on a tick.' I can hear him scrambling around but I'm not sure what he's doing. 'Oh, sorry. I must have missed the message.' There's a long pause as we both digest the implications of this. 'You know, Eva, you're really losing it. It's one thing losing your shit personally but now it's affecting your children. You know I'm the only person in the world who will tell you as it is, and you need to get a grip.'

So much for brotherly love. Stephen has always been to the point, abrupt even, but this is just hurtful.

'When you find your kids, I'll have them to stay again so you can go to the doctor and get yourself fixed.'

'Thanks,' I say, although Stephen's words sting bitterly. 'But Riley is with Mum, so she's okay. It's just Alfie who seems to have disappeared.'

'Dear God, Eva,' Stephen says. I can envisage him rolling his eyes and shaking his head as if I'm the most useless mother ever. Which I probably am. 'Leave everything to me. I'll help out.' He hangs up.

My next call is to Kalah but she doesn't answer. Terror makes it hard to think straight. Kalah must have Alfie, surely? Except she and I need to have words and sort out what really went on between Riley and Autumn. I reverse out of the parking space and head to the exit of the leisure centre, trying to keep myself calm as I drive towards Kalah's house. The relief at seeing her BMW in their drive is almost overwhelming. I park haphazardly next to her car and run up to the door, jamming my finger on the buzzer.

The door swings open a couple of long moments later. 'Here you are,' Kalah says, folding a tea towel.

'Have you got Alfie?'

'Yes,' she replies with an edge of sarcasm. 'It's not like I could just leave him at the pool, could I? I postponed Autumn's dentist appointment. We may have our differences over the girls' fight but I care about you and your kids. So what's with the disappearing act?'

'Thank you so much,' I say. I would like to fling my arms around Kalah, but something has shifted between us. A sense of disquiet and mistrust. Kalah seems tense and takes a step backwards, giving me a wide birth as I pass her. I suppose I look a fright, with creased clothes and a lingering, sour scent of sweat from my hours at the police station. 'I've had the day from hell,' I mutter.

Kalah sighs. 'You'd better come and have a cuppa then.'

I follow her through the open hallway down the corridor but rather than going into the kitchen where I can hear chattering of a television, she gestures for me to follow her into the small bookcase-lined room she calls the snug. I ignore her and pop my head around the door to the kitchen. To my utter relief, Alfie is sitting at the kitchen table. I turn around and follow Kalah into the snug. She shuts the door behind us.

'Have a seat.' She points to the saggy green sofa.

I collapse into it, grateful for its comfort.

'Have you seen your doctor?' Kalah asks as she smooths down her skirt before sitting neatly in the chair opposite me.

'No. I haven't had time and I don't need to.'

'I disagree.'

Annoyance bubbles inside me. Who is Kalah to judge me? She has absolutely no idea what hell I've been going through.

'It's one thing you behaving irrationally, but now it's

affecting your children, Eva. You must be able to see that. And today, you completely forgot about Alfie.'

'I didn't. I asked Stephen to help.'

Kalah ignores me. 'And the way Riley hit Autumn yesterday, it's completely unacceptable. I could have pressed charges, you know. Xavier wanted us to.'

'What, press charges against an eleven-year-old girl? Besides, Riley told me what really happened. Did you know that Autumn was goading her, telling her that I was sick in the head and that Samuel is in love with another woman? Autumn told Riley that Samuel is going to have kids with another woman and he's done something really bad. Where did she get that information from, Kalah? What rubbish have you fed your daughter, or what have you been gossiping about to lead her to say such vile things to her best friend?'

Kalah jumps up from her chair. 'Do not put this on me!' she says, jabbing a French-manicured finger in my direction. I'm surprised she's being so fiery; I haven't seen this version of Kalah in years. 'It wasn't your daughter who returned home with an egg-sized bump on her skull and cuts all down her legs. There's something very wrong with you at the moment and it's affecting your children. I've known your kids since they were babies and I've never seen them so worried and unhappy. This has got to change – for every-one's good.'

'It's fine for you to say that, locked away in your ivory tower. You've no idea of the stress I've been going thorough.'

'It's obvious for everyone to see that something is badly wrong, Eva, but you can't let it affect your kids. I'm sorry that Samuel has left you but you need to get a grip.'

I'm angry now. Kalah is being holier than thou and she doesn't know the facts. Yes, I can see how from the outside it looks as if I'm dropping plates left right and centre, except I'm not. I'm just trying to navigate this hellish situation the best I can. I stand up abruptly.

'Thanks for your concern and thanks for looking after Alfie, but I'm taking him home now. Riley is sorry for the fight with Autumn, but she was provoked and Autumn tripped and hurt herself. Riley didn't push her.'

Kalah swivels towards me. 'No,' she says.

'What do you mean, no?' I glower at her.

'I don't think you're in the right frame of mind to take Alfie home. And where is Riley, anyway?'

'She's with my mum.'

'What, the mum you're always complaining about?' I deeply regret bitching about Mum to her; it wasn't fair of me. 'For the sake of all of the kids, we forgive Riley for her behaviour. I'm really worried about you, Eva, and I think it would be best if your two stay here for a couple of nights.'

I'm dumbstruck. Absolutely not. I have no idea what stories Kalah has been spreading about me, and why, and despite rescuing Alfie this afternoon, I no longer trust her.

'Thank you, that's kind of you,' I say with zero conviction. 'I'm perfectly able to look after my children.'

'I really don't think that's a good idea.'

I interrupt her. 'Or what? Are you going to call social services?' My tone is biting.

'Of course not. I'm just trying to be your friend,' Kalah says.

'I have family to help me,' I reply. I edge past her and at the door, I turn the knob and swing it open. I stride towards the kitchen and my heart warms as I see Alfie and Autumn kneeling on kitchen chairs, their heads together, peering at something on the table.

'Alfie, it's time to go home now.'

My son jumps down from his chair and throws me his massive, cheeky grin, the smile that I love so very much. I turn to see Kalah right behind me.

'Look,' I say in a whisper, 'I really appreciate your concern, and I'm sorry I was so rude to you. And Riley is genuinely sorry for Autumn's injuries. My brother Stephen can look after the kids for a couple of days. They're used to staying with him.'

Kalah nods, but there's no warmth in her expression.

CHAPTER TWENTY-SIX

THE LOVER

When Eva rang for the second time I was just finishing up cleaning a lovely period house, a house which would be perfect if it didn't have so many spiders. I've lost count of how many I've crushed under the heel of my trainer. When we were kids, Eva used to rescue every little creepy-crawly she came across. She even tried to set free a mosquito once, when it had landed on her shin. I slapped it dead with a book. I'm not sure whether her tears were because the book left a red welt on her leg or because I killed the insect, but she didn't seem worried that the blighter was going to spear her skin and suck her blood. Anyway, the old beams in this house are free from cobwebs now and I'm just having a quick rifle through the drawers in the living room to see if there's anything worth removing as a keepsake. Then my phone rings and it's my sister herself.

'Did you get my earlier message about collecting Alfie from school?'

I pause a moment, pretending to look at my phone.

'Goodness, no. I'm so sorry, Eva. I must have missed that. Is Alfie alright?'

'My friend Kalah collected him. She seems to think I'm losing it and need to see a doctor, but of course, she doesn't know the truth.'

'I know the truth, *and* I agree with her,' I say, biting my lip to stop the smile sounding in my voice. 'Would you like me to have the kids tonight?'

Eva hesitates.

'You need to do whatever will keep your children safe,' I say. 'I'm sorry I couldn't have them last night, but the next couple of days I'm much freer.'

'Thank you, Stephen.' Eva audibly exhales. 'I'll collect Riley from Mum's and bring her over to yours.'

Eva looks terrible when she arrives, pale faced, with grey bags under her eyes, and the kids are grumpy and incommunicative.

They're each holding a bag from MacDonald's and I can't believe she thinks it's okay to feed them on junk food. But at least it means I don't have to feed them. Eva is so self-obsessed, she's never even considered the fact that my shopping bills have gone up dramatically having her children to stay. At the very least she should be offering to refund me.

'What's up, Eva?' I ask, as the children file past me into the kitchen.

'Can we have a quiet word?' she whispers. I sigh. I can really do without Eva's drama this evening. I'm livid that I've had to cancel my plans. I had intended to return to the cottage to be with my love this evening. I hope Samuel won't be too worried if I'm not back when I said I would, and the poor man will be hungry, waiting for his supper. That's the big disadvantage of my no-phones policy.

Maybe I'll leave the children alone tonight as I did last time.

'What is it?' I ask, as I usher her into the living room. She shuts the door behind us and I stand there with my arms crossed. Eva can't bring herself to look at me.

'I've spent the best part of the day in the police station.'

I freeze. It feels like my heart is stopping.

'What were you doing in the police station?' I ask, trying to keep my voice level.

'There's so much I haven't told you.' She hiccups, before collapsing onto the sofa. Her leg jiggles as she talks and she clenches and unclenches her fingers. 'The thing is, I wonder if I really am having a breakdown.'

'Why were you at the police station?' I ask again, more curtly this time.

'I was reporting Ian and Samuel missing but it was like they didn't believe me and they thought I was behind their disappearance.'

A smile curves my lips upwards, which I immediately quell, but I let my shoulders relax. This is hilarious.

'What, they're both missing?' I exclaim, pretending to be horrified, as my eyes widen and my hand covers my mouth. 'Poor you. You're really going through the mill at the moment.'

And then Eva bursts into tears, her shoulders juddering. She sobs loudly, that hiccupping and sniffing sound that grates on my nerves and makes my teeth tingle. I can't bear the racket of people crying. I think of the locked basement, the key hidden in my trouser pocket, and the man who is down there.

'You'll get through this,' I say, without much conviction. I know I should comfort her, put my arm around her shoulders, except Eva and I have never been the type of siblings to have a physical connection. Instead I hand her a tissue that may or may not be clean. After a couple of minutes, I get her a glass of water and she calms down, wiping her eyes and apologising for getting so upset.

'Go and see your doctor,' I say again. Eva nods.

Back in the kitchen it stinks of cheap fast food and I tell Riley to take their leftover packaging and put it in the bin outside. She throws me a filthy look. If Eva wasn't in the house, I'd give the girl a slap for being so obnoxious.

'Have you got any homework?' I ask the kids.

They both nod. 'Up to your rooms then, please, and get it finished.'

Eva walks in, her face still blotchy. 'Right, kiddos, I'm leaving now.' She speaks with a false brightness which even an idiot would see through.

'I want to come home with you.' Alfie clutches his mum like a toddler.

'I'll see you tomorrow,' she promises. 'I'll take you to school.' She kisses the top of his head.

'I don't understand why we can't come home,' the boy wails, whilst his sister stands there with crossed arms and a livid expression.

'Sorry, guys,' Eva says. 'It's just for tonight.'

'Come on, Alfie,' I say. 'Let's have a look upstairs and see if I've got a present for you hidden away in a drawer.' I don't, but it'll keep him occupied for a few minutes so that Eva can leave.

'Thanks,' she mouths at me, before hugging both her children again and then slinking towards the front door.

I tell the kids to get themselves to bed and then I go downstairs, make myself a quick pasta and pour a large glass of red wine. Poor Samuel. He must be starving, but there's nothing I can do. I take my bowl and glass into the living room and settle down in front of the television, catching the end of the evening news. Next up is the local news and, to my dismay, Ian Oakley's disappearance has made the headlines.

They've used a formal photo of Ian, probably taken off his tech company's website. He looks older than his years and much more serious.

'Forty-two-year-old tech mogul Ian Oakley has been missing since the weekend. His disappearance is completely out of character, his brother said. Oakley, who is unmarried, set up his highly successful business a decade ago, and the business floated last year netting Oakley approximately fifty million. A 40-year-old woman has been helping the police with their enquiries but she's been released without charge. If anyone has any information or has seen Ian Oakley, please contact the police on the following number.'

When the newsreader mentions the 40-year-old woman, I almost split my sides laughing. I'm sure that Eva never expected to gain notoriety over the disappearance of a friend. I wonder whether I should leak her name to the press or just mention her on social media. That could set off quite the tsunami of suspicion and, in Eva's vulnerable state, could really tip her over the edge. It would certainly undermine her charity, Leap Ahead. I'm also so very tempted to tele-phone Mum and tell her that Eva, her prodigal daughter, isn't quite as perfect as she assumes. Except I won't. The sole time I'll have anything to do with Mum is when she's dead. It's only when I've switched the news off and lean back against my soft, velour sofa that I shiver. As the expression goes, I'm walking a tightrope. The police are investigating

Ian, and thank goodness nothing has yet been mentioned about Samuel, but even so, I can't be complacent. Ian was a complication I hadn't foreseen, but I can think on my feet and the problem will be sorted. I always knew this part of the plan would be the most dangerous and I'm going to need to tread very carefully.

Just before 10 p.m. I check on the children. They're both fast asleep and look almost angelic in their slumber. Unfortunately they're not. I also nip down to the basement before returning upstairs, locking and bolting the door. I slip the key into my coat pocket and head out of the house, locking the front door behind me. I start up my car, then wait for a moment to see if any lights come on in my house, but when they don't I drive away, heading along the now very familiar route to my love, making sure I stick within the speed limits and don't bring any attention to myself. I spend a heavenly five hours in the cottage before heading back just as dawn is beginning to break.

CHAPTER TWENTY-SEVEN

THE WIFE

Angela calls me. 'What the hell, Eva! Damien Caulder told me you were questioned by the police. What's going on?'

I sigh. 'They seem to think that I have something to do with Ian and Samuel's disappearance.'

'Do you?'

'Of course not!'

'Damien wouldn't give me the detail because of client confidentiality but do you want to fill me in?'

The next morning, I'm at Stephen's for 8 a.m. to collect the children and take them to school. Once again, I barely slept, and with my greasy hair and grey face, I know I look a mess.

Stephen peers at me with a look of concern. 'Oh Eva,' he sighs dramatically, 'you really need to see a doctor. The strain of everything is clearly too much for you. You look awful, as if you've got the flu or something and you can barely keep your eyes open. In fact, should you even be driving? Is it safe for you to take the kids in the car? I can do the school run for you if you like.'

Stephen's always been surprisingly observant, more so than any other men I know. I hesitate because I'm sure he means well, but he's not helping my confidence. I shake my head. 'I'll be fine. But thanks anyway.'

Alfie and Riley are quiet in the car.

'Did you sleep well?' I ask them.

Alfie offers me a grunt. Riley is silent.

'Are you worried about seeing Autumn?' I ask Riley.

'No,' she says indignantly. 'She was the one goading me and it was an accident.'

'But you'll still need to apologise to her. You will do that, won't you?'

Riley grunts. 'It's so unfair.'

I sigh. 'Sometimes life is.'

We're just five minutes from school, when Riley screeches. I slam my foot on the brake.

'What's the matter?' I ask, glancing around and seeing nothing to warrant me stopping the car. I'm so on edge, her screech has put every nerve ending on high alert.

'I've forgotten my homework. I left it on the floor of my bedroom at Uncle Stephen's house. We have to go back.'

'No.' I shake my head and carry on driving. 'We're not turning around. We're nearly at school.'

'No, Mum! You don't understand. It's the big project I've been working on for history and it has to be handed in this morning. I'll get a detention if I don't. And what with my suspension, I can't get into any more trouble.'

'I'm sure you won't, darling. I can talk to your teacher.'

'Mum!' Riley shouts. She's trembling now, as if this really is the worst thing in the world that could have happened to her. 'Please, we have to go back. It doesn't matter if I'm late for school but if I don't hand this in it'll be the end of the world. Mum, you've got to understand! I worked so hard on it and Mrs Planter said she'd give a fail to anyone who was late handing it in.' And then my strong, mature Riley bursts into tears.

I relent. She's always been so conscientious, yet I'm very conscious of the fight with Autumn. I can't have Riley unravel any further. It's indisputable that our family situation is taking its toll on the kids, and I need to minimise that. All this upheaval of moving between home and Stephen's and not being able to tell them the truth about Samuel is horrible for us all.

I indicate and turn the car around.

'But I'm going to be late for school too,' Alfie moans.

'I'll speak to both of your form teachers and explain we had a problem at home.'

'Thanks, Mum,' Riley says, sniffing.

By the time we're back at Stephen's we've had to navigate road works and being held up by a painfully slow tractor. My heart sinks as we pull up to his front door. Stephen's car has gone. Riley races out of the car before I've had the chance to switch off the engine. By the time I'm out of the car, followed reluctantly by Alfie, she's tugging on the front door and ringing the bell, hopping from foot to foot.

'I'm not sure we'll get in,' I say. 'Stephen's already left for work.'

Riley runs around the side of the house and tries the back door, returning with tears in her eyes. 'We've got to get in. Or can you ring Uncle Stephen and ask him to come home?'

'No, I'm not doing that.'

'But I need to get into the house!' Riley screeches.

'I am not going to break into a house just because of some

homework,' I pronounce. And then Riley becomes completely hysterical. I haven't seen her lose it like this since she was a toddler.

'Sweetheart,' I say, trying to pull her into my arms, 'it really isn't that important.' Except to Riley, it clearly is. I'm horrified how severely my situation is affecting the children.

'Let's think,' I say, as I hold Alfie's hand. Riley has shrugged away and is crouched on the garden path, her arms wrapped around herself. I remember how Mum used to leave a spare key in her wellington boots. I do the same, shoving it deep into the toe of my left boot, placing the boots in the wood storage box by the back door. We're creatures of habit, so I wonder whether Stephen might do the same thing. There's a small wooden bench to the side of his back door and underneath it is a pair of old green wellington boots. I pull them out and tip one of the boots upside down. A large spider scuttles out and I shiver. I do the same to the other boot. Nothing comes out but I can hear something jangling. I put my arm deep inside and pull out a key wrapped with a tightly spun cobweb. Clearly Stephen hasn't worn these boots or used his spare key in a very long time.

'We might be in luck,' I say to Riley, holding up the brass key. 'I'm sure Uncle Stephen won't mind.' Although I wonder if he will. Stephen is the private type and I don't think he'll be thrilled that we've let ourselves in. Perhaps he never needs to know. Riley jumps to her feet and hurries to my side. I slot the key into the back door. It turns easily and the door opens.

'Do you know exactly where you left your homework?' I ask, following Riley as she hurries through the kitchen.

'It'll be on the floor, unless Uncle Stephen tided it away.' Riley's footsteps clatter through the house but I'm not far behind her as she runs upstairs. She pushes the bedroom door open and I step inside behind her.

What the hell! I don't think I say it out loud, but I'm shocked. I lean against the door frame and let my eyes travel around the small room. It's lined with a navy-blue wallpaper and there are posters all over the walls, pictures of Riley's favourite pop stars. The bed is made up with a smart navy patterned duvet and there's a desk to its side that looks as if it's been built in. Under the window is a kidney-shaped dressing table with a mirror lit up by those big bulbs found in actors' dressing rooms. There are several glass pots, one of which holds cotton wool, and two lipsticks inside another.

'Since when did the room look like this?' I ask.

Riley is kneeling on the floor, pulling together some papers. 'Uncle Stephen let me and Alfie redecorate our rooms. He let us choose anything we wanted; the walls, curtains, bedding, posters and everything. It's cool, isn't it? I've even got a makeup table.'

I don't answer and instead head for the second spare room, which evidently is now Alfie's. This is a teenage boy's nirvana, with a big computer and games console on the far desk and smart grey and yellow decor. Why on earth has Stephen spent all of this money on redecorating his spare rooms for my children? Them staying with him was just a temporary arrangement. It doesn't make any sense, especially as Stephen is forever going on about how little money he has.

'When were these redecorated?' I ask Riley, who is now heading down the stairs.

'Dunno. A couple of weeks ago, maybe,' she says. 'I prefer being at home but my room here is sick too.'

I'm floored and for a moment just stand in the corridor.

And then something compels me to open the final bedroom door: Stephen's room. I can't remember the last time I was in here, but unlike the other two bedrooms, this one clearly hasn't been redecorated in a while. There's a queen-sized bed in the middle of the room and simple white bedside tables either side. Adjacent to the door is a wide pine wardrobe and a matching chest of drawers sits underneath the curved window. I step inside and breathe in the scent of his pine aftershave. I've never liked the cloying smell which reminds me of cleaning fluid. As I slowly glance around, I see a phone lying discarded on one of the bedside tables. A wave of dizziness passes through me and I have to fix my gaze on the pictures on the wall to stop myself from falling over. I let my eyes travel back to the phone. I know this phone. I step towards the bedside table, my heart thudding. It's the latest iPhone in a brown leather case. Gingerly, I pick it up and press it on, my breath catching as the screen saver lights up. It's a picture of me, Riley and Alfie.

This is Samuel's phone.

'Mum!' Riley shouts up the stairs. 'Please hurry because we're going to be really late.'

For a long moment, I'm frozen, staring at the familiar photograph, my brain unable to compute why my missing husband's phone is on my brother's nightstand.

'Please, Mum!'

I shove the phone into my coat pocket and hurry out of Stephen's bedroom, stumbling and almost falling as I run down the stairs.

'We need to go!' Riley wails, forgetting that our tardiness is her fault in the first place.

'Alright,' I say.

Riley and Alfie are already back in my car. I take a quick

look around the hallway, not noticing anything obviously out of place, and then head for the back door, locking it behind me and throwing the key into one of the wellington boots, placing it back under the bench.

Samuel's phone is burning in my pocket. I want nothing more than to take it out, examine it and try to work out why the hell my brother has my husband's mobile phone. With a sickening feeling I realise that Stephen must be hiding something.

I drive carefully, slowly, not listening to the kids' chatter. A lump catches at the back of my throat as I consider whether Stephen, my own brother, might have my husband locked up somewhere. But why? And where? Stephen doesn't have any spare cash. It's not like he can afford to rent another house, or even a lock-up somewhere. Or has he been saving all of these years, squirrelling cash away for the very purpose of obtaining a property to hide Samuel? It makes absolutely no sense. We may have our differences, but why would Stephen want to hurt me? What does he want with Samuel?

As we pull up in front of the kids' school, Alfie says, 'Will you come in so we don't get into trouble because we're late?'

'Yes,' I say, unclipping my seat belt and getting out of the car. My focus isn't on my children. I buzz the intercom and we're let inside, the two kids hurrying to their respective classrooms, with me promising to take the blame for our tardiness. I hurry to the school secretary's office, where I apologise for delivering the kids to school so late and explain that we had a problem with my car. The secretary looks at me dubiously but accepts my excuse.

I need to go back to the police, to hand in Samuel's

phone and explain that I found it in my brother's bedroom. But what will the implications of that be? The police think that I'm behind Ian and Samuel's disappearance. Magically producing my husband's phone is hardly going to support my case. They'll assume that I've had it all along. His phone isn't evidence of anything. Except in my heart of hearts I know something is very, very wrong. Stephen has Samuel's phone and he's redecorated his two spare rooms to make them perfect for my children. What the hell is he playing at?

CHAPTER TWENTY-EIGHT

THE LOVER

I'm feeling tired as I start the first job of my morning, cleaning a modern five-bedroom house on the edge of a neat little village. My phone rings and it's a withheld number.

'Good morning. Is this Stephen Winter?'

I hesitate before answering yes.

'My name is Detective Sergeant Suraya Braemore and we're investigating the disappearance of Ian Oakley and Samuel Simmons. We understand that Samuel is your brother-in-law and Ian Oakley a friend. We'd very much like to have a quick chat with you. Could we come to you or would it be more convenient for you to come into the station?'

I hesitate. I really don't want to talk to them and I certainly don't want to go to the police station.

'Is it urgent?' I ask.

'Yes. Ideally we'd like to speak with you this morning.'

'In which case, come here. I'm at work.' I reel off the address of this house and then when I put the phone down, I worry whether any cameras might pick up the police visiting. The owners of this place won't be happy.

Just twenty minutes later, the doorbell rings and I approach it with caution. Looking through the peephole, I see two people standing there. They're not in uniform but it's obvious they're police. It must be the way they're standing, their officious demeanour, and it punches me in the gut. For a moment, I consider not opening the door, but then I change my mind. They'll track me down whatever.

'Good morning,' I say brightly as I swing the door open.

'Hello. Are you Stephen Winter?' the woman asks.

'Yes. Please come in.'

'I'm Detective Sergeant Suraya Braemore and this is my colleague DS Will Nguyen.' They both hold up their police badges. 'This is a lovely house. It's not yours, is it?'

My laugh sounds shrill. 'If only. No, I'm the family's personal assistant and just work here.'

My knees are literally trembling as I stand back to let the officers pass me. I lead them into the spacious living room and gesture for them to sit down on the pristine sofas, hoping they put my nervousness down to me being in my place of work. I perch on an armchair opposite them.

'As I mentioned, we're investigating the disappearance of Samuel Simmons and Ian Oakley. We understand Ian is a friend.'

'Well, more my sister's friend really. I haven't seen him in years,' I say and then immediately regret my words. What if he was caught on a CCTV or doorbell video entering my house, or what if his phone placed him there as the last known location? Thank goodness we're not at my house. I think of Ian's smashed phone and the fact that there would only be some old floorboards between Ian and these officers if we were in my living room. I wonder if they're like dogs and can sniff a place out. 'Why are you asking anyway?' I say, feigning innocence.

'Have you not spoken to your sister or seen the news?'

'Um, no. Eva's kids stayed with me last night because she's so stressed at the moment. But I haven't had the chance to really find out what's going on. I think my sister might be having a nervous breakdown. It's not the first time she's struggled with her mental health.'

Can they see my nerves? I think I'm good at acting but it is so difficult to remain calm and collected.

'What prior issues has she had?' Suraya Braemore leans forwards, placing her hands on her knees. Her colleague scribbles in a little notebook.

'She suffered with post-natal depression, but long before that she developed these weird phobias, about water in particular. She won't go near water, even to this day.'

'Do you think your sister is capable of hurting someone?' Suraya Braemore asks. Her gaze is steady and quite unnerving.

I sigh. 'Unfortunately, yes. She was the sort of kid who wouldn't think twice about hurting animals, and to be honest, I was surprised when she and Samuel had children. I didn't think she had it in her.'

Suraya Braemore's right eyebrow shoots towards her hairline. 'We haven't had any incidents involving social services. Are you suggesting her children might be at risk?'

'Good heavens, no!' I exclaim. 'I don't think she'd hurt her kids knowingly, it's just that she's been behaving really erratically recently. I think she might have borderline personality disorder, because she's been changing her appearance and making up all these weird allegations. Has she mentioned anything about Samuel being kidnapped? I mean, that's one of the reasons I insisted that Riley and Alfie stay at my place. I want to keep an eye on them, just in case.'

'What has she told you about the alleged kidnapping?'

I'm feeling my way here and need to be careful not to say too much.

'Very little. She told me this crazy stuff about getting messages telling her to go on dates and to cut off her hair, but when I asked for evidence, she didn't have any. Is that what she's been telling you?'

DS Will Nguyen's nod is almost imperceptible but I see it. So they don't believe her either. Bingo.

'Honestly, I've been trying to get her to see a doctor, but she won't go. I love my sister and I want her to get the help she needs.'

'Is Eva the elder sister?' Will Nguyen asks.

That puts a smile on my face. I know I'm looking good at the moment, because that's what love does to you, and of course, Eva is a mess with her dreadful haircut and grey complexion. She's put on weight over the years too, really let herself go considering she's only just turned forty. 'No, actually. I'm the older sibling.'

'And how was your upbringing?' Suraya Braemore asks. I'm not sure what that's got to do with them but I'm happy to throw in some context.

'It was a strange childhood for both of us. We were loved, but Eva was always the chosen one. Our mother struggled with miscarriages, so they adopted me and then four years later Mum fell pregnant and Eva was born. Our parents had very high expectations of Eva whereas I was always the disappointment, the child they wouldn't have bothered having if they'd known they could conceive naturally.'

'And how is the relationship with your parents now?'

'Dad died some years ago. Eva sees Mum regularly. I don't. We had a falling out.'

'What is your relationship like with your sister?' Suraya Braemore asks.

'I love my sister. She's the most important person in my life and I'd do anything for her.'

'So the fact you were adopted and she wasn't has never caused issues between you?'

I wonder how honest I should be here. 'Sure, when we were kids, I was jealous of her because she was the real child and I wasn't. Our parents definitely favoured her, but as we grew up, I realised what a wonderful person Eva is. So selfless even if she is troubled. If our parents didn't treat us equally, she always made sure I got a fair share. And she runs a charity, which you probably know about. I really love my sister and that's why I'm so worried about her now.'

'And as far as you know, how was Eva's relationship with Samuel, her husband?'

'I assumed that Samuel left Eva because she was clingy and demanding. She was never like that around me, but with Samuel, gosh, she pushed him so far, anyone would have cracked. I'm surprised he didn't leave her years ago. I thought he'd gone off somewhere to get his head straight, put some space between them. I told her on numerous occasions that she was being too needy. Where is Samuel, anyway?'

'We don't know and we're concerned that Samuel might have come to harm.'

I pretend to gasp. 'What, you think Eva might have hurt him?' I pause, pretending to give that some serious consideration and I'm about to say yes, I think that could be a distinct possibility when I remember that Samuel is going to have to come back after the plan is fully completed, so that he, I and the kids can live a normal life. So no, I want the police to think that Eva is deranged but not evil.

'Honestly, I don't think Eva is capable of murder. I just think she's having a major breakdown. I'm more scared that she's going to do something to harm herself.'

'Are you saying that she's a danger to herself?' Suraya Braemore frowns at me.

I have to be so careful here, treading a very fine line. I want to suggest that Eva is fragile, so that when she dies, her suicide doesn't come as a shock, but I don't want her committed.

'No,' I say, gazing at the far wall. 'If I thought she was a danger to herself or her children, I would take action. I love my sister. But I do think she needs some therapy or medication.'

'And what was her relationship with Ian Oakley?'

'She used to go out with him before she married Samuel. But other than him being a trustee for Leap Ahead, I wasn't aware she had a relationship with him. It was such a shock when she told me just the other day that she's unofficially engaged to him. Do you know what's happened to Ian? I was horrified to see his face on the news. You don't think Eva has anything to do with that, do you?'

'We are investigating his disappearance,' Suraya Braemore confirms.

'Well, I hope you find him soon.'

The police officers glance at each other, and then Suraya Braemore stands up. She pats down her trousers and turns towards me. 'Thank you for sharing that information with us. If you think of anything else that might help us find either Samuel Simmons or Ian Oakley, please get in touch. The very smallest, insignificant thing might just be of help.' She hands me a business card. I see the officers out and watch through the peep hole as they walk along the road, getting into a black sedan car and slowly driving away. I go back into the living room and start laughing. I laugh so hard, my laughter edges into hysteria and I have to sit down to control the shaking. Wiping my face with my sleeve, I lean back into the armchair and think. I did really well there. No, better than that. I gave the performance of a lifetime. And now my thoughts turn to Eva. I wish I could have given her a task that included swimming in the English Channel, or at least doing a hundred lengths in the local pool. Now that really would have been a bucket-list item. Except I couldn't, because only Eva's closest friends and family know about her water phobia. Such a shame. I think back to all of those years ago when the phobia started. What would have happened if we hadn't saved Eva? I've often wondered that. Would Mum and Dad have refocused their love on me? Would they have treated me better? And would Samuel have been with me instead? I'll never know, of course, but my current plan rights all of those wrongs.

I stand up and start shaking out some of the cushions, removing the indentations from where the officers sat.

Before, I didn't want there to be a police investigation, but now I'm glad that they're probing into Eva's life. It paves the way for the next step in my plan: getting rid of Eva permanently so that Samuel, Riley, Alfie and I can live together happily ever after. I'm hoping that with a little further encouragement, Eva will take her own life, but if she doesn't, a tragic drowning accident would be just perfect.

CHAPTER TWENTY-NINE

THE WIFE

I sit in the car outside the children's school passing Samuel's phone from one hand to the other. The phone is fully charged, which doesn't make sense, and I wonder if Stephen has been using it for something. I punch in Samuel's pin, except it doesn't work. When did he change it? The same time he changed his banking code? And why? What is it that he wanted to stop me from seeing? I try a few other potential pins: the obvious ones of our birthdays and wedding anniversary, but I'm locked out. And then I wonder if I should call Stephen, demand to meet him and ask straight out why he has my husband's phone, and why he's decorated his spare rooms for Riley and Alfie without telling me. Except I don't. I've always been just a little scared of Stephen. Years ago I assumed it was because I was in awe of my older, stronger brother, except now, I'm not so sure. He's always had an edge of cruelty which was directed towards me. I assumed it was jealousy, the fact that I'm our parents' biological child and he's not, except when we were young Mum and Dad went out of their way to make sure they treated us equally. It was

Stephen's fault that he had a massive bust-up with them when Dad sold his business. He wanted a payout, arguing that he needed the money then, when he was young, not upon our parents' deaths, when we'd be incurring huge inheritance tax bills and hopefully were settled in life. And he didn't want Dad to inject so much money into the charity. Dad was livid, called him avaricious and not of his loins, or something equally unpleasant. He never spoke to Dad again. Mum tried so hard to reconcile our broken family, reaching out to Stephen behind Dad's back, and they did have a relationship for a bit. But when Dad died suddenly of a massive heart attack, Stephen refused to attend his funeral. Mum was completely devastated. Against my advice, she wrote to Stephen and told him that Stephen owed his parents everything, that they rescued him from a childhood in care, that his mother was a druggie who didn't want him. And Mum told him that she had changed her will and everything was being left to me.

I tried very hard to change Mum's mind. Yes, Mum was really hurt by Stephen's behaviour, but I didn't think it was fair to cut him out completely. I still don't think it's right and I have every intention of giving Stephen part of my inheritance when the time comes. Having said that, he's so proud he probably won't accept it.

Stephen may owe his life to our parents, except he didn't have any choice in the matter. They chose him when he was a baby. On the other hand, I really do owe Stephen my life. It's been years since I've thought about how he rescued me from the river. It's not something I like to dwell on, as it only compounds my fear of water, but I'll never forget that horrendous afternoon. We should never have been by the river that day. It was swollen and rapid following weeks of unseasonably heavy rain, but the seclusion was too tempting for a bunch of rebellious sixth-formers with nothing else to do on a summer's day. My recurring nightmares all stem from my near drowning in the river, yet I try to block out the terror, the voice that I think I heard, yet surely I didn't.

'Just leave her.' That's what Stephen says in my nightmares. *Just leave her.* Except when I came to in the derelict game keeper's cottage, vomit on the floor next to me, a man and a woman dressed in green and white uniforms, I was so confused.

'Hello, Eva,' the female paramedic said to me. 'You're a very lucky girl. You nearly drowned in the river and it's only thanks to your quick-thinking brother that you were saved.'

Stephen was standing next to me, his arms covered in goosebumps, his clothes sopping wet. He was looking everywhere except at me. The male paramedic handed him a silver sheet, which he wrapped around his shoulders. I tried to talk, to ask what happened, except my voice wasn't working.

'We're going to take you to the hospital,' the female paramedic said. 'Just to get you checked out.'

As they levered me onto a stretcher and carried me towards the ambulance, I looked all around but I couldn't see any of Stephen's friends. They had gone.

I have never returned to that stretch of the river and I don't think we had any family picnics after that horrendous day. But Dad was right about one thing. He sold off twenty acres of that land to a housing developer and made a small fortune. As far as I know, Mum still owns the rest of the land and the keeper's cottage that stood just a few couple of hundred metres back from the river. I can't imagine what state it's in now, even if it's still standing. Later, Stephen boasted that he lost his virginity in that cottage and it makes me wonder, does he still go there?

I telephone Mum.

'How's Riley doing? We had a good heart to heart.'

'Thank you, she's fine. Hopefully she's made up with Autumn. I was calling to ask about the game keeper's cottage near the river where we used to go.'

'Where Stephen nearly got you killed, you mean,' she interjects.

'Was it sold off after Dad died or do you still have it?'

'Goodness,' she says. 'No. I've done nothing with it. It's boarded up and falling to pieces and needs knocking down. I haven't been there for years. Why on earth are you asking about that old place?'

'It came to me in a nightmare,' I say.

'Oh, Eva.' Mum sighs. 'I've been telling you for ages to go and see a shrink. This phobia of yours seems to be getting worse rather than better and it's no good for your children.'

I do not need a lecture from Mum at this point.

'You're right,' I say. 'Anyway, I must be going. I'll call again soon.'

I head towards Mum's house, recalling that the turning off to the cottage was somewhere approximately six or seven miles down a narrow country lane between the quaint villages of Wickley and Torchingham. I drive slowly, getting hooted at by impatient van drivers and almost pushed off the road by a man in a black Porsche. Every time I think I've found the turning, it's a gate that leads into a field or a farmhouse set back from the road. I wonder if the track even exists anymore, the cottage only accessible on foot. Just when I'm about to give up, I see a woman wearing a waxed jacket walking a black Labrador. I indicate and pull up next to her, winding down my window.

'Sorry to disturb you but I'm trying to find a derelict cottage somewhere around here. Have you lived here long?'

'Coming up for fifty years. Does that qualify?' She beams at me and then peers closer through the open window.

'Good heavens. Are you Dorothy Winter's wee lass?'

'Yes, Dorothy's my mum. Do you know her?'

'My husband, Fred, said that you were doing up the game keeper's cottage. Such a lovely spot up there secluded in the woods. I'm sorry to hear that your father passed away but how is your mother?'

'Um, she's fine,' I say. I haven't got a clue who this woman is or what she means about the cottage, although I am starting to wonder...

'Your family weren't too popular when you sold off all that land for development, but people have short memories. You're forgiven now. If you're spending more time here, you should pop in for a cuppa sometimes. Our place, Purnell's Farm, is two turnings on the left, one turning beyond the track down to your place.'

'Thank you,' I say, relieved that this lady has inadvertently given me directions.

'Don't forget to stop in for a cuppa next time you're here,' she says, before stepping backwards and giving me a wave. I close the car window and drive away, very slowly. And there it is. A small track between two oak trees. I turn left and follow the track, driving very carefully over the potholes and mud. There are tyre tracks along here, suggesting that this narrow country track has been having regular use, but it's uneven and the car bounces as it rocks from side to side. After a few hundred metres of driving between hedges and dodging low-hanging branches of overgrown trees, the track peters out and in front of me is a broken wooden gate set in a fence made from barbed wire. I do a three-point turn, which turns into more like a nine-point turn, and drive the car a little way back in the direction I came. To my right is a clearing between trees, so I edge the car there and park it in such a way that it's barely visible from the track. At least I'm pointing in the right direction now, should I need to get away in a hurry.

Nerves flicker in the base of my stomach as I tug on my old wellington boots and do up my long navy parka. My boots squelch as I follow the muddy tyre tracks, keeping as far to the right as possible, under the shadows of the heavy, dark branches of oak and hornbeam trees. The old gate opens with a squeak and I see that there's a single line in the grass where it is flattened. Someone has been walking up and down here regularly, in-between the sprawling rhododendron bushes. With a thudding heart, I continue walking. And then I see it. A thin plume of smoke rising above the trees. I tiptoe forwards. The terrifying cottage of my dreams is right here in front of me, except it doesn't look nearly as run down as Mum portrayed it and it certainly isn't boarded up. Some of the wooden panels on the front of the building have cracked and buckled and there are weeds growing all around it, ivy clinging around the paint-peeling window frames. There are just two windows either side of the front door and both have curtains blocking out the interior. I creep around the whole building once. It's not much more than a shed. But someone is inside. Someone is living here. I stand to the side of the first window, trying to peek in through the tiny gap in the curtain. I can't see a thing.

Is Samuel being held inside, kept captive by Stephen? I

tiptoe the whole way around once again, my heart as loud as the singing birds. There's no car here but that's not surprising, as Stephen must be at work at this time of day. It's a relief; it means I'll be able to rescue Samuel unimpeded. For the first time in three weeks, I feel hope. I can save my husband. Frustratingly, there are no old gardening implements or pieces of wood lying around which I can use to force open the front door. I take a deep breath and walk up the short path to the front door, ready to try the handle, ready to start banging on the door. And then I freeze.

There's the sound of a car engine. The slamming of a car door. I scud towards the side of the building but I'm too late.

'Eva?'

I swivel around and come face to face with my brother. Stephen is holding two bulging Tesco carrier bags which he drops with a thud to the ground. He looks different somehow. Perhaps it's the red scarf around his neck, a scarf that looks just like one that I have at home.

'What are you doing here?' I ask. 'What's going on?'

There's a long pause before he replies, 'You need to leave.'

I take a step towards him. Stephen's face is impassive. I've always found it so difficult to read him, and that's likely why he always got the upper hand in our sibling fights.

'Have you got Samuel?' I ask.

He just stares at me, his pupils like black pinpricks, his lips a tight straight line.

'Stephen, talk to me,' I say, taking a step towards him, even though I'm scared. My brother could overpower me so easily.

And then he sighs, and his face seems to soften. 'You're

right, we need to talk. The sun is shining, so let's go for a walk and I'll tell you everything.'

'Who's in the cottage?' I ask. He steps away from the shopping bags and walks towards me. Suddenly, I feel a cold fear swim through my veins and take a step backwards, but Stephen slips his arm into mine and starts striding forwards, pulling me with him.

'Relax!' His laugh sounds brittle and despite him telling me to relax, there is tension in his neck and a little nerve flutters at his temple. 'You know, I'm glad you're here. It'll give us time to have a heart to heart.'

'Mum said this place is derelict,' I say. Stephen is walking briskly and my boots slurp in puddles as I try to keep up with his long strides.

'As you can see, I've done some work on it, so no, it's not derelict. I've been using it as a weekend cottage, a place where I can get away from the world and have some privacy.'

'Is there someone in the cottage with you?' I ask.

'So many questions, Eva. So many questions. I've put a bench under the willow tree. We can sit there and I'll explain everything.'

He's right, I have so many questions, yet it's evident that Stephen will only answer them on his terms. It hits me how that is nothing new. He's pacing quickly and I'm struggling to keep up with him, but his arm through mine is pulling me along. I hear the sound of the rushing river long before I see it. Fear flutters in my stomach and I stand still, tugging my arm free of his.

'Don't be silly,' Stephen says, placing a heavy hand on my arm. It's then that I see a simple gold band on the ring finger of his left hand. What does that signify? Why haven't I seen that before? But before I can open my mouth, Stephen speaks. 'You're an adult now, with children, and we're not going down to the river's edge. This is my happy place and I want to share it with you.'

'What?' I scoff. 'The spot where I nearly drowned?'

'You're being melodramatic. Firstly, you didn't drown because I saved you, and secondly, you're not going to fall into the river. It's very beautiful there, where I like to come to think. Not everything is all about you, Eva.'

'Just tell me what's going on,' I demand.

'Nope.' Stephen clamps his lips together and carries on walking. I have a choice. Turn back towards the cottage or follow him. Every nerve ending in my body is telling me to get away from him, but my brain is shouting, *this is your brother; you need to know what he has to say*. I swallow hard and hurry to catch up with him.

I don't recognise it here, but then again I haven't been to this place in over twenty-five years and the vegetation will be all different. Except the river is roaring and every step we take closer to the bellowing of the water, another bolt of fear drives through me. Stephen comes to a full stop. We're high above the river and I don't see the grassy verge or the willow tree where we used to come.

'It looks different,' I mutter.

Stephen takes a step forwards and stares down at the rushing water, his hands on his hips. How can he stand there and be so fearless?

'Where's the bench?' I ask.

'Over there,' he says without gesticulating so it could be anywhere. I follow his gaze down to the swirling river and take a step backwards. The fear is choking me.

'Have you got Samuel?' I ask.

Stephen turns towards me very slowly and then he

reaches for my hand. His palm feels icy cold and I want nothing more than to pull my flesh away from his. 'I love Samuel,' Stephen says, his steely eyes locked onto mine, his face bizarrely expressionless. 'I'm sorry, but I love him. I always have done and now it's our time to be together.'

'What?' I exclaim, unable to make sense of that statement.

'You've taken everything from me, Eva. And you owe me every breath you take.' And then he shoves me, so hard, so unexpectedly. I feel my feet slip from under me but instinctively I grab for whatever I can and I clutch the red scarf that is tied around Stephen's neck. His eyes widen, reflecting my fear, and together we tumble downwards, and due to his larger size and weight, he barrels into my body, knocking me further away. I hear a scream and then I hit something. But unlike last time, my legs slam into a spider's web of thick tree roots, my left foot catching hard so my ankle flips the wrong way, causing a bolt of pain to scream up my leg, my other foot scrambling uselessly in the mud on the side of the bank. Instinctively, I fling my arms upwards, grabbing onto the trunk of an overhanging tree. I'm just inches from the rushing water, but I'm completely dry. In that split second I feel bizarrely calm, with a deep instinctual belief that today it's not my time.

And then I see a flash of red: Stephen's scarf is being dragged downwards, disappearing into the swirling water, and then his head surfaces, a look of pure terror on his face, his dark hair flat against his scalp. Stephen can swim. Surely he can rescue himself? An arm reaches out towards me but he's too far away and despite trying to lean across the river, I can't reach him. The water is so fast and strong, he's swept underneath it, the brown murky water surging all around until there's no sight of any life. I watch the water with a sense of horror as I slowly absorb what has just happened; what is happening right now. Stephen pushed me. I saw such hatred in his eyes, and yet it is him who has been taken by the river. I start trembling violently and haul myself upwards. It's hard because my left ankle is throbbing with agony and my right foot struggles to gain traction in the sheer muddy bank. My body feels so very heavy. Somehow, I crawl upwards, hauling myself towards the top by grappling with tree roots and thick blades of grass, forcing my way through the pain. All the time, in my mind's eye, I see Samuel lying on a strange bed, a knife at his throat, and I see Riley and Alfie. If I don't get out of here, then my children might be parentless. It's up to me to save my family. I throw myself onto the bank of grass at the top, panting heavily, and then lever myself up to a sitting position.

Stephen. Where is he? I scan the river, the swirling, frothy water, the dark brown depths. It's as if all trace of him has completely vanished. I try to get my breath, fumbling in my jeans pocket for my phone. My mud-covered, bleeding hands come out empty. My phone has gone. I dig into the pockets of my coat, and feel relief as my sore right palm clasps my car keys.

Very carefully, I ease myself up to standing, avoiding putting too much weight on my left ankle. 'Stephen!' I shout, but my voice is picked up by the wind and the deafening roar of the river. I know it's futile. And then I start hopping, running as best I can, despite the pain. I need to call for help and I remember that I've left Samuel's phone in the car. I force myself to run blindly along the path that we walked along just five minutes ago when I followed Stephen to the river's edge, the panic of losing Stephen dampening the pain of my twisted ankle. My lungs are burning but I'm not the one in the water. I have air. I trip, my arms and legs are scratched and bruised but this is life or death. I stop for a moment to give my ankle a break, to catch my breath and recall what just happened: Stephen pushed me. He actually put his hand on my chest and shoved me backwards towards the river. Did he want me to die? And what did he say? That he loves Samuel. I didn't even know he liked men, let alone Samuel. But does he deserve to drown in the river? No. I have to save my brother. I hobble along the path, reaching the cottage first, tugging at the door, but it's firmly locked. I bang my fists on the glass of the windows, shouting, 'Help! If there's anyone in there, call for an ambulance!' And then I see Stephen's car and hop towards it, tugging at the doors, but they're locked. Yelping with pain and frustration I jog to my car, forcing myself to ignore the burning, trying not to think.

With a scream of relief, I point the key fob at the car. The doors click and I fling open the passenger door and grab Samuel's phone, pressing down the two buttons on the sides until the emergency SOS number appears on the screen.

'You need to help us!' I cry. 'My brother has been swept down the river and I don't know if he'll survive.'

CHAPTER THIRTY

THE WIFE – THE NEXT DAY

Stephen hasn't been found. The consensus is he'll either have been swept out to sea and eventually his decomposed body might make its way back to shore, or he's been caught at the side of the river, held fast underneath the fast-flowing water by detritus.

The police and the coastguard have been amazing. They sent up a helicopter which hovered up and down the river, desperately seeking any sign of life. They've launched boats to scour the estuary and spoken to experts about the currents and tides and the trajectory a human body might take. Police dogs have sniffed along the river banks. But there's been no trace of him; no sign of that red scarf; no battered body or bloated face. The water has taken him in exactly the way that he wanted it to take me.

Samuel has been kept in hospital overnight and this morning he is at the police station being interviewed. The police presence has been overwhelming, although fortunately they've managed to keep the media at bay – for now, at least.

I brought the children to see their dad last night, and our tears of joy and relief all mingled together. What I haven't had is a proper debrief with Samuel, the chance to really find out what Stephen did. The police have that prerogative.

Now I'm waiting outside the police station for Samuel to emerge. The sun is warm on my cheeks and I'm in pain from my sprained ankle, but there's also a chasm in my heart. My brother is almost certainly dead.

Samuel emerges from the wide front door, blinking slightly as his eyes adjust to the bright light. I wave at him, and he nods as he walks forwards. He is pale and he has shaven off his beard, leaving just a darkening of a day or two's facial stubble. My husband looks different, as if the past three weeks have fundamentally changed him in a profound way. I hate to think how Stephen treated him, chained up to a bed, how terrified he must have been and shocked. I think that will be the hardest thing to process: the shock that my deranged brother kidnapped his brother-in-law, and in some totally delusional way, believed that he could take everything that is mine: my husband, my children, my home.

'How are you?' I ask as he steps towards the car. He shrugs his shoulders. I move as if to get into the driver's seat but he holds his hand out. 'I'd like to drive,' he says.

'Are you fit to drive?'

'I'm perfectly fine.'

I raise an eyebrow but hand him the key, then hobble to the passenger door.

'How are you, darling?' I ask, as Samuel settles into the driver's seat. I place my hand on top of his wrist.

'I need to drive,' he says, pulling his arm away.

'I can't begin to imagine what horrors you've been through.'

Samuel doesn't answer but starts up the engine. I get that he wants to drive. It must have been unimaginably horrific losing all control, being kept chained to the bed for the past three weeks. I'll never forget that look of animal fear in his eyes when the police, swiftly followed by me, even though they wanted to keep me back, swept into the bedroom and found him, his wrists and ankles chained to that bed. I threw myself at him and sobbed.

'Were the police good to you?' I ask. He grunts in response and I turn to stare at him. Samuel's eyes are firmly fixed on the road ahead but there's tension in his neck. I guess he has so much to process and I wonder if he's going to suffer from post-traumatic stress disorder.

'I'm so sorry that you've been through this,' I say. 'I know I had no control over him, but Stephen was still my brother. I feel like I'm responsible in some way even though I'm not. I had no idea he was so unhinged. I feel terrible that I didn't realise he was gay and that he became fixated on you. Why didn't he just tell me that he preferred men? Some of my best friends are queer, and the whole family would have been completely supportive of him. We may be many things, but no one in our family has ever been homophobic.'

Still Samuel doesn't respond and I feel like there's a shield between us, something that I'm going to have to break down gradually. He indicates to the left and turns the car towards the motorway. It's a shorter way home, but we rarely go this way, preferring the gentler country roads. I don't say anything.

The motorway is busy with three lanes of traffic, mostly heavy lorries heading towards the coast, but Samuel drives confidently and soon we're in the outside lane, driving at 70 mph. When my phone rings, I'm startled. I fumble for it in my bag, my heart jumping when I see that it's Riley and Alfie's school. Please, not another drama, I think, at the same time grateful that I'd only temporarily misplaced it and not lost it in the river the day before. I jab the call accept button.

'Hello, is this Mrs Simmons?'

'Yes,' I confirm. 'Is everything alright?'

'Yes, just calling to –' And then the line goes dead. I glance at the phone assuming we've lost reception but then I notice that my phone is completely out of battery. I groan.

'It's the school and my phone died,' I tell Samuel, whose face remains impassive. 'I hope there's no emergency.' Then I remember I still have Samuel's phone in my bag.

'I found your phone at Stephen's house,' I say as I remove it. 'He must have stolen it from you. Can I use it to call school back?'

'Suppose so,' Samuel says, almost begrudgingly. He really is acting strangely.

'I don't know the pin. You changed the code.'

'It's 5549,' he says.

That number means nothing to me but I don't question it. I type in the pin and sure enough, the phone unlocks. I call the children's school and speak to the secretary.

'I just missed your call,' I say, anxiety knotting inside me. 'Is everything alright?'

'Oh, I'm sorry to have worried you, Mrs Simmons. Alfie is very upset because he left his trainers at home and he was wondering if you could drop them in.' What, Alfie has left his trainers behind yet again? What is it with my son and his shoes?

'Yes, of course I can drop them off, but it won't be for another hour or so.'

'That should be fine, Mrs Simmons.'

I end the call and let out a breath. 'Nothing to worry about,' I say to Samuel, but still my husband remains expressionless. He hasn't even asked about the children, which is mighty strange.

I glance down at his phone. And then look again. There's a strange app on the front screen, wedged between WhatsApp and the phone icon, a picture of a cartoon face with a microphone in front of it. I click on it. The app opens up and, with dismay, I realise that it's a voice-changing app. Why is this on Samuel's phone? Was Stephen using it? I recall that dalek-like voice which sounded like a man. And then I wonder how Stephen got the pin for Samuel's phone. Did he force my husband to hand it over, running the blade of the knife along his neck until he gave it to him? Was my brother really that much of a psycho? Or did he perhaps use facial recognition when Samuel was asleep? I'd like to ask Samuel, except from the setting of his jaw and the tension emanating from his every pore, I know that now is not the right time.

The car jolts slightly and I look up. Samuel is looking at me.

'Watch out!' I yell, as the car swerves towards the central reservation. Samuel yanks the steering wheel the opposite way and a lorry hoots at us. 'Please be careful,' I say, as Samuel indicates to the left and pulls across two lanes into the slow lane.

'Give me that,' he says, taking his left hand off the steering wheel and grabbing his phone. He shoves the phone into the side pocket of the driver's door, where I can't reach it.

'What's going on, Samuel?' I ask, confusion making my head hurt. 'Did you know what Stephen was doing? He told me that he loved you. He completely lost a grip on reality.'

'No, Eva. It's you. You have ruined everything, with your holier than thou attitude. You killed Stephen!'

'What?' I exclaim, my thoughts a whirl of confusion. 'He tried to push me into the river, but he slipped in the process.'

'You've always thought you were better than him, haven't you? Just because you were the real child and he was adopted. But you're not better than him. He was everything that you're not.'

Bile rushes up my throat into my mouth. 'What?' I gasp. My brain is unable to make sense of what Samuel is saying.

'Are you... Did you...' I can't get my words out. 'Were you having an affair with Stephen?'

'It wasn't a bloody affair, Eva! It was love. I love Stephen and he loves me back. Unconditionally. We've always loved each other. It's just for so many years, we tried to suppress it. And now you've killed him! You've killed my only true chance of happiness.'

I shake my head repeatedly, as if the motion is somehow going to make sense of what my husband is saying.

'Were you *with* Stephen? You mean you weren't being held captive?'

Samuel laughs. It's a dark, bitter laugh, more like a bark, and it sends shivers through me. 'We love each other, Eva.'

'I don't understand,' I murmur. My left hand is gripping the door handle, my head is throbbing. 'Have you always been gay? Has the whole of our marriage been a sham?'

'It's constantly about you, isn't it, Eva? Always about you.' He pauses for a moment and then his words spit out like pellets. 'I heard you outside the cottage and assumed you were the police. It was easy to stage the scene, attaching the chains firstly to my ankles and the bedposts, and then swallowing several sleeping pills, before slipping my wrists into the chains and fixing them. And because the police didn't tip up until later, I was completely groggy when you all stormed in. That was genuine. But I've got to live with the guilt, Eva.'

'What guilt?' I whisper. The guilt of cheating on me? The guilt of blackmailing me? The guilt of pretending to be someone he isn't?

Samuel slams his foot harder on the accelerator and the car leaps forwards.

'If I'd come outside when I first heard you, I would have realised that it was you who was there, not the police. I could have gone with you and Stephen to the riverside so it would have been two against one. It would be you who was dead, swept away by the current, not Stephen. It should have been you.' He lets out a sob and I stare at this man, his jaw tense, his eyes flashing with anger, the man whom I thought I knew so well. I realise I don't know him at all. 'If only you'd killed yourself as you should have done, Stephen would still be alive!' He's shouting at me now, pummelling his fists on the steering wheel, despite the speed we're driving. 'We'd have custody of the kids, our lives would be perfect! But no, you're so entitled, Eva. Everything always goes your way.'

'What are you talking about?' I whisper. My knuckles are white as I grab the sides of the seat. 'Please slow down, Samuel.'

'We planned it all together. The bucket list, every task

designed to make you look increasingly deranged, to show the world that it was you who broke our marriage, it was you who is crazy. And when I was ill, Stephen cared for me better than the most loving nurse.' He's jabbing the steering wheel with his left fist, his left knee jangling up and down.

'Slow down, Samuel!' I yell at him. 'You're going to kill us and then the kids will be orphaned. Is that what you want?'

And suddenly, he slams his foot on the brakes and swerves the car into the hard shoulder, eliciting another hooting of the horn by a massive articulated lorry that misses us by about a centimetre. My heart feels like it's jumped up into my throat. The car shudders to a halt. Instinctively I lean across and switch the hazard lights on.

'Even now, you're trying to control things,' Samuel says, spitting out his words as if they're individual daggers, pointing at the flashing light on the dashboard.

'I don't understand,' I murmur, unable to look at him.

'What is there not to understand? Stephen and I were doing this together. We wanted to be together to spend the rest of our lives as a happy family. But I've failed him. If I'd come out of the cottage when I first heard you, you would be dead, not Stephen. I've completely failed him.' He swallows a sob.

'But why didn't you just ask for a divorce? Why weren't you honest with me? It would have hurt, but I would have understood. I would have wanted you both to be happy.' My voice is jittery and despite the warmth in the car, I'm shivering. The car rocks every time a lorry speeds past us.

He scoffs. 'The prenup. The fucking prenup, Eva. If I'd left you, I would have walked away with nothing. And

Stephen had already been cut out of your parents' lives and will. Simmons Edge will go down the pan if we don't keep the Pellangica account, and then we'll have nothing. But if you die, then the children and I get everything – the house, your inheritance. I thought you truly loved your children, that you'd be willing to die for them, except no. You're too much of a narcissist.'

'You did this for money?' I stare at this stranger, the supposedly loving father to our children, the man I've shared a bed with for the past fifteen years. 'Why didn't you tell me you were unhappy? Why didn't you tell me you prefer men to women?'

'And here we go again,' Samuel mocks. 'You never listen, do you, Eva? The prenup. I deserved more, yet Stephen and I would have got nothing. Nothing!'

'The bucket list, all the extortion, that was both of you?' I am completely stunned. 'You mean you weren't being kept captive after all?'

'We did it together. Always together. But you've ruined it, Eva, like you ruin everything.'

He turns to look at me with such hatred in his eyes, in that split second, some animal instinct kicks in. I fling open the passenger door and leap out of the car, the force of a passing lorry just centimetres from my face flinging me back against the metal of the car with a thump. But I squeeze around to the front of the car and run. I've got to get out of here. There's a steep embankment to my right and I start clambering up it, grabbing big tufts of grass just as I did yesterday, except here there's no water, just the incessant roar of traffic and the choking engine fumes. I haul myself upwards and upwards, the pain in my ankle numbed by sheer terror. Samuel is just inches from me, moving faster, nimbler, his face now level with mine. An arm snakes out and grips me around my throat.

'Don't, Samuel!' I cry. 'Think of Riley and Alfie. They love us both. You'll go to prison for life.'

I'm waving my arms around manically. Why doesn't anyone stop to help? Surely the passing motorists can see that I'm in trouble. But everyone is driving by too quickly, all in their own little worlds, oblivious to my sheer terror. Samuel's grip around my neck is getting tighter, stronger.

'Please, Samuel,' I croak. My voice is fading as he squeezes, the air in my chest being pushed out, my lungs burning. I kick at him but he punches me in the stomach with his spare hand and it feels like my insides have been pushed out. For a brief second I lose consciousness, except then there's the sound of a horn, and images of Riley and Alfie laughing, playing in the garden, their innocent faces smiling up at me, hurtle me back into the here and now. I have to fight. This is life or death, the future for my children. I kick outwards, catching Samuel in the back of his knee, and for a fleeting moment he releases the grip around my neck. I look downwards. We're perched so precariously on this bank, just one wrong move and I'll be tumbling down into the path of the passing traffic. He tightens his grip again but I use my spare fist to punch him in the nose and he grunts, swearing violently. And in that millisecond I knee him in the groin. Quite how I manage the manoeuvre I don't know, but his arm slips away from my neck, and with both hands I push him. He's not expecting it and he slips downwards, before the steep incline gives him no traction and he's falling. He looks up at me, his eyes wide with terror, those eyes I loved so very much. And in those pupils I see overwhelming hatred, a look I know I will never forget. He screams then, a bloodcurdling cry as gravity sends him tumbling over and over. If we were just a metre to the left his fall would have been broken by my car. But he's not. He rolls downwards into the road and the scream gets lost as my husband disappears under the wheels of a monstrous articulated lorry.

CHAPTER THIRTY-ONE

THE WIFE – A FEW MONTHS LATER

'Do I need to take the sausage rolls out of the oven?' Riley asks. My girl has grown up so much in the past few months, and not just because she's moved to a new senior school.

'Check to see if they're brown,' I say. I'm cutting the crusts off sandwiches on the island unit in the kitchen. I glance around the room. It's very different to the one in our old house, smaller and more modest. We're in a new build on the edge of Horsham. We are part of a community and have neighbours, many of whom I'm hoping will be joining us for our drinks party this evening. I couldn't stay in our old house; there were too many memories, mostly happy ones, which have now been tainted with the knowledge that Samuel wasn't the man I thought he was. I've spent hours and hours poring over all the pointers I must have missed, wondering what Stephen had that I didn't and why they were so cruel towards me. I can understand that they fell in love with each other – these things happen – but what I can't understand are the layers of deception, the greed and the viciousness towards me. I don't have any answers and I am slowly coming to accept that I never will.

When the emergency services first arrived at the scene of Samuel's death, they initially thought he had slipped down the bank. But then it turns out the police received three phone calls from strangers reporting an altercation on the embankment. Some fast-thinking stranger got a blurry shot of Samuel with his arm around my neck. Various witnesses stepped forwards, explaining how they couldn't stop because they were driving too fast on the motorway. For me, that has been one baby step to regaining hope in my fellow human beings. We weren't being ignored; it was just impossible for anyone to step in in the moment.

Samuel's funeral was terrible. I wanted to grieve, we all did, but how is that possible in the knowledge that my husband was trying to kill me? In the end, I grieved for the husband I thought I had, and that process may well last a lifetime.

Most people know the truth now, that Stephen and Samuel died in their quest to kill me. But how do you explain such a horror to your children? I don't want Riley and Alfie to remember their dad as anything except a good father, because he was a good father. Despite everything, he wanted the best for them, even if he couldn't see that they needed their mother as well as their father. It all could have been so different. Yes, I would have been heartbroken to discover Stephen and Samuel were in love. I would have felt betrayed, but I genuinely believe I could have forgiven them eventually. I've thought back over the years, trying to remember clues that I might have missed to suggest that they were in love with each other, yet I can't recall a single thing that might have given rise to suspicion. And yes, under the terms of our prenup, Samuel wouldn't have received any of my money. But I would never want the children to suffer, so I would have made sure that Samuel and Stephen were financially sound. They misjudged me. I still can't believe that they really thought forcing me to complete some crazy bucket list would work. They'd have been better off extorting money from me to enable them to set up their new life. But it's impossible to get into the heads of other people, even those you think you know the best. That's what has shocked me. I really didn't know either my brother or my husband. I was chugging along in my own little world and never took the time to ask them how they really were. I'm not completely blameless in all of this.

I read Stephen's journal from front to back. It was shocking to learn how long he's been in love with Samuel, how for most of his life he pretended he was straight, even getting married to Kylie. It broke my heart that in today's day and age, he still felt the need for pretence. His diary entries suggest that he first came out to Samuel when they were at school, but Samuel rejected him. That must have hurt, bitterly, and I wonder if that led him to the years of pretence. And then over the past few years, he wooed Samuel with a long, steady campaign and it paid off. Although Samuel was far from being Stephen's prey. He was a willing participant. I think of the diamond necklace I found hidden in Samuel's wardrobe, and realise it was for me after all. Except it had no meaning. It was a decoy. I haven't got around to it yet, but I shall sell the necklace and give the proceeds to Leap Ahead. Samuel probably used my money to buy it, anyway.

I'm not sure that the children will ever truly under-stand what happened, and in a way I'd rather that is the case. They're both having counselling, and considering the horrendous circumstances and life-shattering changes, Riley has settled in well at her new school. Her friendship with Autumn has never truly recovered and they're at different secondary schools now anyway, which is possibly a good thing. Alfie has taken up diving and is excelling in it. He's naturally bright and fundamentally lazy, so I'm forever having to nag him to do his school work, but he's remarkably well adjusted considering all our life upheavals.

I'm also seeing a therapist, the one that Kalah recommended. She's grounded and nothing seems to shock her. We've gone right back to that drowning episode when I was thirteen. I'm now quite convinced that the words that come to me in my nightmare, *Just leave her,* were spoken by Stephen. I reached out to some of his old school friends, finding them on his friend list on Facebook, and it turns out that it was the driver of the car, a man called Ben, who dived into the river and pulled me to safety, that it was he who resuscitated me, not Stephen, who just stood on and stared. Apparently, Stephen begged Ben to tell the authorities that it was him, Stephen, who was my saviour, that if Ben didn't, Stephen would be in such trouble with our parents he'd be banned from going out with his friends ever again. It shocks me to think that Stephen harboured hatred and jealousy towards me my whole life.

My big win is I went for my very first swimming lesson last week. I'd be lying to say that I enjoyed it; in fact, my heart was racing so hard I'm surprised it didn't cause waves in the water. But the fact is, I pulled on a swimming costume and I actually got into the water. For me, that is a minor miracle.

The doorbell chimes. 'I'll go,' I say to Riley as I wipe my

hands on a tea towel. I stride to the front door and pull it open with a smile.

'Hello, gorgeous!' Ian bends down and places a kiss on my cheek. He looks different these days. The wire-rimmed glasses have been replaced with rectangular tortoiseshell frames and there's a scar on his right temple, a visible reminder of the horrors he experienced at Stephen's hands.

'You're bright and early,' I say.

'Thought you might need a little help with the barbecue.' He grins before following me through to the kitchen and removing four bottles of champagne from a bag.

'Ian!' Alfie runs into the kitchen. 'Can we play Minecraft?'

'Sorry, mate,' he replies. 'It's party day today, but if your mum will let me stay after everyone's gone, we can have a game then. What do you reckon?' He holds his fist out and Alfie and Ian do a fist pump.

It was me who found Ian. The day after Samuel died, I went to Stephen's house, ostensibly to collect the children's belongings but also because I wanted to search the place, to find out if there were any clues as to how long he and Samuel had been having an affair. I used the spare key in the wellington boot and crept inside. There was a spookiness to the house, like a stillness, as if it had turned into some sort of a mausoleum, as if Stephen's ghost might jump out of the shadows and strike me down. I hurried upstairs, chucking the kids' things into their small suitcases and dragging them both down to the hall. Then I returned upstairs to have a nosy through Stephen's bedroom. I found the leather-backed journal in his bedside drawer. I was walking downstairs, intending to flick through it, when I heard a tapping noise. I jumped, my hand flying up to my neck. My first thought was that it was Stephen returning to haunt me. When I calmed myself, I wondered if he had mice in the attic. The tapping came again, except it sounded like it was coming from underneath my feet or in the side wall perhaps. And then I remembered that Stephen's house had a basement. I raced to his small utility room and tugged on the door handle to the basement but it was firmly locked. I searched frantically for a key but I couldn't find one. In the end, I telephoned Detective Sergeant Suraya Braemore.

'I'm in my brother Stephen's house and I've heard a noise,' I said breathlessly.

'Do you think it might be him?' the detective asked. There was concern in her voice.

I didn't think it could be Stephen; I doubt the very strongest of swimmers could have survived the swirling rush of the river. 'No, but it might be Ian Oakley.'

Within half an hour, the police were there with a battering ram, knocking down the door. Suraya Braemore tried to stop me from following her colleagues down the steep stone steps to the basement, but I barged through.

When I first saw Ian, I thought he was dead. His head was a bloody pulp, his lips split, his wrists attached with chains to a down pipe by the far wall. There were three empty plastic bottles of water at his side and the place stank of excrement. I cried out and Ian's eyes flickered open, and then I was ushered away. Paramedics arrived and spent a long time with Ian. All the while I kept asking Suraya Braemore if he was going to survive. Eventually he was stretchered out of the house, an oxygen mask over his ghostly white face.

He was severely dehydrated and had suffered major concussion, cuts and bruises, not to mention some horrible ill effects, having been pumped with medication that kept him largely unconscious. But Ian is a fighter and after ten days in hospital, he was released. He confirmed that Stephen had drugged him and kept him hostage after he got suspicious about him and visited him at home. All of that happened because of me. I wouldn't have blamed Ian for wanting nothing to do with me ever again. I visited him daily in hospital and he was by my side when we buried Samuel. We haven't had a funeral for Stephen yet, because his body hasn't been found. Mum says he doesn't deserve a funeral. I hope that his body will wash up on a shore someday because we all need closure.

The doorbell chimes again. I hurry to the front of the house and swing open the door. It's Kalah and Autumn, with Hunter and Angela standing behind them. My smile is coy because we still have some way to go before fully mending our friendships, but Angela steps forwards and throws her arms around me. 'Are you going to invite us in, then?' She laughs, shoving a bottle of wine and a bunch of flowers into my hands.

Kalah smiles at me tightly as she hands me a big box of chocolates. 'For you and the kids,' she says. I haven't been the only one who has suffered these past months. According to Angela, everything that happened to me gave Kalah some strange strength. At long last, she has split up from Xavier. He's now living in a small flat in Horsham while they sort out their divorce. Angela might have lost me as a client but she's gained Kalah. And Nicolette – she can't be here today. She is on the Amalfi coast with her new man, and no, he's not married. I feel particularly bad about the way I treated Nicolette, condemning her as the key suspect. She's been surprisingly forgiving. In fact, when my friends discovered the truth about Samuel's disappearance and the bucket list, they couldn't have been more supportive. They were there for me when we buried Samuel. They were there for me when I put our house on the market and found this new home, and I have no doubt they will be there for me through whatever life challenges I face in the future. Because that is what our best friends are for: to support us without judgment through the ups and downs.

I shut the door and hurry after Kalah, catching up with her and sliding my arm into hers. I know now that she was genuinely worried about me and that what I perceived as her annoying interference came from a kind place.

'How are things going with Ian?' she whispers.

I nudge her gently in the ribs. 'They're not,' I say. For sure, I'm grateful for his support and enjoy his company, and whereas in the past I used to think he was all about living life too fast, now I realise that the crazy fun-loving side is a mask and he's steadier than I had assumed. The kids like him too, especially because he's such a whizz with the computer, but I'm not ready for a relationship, and I'm not sure I ever will be. My trust has been well and truly shattered. Ian says he understands that, so we'll just have to wait and see what happens.

A LETTER FROM MIRANDA

Thank you so much for reading *Every Breath You Take*. The idea for this book came about when I was clearing our attic and discovered my workbooks from when I was at primary school. The English Language stories were the most fun as they gave a running commentary of our family life. (I now realise just how much teachers get to know about their pupils' families!) Aged eight, I wrote a story about my ideal home – a chalet in the mountains – and my ideal job: being a writer. This led me to think about the concept of a bucket list. What if it wasn't a lovely list of things to do but rather a list of demands?

I had wanted this book to be called The Bucket List, however when it was mooted with my publishers, it soon became apparent that a picture of a bucket on the front of a book, wasn't the best idea!

If you would like the chance to name characters in my future books, I'd love it if you could join my Facebook Group,

Miranda Rijks Thriller Readers' Group, where I post details of giveaways and bookish news. https://www.facebook.com/groups/mirandarijks

The following people loaned their names, or the names of their loved ones for *Every Breath You Take*. Thank you to you all! Katie Butterworth, Reneee Denis Simmons, Kalah Eltogonde, Christina Faris, Francesca Green, Jen James, Mark Jenkins, Vina Leekha, Denise Little, Jackie May, Deb Morris, @MyBookReviewFreedom, Nicolette Reite and Sharon Richert. And special thanks to Daniel Blewitt.

None of this would have been possible without Inkubator Books. Thank you to Brian Lynch, Garret Ryan, Stephen Ryan, Jan Smith, Alice Latchford, Claire Milto, Elizabeth Bayliss, Ella and the rest of the team.

A huge thanks to the book blogging community who take the time to review my psychological thrillers, share my cover reveals and talk about my books on social media. I am so grateful for your support.

Finally, and most importantly, thank *you*. If you have a moment to leave a review on Amazon and Goodreads, this helps other people discover my novels and I'd be massively grateful.

My warmest wishes,

Miranda

www.mirandarijks.com

ALSO BY MIRANDA RIJKS

Inkubator Books Titles

Psychological Thrillers

THE VISITORS

I WANT YOU GONE

DESERVE TO DIE

YOU ARE MINE

ROSES ARE RED

THE ARRANGEMENT

THE INFLUENCER

WHAT SHE KNEW

THE ONLY CHILD

THE NEW NEIGHBOUR

THE SECOND WIFE

THE INSOMNIAC

FORGET ME NOT

THE CONCIERGE

THE OTHER MOTHER

THE LODGE

THE HOMEMAKER

MAKE HER PAY

THE GODCHILD

EVERY BREATH YOU TAKE

Printed in Great Britain
by Amazon

44457228R00152